Parental Advocacy

Parental Advocacy

Empowering Parents to Take Action in Challenging Times on Behalf of Their Children

D. Robert Kennedy
&
S. June Kennedy

Copyright © D. Robert Kennedy & S. June Kennedy.

Cover designed by Global Summit House

All rights reserved. No part of this book may be reproduced in any form or by any electronic or mechanical means, including information storage and retrieval systems, without permission in writing from the publisher, except by reviewers, who may quote brief passages in a review.

ISBN: 978-1-64945-367-9 (Paperback Edition)
ISBN: 978-1-64945-368-6 (Hardcover Edition)
ISBN: 978-1-64945-366-2 (E-book Edition)

Scripture taken from the Holy Bible, King James Version (Authorized Version). First published in 1611. Quoted from the KJV Classic Reference Bible, Copyright © 1983 by The Zondervan Corporation.

Scripture taken from Holy Bible, New International Version®, NIV® Copyright ©1973, 1978, 1984, 2011 by Biblica, Inc.® Used by permission. All rights reserved worldwide.

Scripture taken from the New King James Version®. Copyright © 1982 by Thomas Nelson, Inc. Used by permission. All rights reserved.

Book Ordering Information

Phone Number: 347-901-4929 or 347-901-4920
Email: info@globalsummithouse.com
Global Summit House
www.globalsummithouse.com

Printed in the United States of America

DEDICATED

To our sons, Robert III, Leighton, and Sheldon, our daughters in law Nadia, Jessica and Elaine and our seven grandchildren, Jehlyssa, Brittani, Leighvanni, Robert IV, Jayden, Darius, and Cameron through whom we have learned to be more effective parents and grandparents. We are constantly being made aware that we are not perfect, but wish to thank God for his grace in watching our intensions and filling our imperfections. As we think of our blessings, we also share the burden of the many parents who are being challenged by their children, and we are praying that God will bless them in the ways we have been blessed.

CONTENTS

Introduction xiii

Part I Challenges Facing Parents & Children Today 1
   1. Challenges Facing Parents and Children Today 3
   2. Do You Know Where Your Children Are? 9
   3. Do You Know Who Your Children Are? 56
   4. How To Parent In A Digital Age 68
   5. Parenting In A Culture Of Violence 87
   6. Parenting and The Sexualization of Our Children 104
   7. Parenting In A Culture Of Uprootedness 124
   8. Parenting Through A Pandemic 143

Part II The Tools Of Advocacy 149
   9. Parenting as Advocacy 151
  10. Understanding the Rules of the Game for Effective Advocacy 164
  11. How to do Educational Advocacy 179
  12. Dealing with the Church as an Agency of Advocacy ... 205
  13. Using Scripture as a Tool for Advocacy 215
  14. Using Prayer as a Tool of Advocacy 224
  15. Using Counseling for Advocacy 250
  16. Going Beyond the Rules of the Game for Successful Advocacy 256

Conclusion 267
Appendix I 273
Appendix II 313
Helpful research resources for effective parenting 315

THE WISDOM OF PARENTAL ADVOCACY

For more than thirty years I have worked as an elementary school teacher. My involvement with parents and their children has convinced me that some parents are not prepared for parenting. They do not know how to advocate for their children in their every day living, and from my perspective their lack of understanding is profoundly expressed in the area of academics. It can be argued that in many instances the children direct the parents on how problems should be solved and this has placed much stress on the parents.

The call given by Drs. D. Robert and S. June Kennedy for parents to shoulder their responsibilities cannot be overstated. Together they hope that parents can have some help at their finger tips to guide in the knowledge that is needed to direct their children in their social, educational, spiritual, emotional, and physical development. The younger the child/ren the greater the responsibility for training needs to be taken. Some parents shirk their responsibility too early and force their child/ren to become independent long before they are able to make mature decisions. One consequence that results from this shirking of parental responsibility is that children make wrong decisions that lead to the kinds of breakdowns we are seeing in our contemporary society.

All parents need to advocate for their children. Only then can our children become positive leaders for the future. When I see children with multiple addictions, I often say to myself 'there goes another child without an advocate.' And I wished that something could be done for the parents as is being done for the children. The point is that we give so much attention to head start education and other programs for children development when the real problem has more to do with the parents than with the children. Multiple programs are in place for parental support and empowerment; however, many parents fail to access these programs, like because of personal and cultural inhibitions, or lake of knowledge on how to mediate the system.

The plea being made in *Parental Advocacy* is for parents to seek to understand the seriousness of their roles as parents and regardless of their preferences to consider as of first importance the impact of their action on the lives of their children. The Native American legend as told by an old sage is quite instructive. It state that every person at birth has two wolves within. The wolves grow with each child and affect their behavior throughout their lives. One wolf is the source of everything evil in life. The other wolf promotes acts of kindness, truthfulness, love and mercy. The two wolves constantly battle each other. Consequently, a person's behavior reflects the wolf that is winning that day. A listener, captivated with this story, asked, "Which of the two wolves will win?" The old sage paused for a few seconds and then responded, "The one that you feed." The story can be interpreted to say that whatever parents focus on in their children's development will to a large extent determine what the children's lives will be. Parents, feed the better nature in your child/ren by being their best advocate.

Eveythe K. Cargill, PhD
Adjunct Professor at Calhoun Community College, Huntsville, Alabama.

Dimensions of parental nurture range from feelings of abject disempowerment to scenes of helicopter parenting. Somewhere in the mix, parents must still be involved in the lives of their children whether they are over or under eighteen. In an era where children are returning home as young adults, a new approach to parenting is needed. Parents must continue to provide a rich resource of wisdom and knowledge

Parental Advocacy

through advocacy on behalf of their children especially when young adult children cannot afford to buy homes, rent apartments or support themselves fully. Empowered and transformational parenting permits parents to develop within children leadership, coping and thinking skills and strategies to complement parental advocacy in these challenging times. Children must attain continued relevance for their lives in a post-modern world, where traditional ethics, morality and spirituality are challenged by a world that centers totally on the self.

In this book Drs. D. Robert and S. June Kennedy argue persuasively for a new approach to parenting, one that is clearly grounded in the social sciences and strong in religious tradition. It is a must-read for all parents, especially those who feel disempowered to act in any meaningful manner. Transformational parental advocacy should be added to any research that parents must carry out in their development. I have been personally encouraged after reading this book that our world still has great possibilities for parents and their children. All that is needed is for them to find that ways of accessing the possibilities.

Sylvan A. Lashley, M.B.A., Ed.D., J.D.
Principal - Greater Atlanta Adventist Academy
Atlanta, Georgia

Everyday, in our work at the Family Success Center of the Oranges we see parents who are filled with fear and frustration. They are struggle through their situations in the development of their children. We see them looking for help, but it is clear that they have very little knowledge of the systems in which they seek to participate. As the Director of the Family Success Center I am convinced that the book Parental Advocacy will be one of the most helpful guides for the many parents who might feel lost and all who seek to be proactive as parental advocates.

Madeline Corredor- Garcia,
Mental Health & Substance Abuse Clinician Rutgers University
New Jersey 07050

INTRODUCTION

Some individuals have argued that "A child is considered anyone living at home under their parents' authority." Of course, if this definition were totally true, then all the young adults who are returning home at age 25 could be considered children. In the current debate across America, there are questions about when a child ceases to be under their parents' authority. Some States declare a child to be an adult at the age of 18, while other States say 21. In our discussions, both of these ages are acceptable to us, since we consider that people have different ages of physical, cognitive and even spiritual development. Not that we expect parents to hover over their children until they reach adulthood, for parents need to learn how and when "to let go." But we also think it important that parents should carefully note the needs of their children, even those that demand advocacy.

Our interest in this volume is to consider issues connected with parental advocacy. Our concern for parental advocacy developed from our work in the field of ethics and education, especially as we focused on parents with youngsters who were suffering with learning challenges. We have seen many children, being treated as disciplinary challenges, who were struggling because of some disability. We have seen parents who have been profoundly anxious because they have seen their children hurt because of misinformation and misunderstanding. We have seen them struggling because they did not know of the resources that were available in the training of their children. We have seen those who have struggled because their children have been subjected to months and years of trial and error to identify the challenges they faced. We have seen all kinds of issues in which the lives of children could have been salvaged if parents knew how to advocate for them.

More than speaking of parental advocacy for those children who have some challenging condition, we should understand that all children need to have parents who are involved in their lives. To be a child is to be vulnerable, and to be a parent is to be one who can aid those who are most vulnerable. The point is that, this book seeks to give insights, steps, tips and advice on how parents can give support, security, and protection to their children. It is not a book on values as we have written in the past. It is a book about parental advocacy. When we asked our sons what they understood by parental advocacy, they said it is "How to stick up for your kids." We said to them that sounds simple, but as we talked about it, we soon admitted that they were right, parents need to "stick up for" or "stand up for" their kids and they need to do it right.

PART I

Challenges Facing Parents & Children Today

CHAPTER I

Challenges Facing Parents and Children Today

We are surely living in a time of grave challenges, challenges confronting both parents and children. One only has to listen/read/watch the news reports and speaks to any medical, social, or human service worker to understand the gravity of the challenges. The common theme emanating from what is heard and seen on the news is the destruction of homes, families, and communities. The destruction of the family has been an ingenious plot of the devil for decades.

"Who is to blame?" Who is responsible for the challenges and the destruction? Some persons blame government policies and political ideologies that seem to disregard the high value of family. Others blame religious extremism, while others blame social permissive. While attending a conference of Black Ministers in New Jersey, some time ago, the issue of blame became more emphatic as Governor Corzine sought to answer questions concerning education and the responsibility of teachers. Some were calling for the firing of teachers whom they claim were destroying their children. The attacks on teachers are sickening, and what is often apparent is that there is a lot of misplaced blame. When parents have abdicated their responsibility for educating and disciplining their children, they blame teachers for the outcome of their children. In reality, one needs to think seriously as to the responsibility of parents in our contemporary culture. Sometimes we find parents who are seeking to absolve themselves from their responsibilities quoting prophetic statements from Scripture. One statement often quoted is found in the words of the Apostle Paul, which says:

> This also know that in the last days, people will be ungrateful, unholy, inhuman, implacable, slanderers, profligates, brutes, haters of good, treacherous, lovers of pleasure rather than lovers of God, holding to the outward form of Godliness but denying the power (2 Tim 3:2-5).

In effect, we gloss over conditions with, "it has been prophesied." However, we need to note that prophecy does not create a situation; it only predicts it or critiques it. Prophecy warns and instructs us. It does not say that we are trapped in any condition. Prophecy offers us wisdom on how to respond to circumstances, so while we may be in front of some of the predicted realities, we are not trapped.

Some time ago, we attended a seminar, where the presenter shared the following statistics with us:

- Every 1 second, a public-school student is suspended.
- Every 9 seconds, a high school student drops out.
- Every 9 seconds, a public-school student is corporally punished.
- Every 16 seconds, a child is arrested.
- Every 25 seconds, a baby is born to an unmarried mother.
- Every 37 seconds, a baby is born to a mother who is not a high school graduate.
- Every 40 seconds, a baby is born into poverty
- Every 1 minute, a baby is born without health insurance.
- Every 1 minute, a baby is born to a teen mother.

- Every 2 minutes, a baby is born with low birth weight (less than 5 lbs., 8 oz.).
- Every 3 minutes, a baby is born to a mother who had late or no prenatal care.
- Every 6 minutes, a child is arrested for a violent crime.
- Every 10 minutes, a baby is born with very low birth weight (less than 3 lbs., 4 oz.).
- Every 18 minutes, a baby dies.
- Every 40 minutes, a child or youth under age 20 dies from an accident
- Every 2 hours, a child or youth under age 20 is killed by a firearm.
- Every 2 hours, a child or youth under age 20 is a homicide victim.
- Every 4 hours, a child or youth under age 20 commits suicide.
- Every 11 hours, a young person under age 25 dies from HIV infection.[1]

Yes, the challenges we face are grave. In a global culture, these challenges should not be seen anymore as just an American phenomenon. As we travel all over the world, we see them. And parents are frustrated for they do not often find themselves with the personal resources to deal with them.

> A national survey by the Pew Research Center conducted Feb.16-March 14, 2007, among 2,020 Americans, finds a widespread belief that today's parents do not measure up to the standard that parents set a generation ago. Mothers are perceived as having a more difficult job and are judged more harshly than fathers. More than half of Americans (56%) say that mothers are doing

---

[1] These statistics came from *The Children's Defense Fund* and are presented quite frequently at workshops as evidence of the multiple challenges that are being faced by parents and children today. Whether they are fictional or factual, we cannot deny the reality that the problems are severe.

a worse job today than mothers did 20 or 30 years ago. By comparison, somewhat fewer people (47%) say fathers are doing a worse job than fathers did 20 or 30 years ago.

Nearly four-in-ten Americans (38%) list societal factors when asked in an open-ended format to name the biggest challenge for parents today. Among the top specific concerns mentioned are drugs and alcohol, peer pressure, and the impact of television and other media.

Beyond societal influences, other perceived challenges in raising children include teaching morals and values, maintaining discipline, handling the financial aspects of childrearing, and dealing with the educational system.

The views of mothers and fathers are similar when it comes to the challenges parents face today. Societal factors - including drugs and alcohol, peer pressure, and entertainment media - are the top concern for mothers and fathers alike[2].

> **The biggest challenge in raising children today, according to parents and non-parents alike, is dealing with the outside influences of society.**

Much more could be stated at this point to outline multiple challenges that parents and their children are facing; however, it is our opinion that anyone who has an interest might find the table in the appendix at the end of the book helpful. The chart seeks to emphasize the significance of the challenges, some data concerning the problems,

---

[2] People-press.org/reports/display.php3?ReportID-The Pew Research Center, Report, May 2, 2007,

some causes of the challenges, and some ways in which resolutions can be reached to deal with the challenges.[3]

We cannot bury our heads in the sand.

The most pervasive challenges facing both parents and children should make us think more seriously about our responsibilities towards our children. We cannot deny that the lives of our children are being destroyed, and when children are destroyed, their adulthood lives are often destroyed. Miracles of transformation do happen, but we cannot just sit back and wait for a miracle. Even in miracles, "An ounce of prevention is [still] worth more than a pound of cure." Here are some pertinent questions we must ask ourselves as parents:

> What happens when we do not care for our children?
> What happens when children are not protected?
> What happens when children are born without families?
> What happens when children are abused?
> What happens to children who are traumatized?
> What happens to children who are subjected to violence?
> What happens when the Department of Social Service gives more considerable attention to our children than the focus of their families?
> What happens when the courts make decisions about our children rather than us making decisions about them?

These are questions that should cause us to become proactive about advocacy. We should not go about life blaming others. Instead, we should search for the correct answers to the challenges we face. And the answers should not just be simplistic but should be based upon well-informed

---

[3] If you wish to have a great sense of urgency regarding parental advocacy, you need to spend a little time looking at the table.

theories of advocacy. Our goal in the follow-up discussions is to help parents who often know little about advocacy, develop skills as to how they can take greater responsibilities for their children who are caught up in systems with the potential to destroy them. What we are asking is that each of us takes more responsibility and stop trusting others to take responsibility that we can carry for ourselves.

QUESTION FOR REFLECTIONS

1. Can you name five of the most significant challenges facing families in general today?
2. What is the significance of being aware of the challenges?
3. How might parents know when it is urgent to stick up for their children?

CHAPTER II

Do You Know Where Your Children Are?

Whenever a parent is unable to find his/her child, such a parent might become hysterical and burdened. Many times, as we go to the mall, we see agitated parents looking frantically for a son or a daughter before the inevitable happens. Many parents take extra precautions and keep a close watch on their children to avoid the woes of searching for a lost child. Sometimes some parents might go to the extreme such as putting a child on a leash, especially when they are in large crowds. Onlookers might characterize the cautious parent as overprotective or even abusive in their efforts to ensure the safety of their child/ren. And yes, an overprotective parent can harm their child/ren, but if the intent is the safety of their children, probably one needs to look at the age of the child, and the context before passing judgment.

On the other hand, some parents are careless or lax about the safety of their children. They leave them to run free, even in circumstances where there are apparent dangers. In between, there are parents who are genuinely caring, and responsible, who do ensure the safety of their child/ren in every circumstance. The Bible records one incident of two parents who might be characterized as careless if we extract the narrative from its cultural context. Luke, chapter 2: 41-52, marks the saga of the frantic search of Mary and Joseph for their son, Jesus.

As the record states, when Jesus was twelve years old, He went up to the Temple in Jerusalem with His parents. At the end of the celebrations, he remained behind and engaged in a debate with the Scribes and Pharisees. While Jesus was comfortably challenging the minds of his hearers with his vast knowledge of Scripture, his parents were on their way home, totally unaware of their son's absence for three days. The parents were fellowshipping and assumed their son was in the company of relatives and friends, as was customary. After three days of traveling, the parents checked to confirm that their son was safe. The worst fear any parent could imagine became a reality - Jesus was not among the crowd. Can you imagine the frustration, anxiety, and fear as Joseph and Mary took the long trek back to Jerusalem? Can you imagine the wild thoughts running through their minds as they thought of the previous efforts made to destroy their child? (Mt. 2:1-8). Had their carelessness now robbed them of their child? Can you hear their prayers asking for forgiveness and, at the same time, asking Divine protection for their child?

On reaching Jerusalem, Mary and Joseph wasted no time in searching everywhere for their lost son. Their quest led them to the Temple, where they carried out a thorough search. After a careful search of various rooms, the anxious parents found Jesus among the Elders, arguing Scriptures. Jesus was quite composed without any sense of being lost and no thought about the anguish his parents were experiencing in his absence.

One can draw many inferences from this incident. In the first place, many could argue that at twelve years old, Jesus should have sought to be in the company of his parents and family at all times. On the other hand, some might argue that it was no fault of Jesus that he was left behind. His parents felt culpable, for they assumed too much. They took it for granted that Jesus was with family members. They began the journey home without assuring themselves that their child was with them; therefore, full responsibility was theirs. Some others might even argue that the religious leaders should bear some responsibility, for they should have been careful enough to check the child as to the whereabouts of his parents. They should not be engaging a child for three long days without knowing about his parents. Of course, all the arguments we posit are plausible when interpreted in our Western thinking and understanding of family and communal structures and relationships.

In our contemporary culture, parents are liable for twelve-year-olds because they are minors. However, whether one chooses to blame the child or the parents is not the issue here; instead, the point is that many parents are like Mary and Joseph - assuming that their child is in the crowd with other relatives and friends, that their child is safe, while the child is missing. Assumptions can be helpful at times, but they often lead to a loss. Merely assuming that our children are safe is reckless parenting. Assumptions often have deadly consequences because they are not based on facts.

> **Assuming our children's safety is reckless parenting.**

Mary and Joseph might be absolved of blame because their cultural context suggested that any family member or neighbor could care for their child. We believe that any parent, irrespective of culture today, should first check that their child is on the journey with them. They should ascertain with which relatives or friends the child is traveling. Today parents cannot afford to take anything for granted because we live in an individualistic culture, where each one looks out for himself/herself. Furthermore, studies have shown that many children are hurt most by individuals they know - individuals who are closest to them. Parents need to be cautious about their assumptions as to the wellbeing and safety of their children when they are left alone.

Lost children and lost parents

Our discussion thus far focused on a question of location - geography, but we wish to note that knowing where your children are is more than a practical question about geography. A child can be lost in many more ways than in locations such as the mall, the church, or school. Here we note that each year, many parents lose their children by one means or the other. It is quite traumatizing and disturbing for any parent, whether a child is lost for a few minutes or long periods. The following statistical chart from the *National Incidence Studies of Missing, Abducted, Runaway, and Thrown away Children* conducted by the U.S. Department of Justice, is a revelation about a grave problem that we encounter in our country and the world. The following is the 2019 report:

Lost, Injured, or Otherwise Missing:	*421,394*
Runaways:	*1.6 -2.8 (each year)*
Family Abductions:	*54,100*
Attempted Non-family Abductions:	*114,600*
Thrown-aways:	*127,100*
Non-family Abductions:	*3,200 to 4,600*

These figures are quite staggering and will be grimmer if the trend is not corrected. The question that many might be asking is, "What can parents do to ensure the safety of their children?" But while we seek answers to such a question, it is interesting to note that many children are lost right in their homes, before their parents' eyes, and many parents do not even know it. Many children are caught up and lost in the high-tech internet world in which they live. One might question how this can be possible. The simple response - through unlimited and unstructured accesses. Many children are lost in the entertainment culture. Many are lost because of overindulgent parents and other adults in their lives. And still many are lost in their developmental stages. It is crucial then for parents and other adults to have a clear understanding of the safety and wellbeing of children.

The concerns voiced by many individuals, the statistics available, and the information presented above should lead every parent to reflect seriously on the question, "Do you know where your children are?" Years ago, when we lived in New York City every night at 10:00 pm, the radio announcer Ted Powers' voice came on the radio. It said, "It is 10 pm; do you know where your children are?" As parents, we always smiled and responded as if Ted could hear us responding, "Yes, we know where our children are. They are in bed."

Parents should not trivialize the question above, and they should not understand it as only asking about the physical whereabouts of their children. The question seeks to ask parents how much information do they have about their children - information which goes beyond the knowledge of shelter, food, and clothing. The question framed in different ways is asking, "Do you know about your children's developmental needs?" Do you know them emotionally? "Do you understand the stages of their physical development?" "Are you aware of their intellectual development?" "Do you understand what they should be accomplishing each year as they get older?" "Do you know where they are in their social development?" "Do you know the kinds of friendships and bonds that they are developing?" "Do you know where your children are in their spiritual development?" "Do you understand their faith development with each passing year?" "Do you understand the challenges to their faith?" "Do you understand the challenges to their spiritual lives?" We hope that none of these questions about children are lost to parents.

No one expects that all parents are to be experts in responding to the questions posed as if they are trained, developmental psychologists. But there are basic things that one needs to have as one thinks of the task of parenting. When we see the impact of the lack of parenting on many children, we often say jokingly, "people need to have a license to have children." To put this more seriously, we are saying that no one should be a parent until such a one has attended parenting classes, for it is truly a tremendous task to be a parent.

Some time ago, we listened to a discourse on the "stewardship of parenting," and the point that the speaker drove home, forcefully, was that "parents who neglect to know their children and provide for them are infidels." Strong words, one might argue, but they are words that should move every parent to evaluate his/her role as parents. In other words, your teenage child is no longer seven. While some parents do not recognize the maturing of their children, there are those parents who force their children into adulthood before they are ready. Both attitudes are destructive and can have lasting consequences on succeeding generations.

Because of these extremes in child-rearing practices, we mention here a few of the things that happen to our children as they grow:

1. Children pass through developmental stages. This effort is to help many parents begin to focus on the things that occur in their children's lives.
2. That parents think of their children differently and understand that as children grow, they mature in various ways.
3. Parents should respond appropriately to the needs of children if they want to have healthy families.

Stages of development

Our progressive development: Human beings pass through several stages of development or changes from birth through the various phases of adulthood. There are significant changes occurring at each stage or level of our development that determines or defines who we will become until death. No one is a baby one day, and then suddenly, the next day they become matured adults. Instead, these changes occur progressively throughout their lifespan. All the faculties –physical, social, mental, emotional- develop at various stages of our lives. We move from being infants to being toddlers, through the varying stages of childhood, through the teen years and adulthood, and as physical changes occur, we mature in most of the other categories. For example, we develop a sense of right and wrong in varying degrees at each level. A child's understanding of right and wrong develops with age. Therefore, an adult's knowledge of right and wrong should be more matured than a child of six years old. As we grow, our attitude toward others is never the same from birth to death. We change our attitudes and perspectives toward various issues throughout our lifespan.

Our society is greatly indebted to social scientists and educators, who, by their intense studies, observations, and experiments have given humanity a better understanding of the stages of development as we journey through our environment. They argue that humans (children) develop in progressive stages, which are predictable.[4] However, factors such as the culture and family background in which individuals are brought up, are determinants of how the traits and characteristics we develop, individuate. While we develop in stages and might exhibit similar traits through them, such stages are not rigid. Not all five, six, or ten-year-olds display the exact characteristics in the same ways. Environmental factors, genetic factors, and other factors impact the rate of development for each child, and these are important for parents to understand how they can guide their children through the developmental maze.

> **One should remember that the stages of human development are not rigid.**

Educators and researchers seek to make it easy for parents and others who work with children, to understand the various stages of development, by reducing them to three broad categories. The three broad categorizations are: (1) early childhood - birth to eight, (2) middle childhood - eight to twelve, and (3) adolescence - twelve to

---

[4] Our comments are grounded in the works of such scholars as Jean Piaget, Erick Erickson, Lawrence Kohlberg, James Fowler, who have carried powerful influences on development theories in a variety of ways. While we have not quoted these authors directly, one can see the importance of their research.

eighteen[5] While such categorization is beneficial, they can also make for superficiality, so other educators offer more categories.[6]

We are using the three categorizations with the provision that, at times, we will go for the greater detail instead of the superficial. We hope our choice will not prevent parents from gaining a clear understanding of the crucial years in the lives of their children. We desire that the knowledge they gain along with their proactive parenting, will make for the most favorable outcomes.

From birth to 5 years old: This time frame is called the Early Years. It encompasses a span from birth to age five. These years are crucial in the development of children, for it is here that the stage is set for adult behavior and how they live their lives later on. These years are also the impressionable years. Children learn from what parents do and say. Who children become in adulthood; they are now beginning. It is during this period that many transformations take place. As one watches the newborn babe move from a stage of helplessness and total dependence to being active, curious, talking, walking, imitating what they see, and becoming independent in many respects, it is incredible. We see rapid increases in the acquisition of language, number recognition and recall, and the ability to recognize, recall, and frame letters into words. During this stage of development, children acquire the necessary skills which set the foundation for future learning. As these changes occur, parents have a once in a lifetime chance to mold the characters of their children and guide them as they navigate through the maze of rapid growth and changes. They have the golden opportunity to teach, seat the values and morals that they wish their children to develop. These, in turn, will help to determine the attitudes of their children later in life. The early stage of development is the opportune time for proactive parenting.

---

[5] https://education.stateuniversity.com/pages1826/Child-Develoopment-Stages-Growth.html

[6] https://education.stateuniversity.com/pages/1826/Child-Development-Stages-Growth.html

Parental Advocacy

Parents should know that although changes occur rapidly, they do not happen in a vacuum. The world around them impacts the development of children. What they see and what they hear shape their characters. In other words, they learn best when they have the opportunity to interact with things, with their peers and other people. Here are some things that parents should understand as their child/ren develop.

1. Children learn about the world through the physical senses of touch, of taste, of smell, of examining things.
2. Children learn by imitating the habits of those around them.
3. Children get meaning through their interactions with people and the varied experiences they encounter.
4. Children are not thinking logically, moving from cause to effect. They are very simplistic in their understanding.
5. Children's understanding develops from the concrete and later to the abstract.
6. Children live from moment to moment, with no sense of timing or thought of tomorrow.
7. Children give very little thought to how they feel
8. Children experience rapid physical growth.

Aside from the list above, there are other notable developmental characteristics that one can observe as children move through the first five years of life. In the first place, many children seem to be **uncoordinated** and **awkward** in their movements. Children often fall, or items in their possession fall and break while they seek to get control of the gross motor skills. Parents should not be overly concerned since, in a typically developing child, such moments are not lasting. We have heard harrowing stories, and many of us might have had negative experiences at that stage of development. Many parents and adults often mischaracterize what is happening to children in this stage. They call the children awkward and clumsy and then punish them for breaking things. Yes, it is an awkward and clumsy period of development, and children have no control over it. Our sister gave us a heart-wrenching story about what happened to her son. She went to work and left her three-year-old son with a sitter who was supposedly a mother of many years. When she returned later that evening, she found her child crying, and the sitter quite enraged. The mother wanted to know why her child was crying. The angry sitter told that she had spanked him because he broke her dish that she treasured so much. The mother was horrified that the sitter spanked her three-year-old son for breaking something. Of course, that was the last day that that sitter earned a living by sitting that child. The perceptive mother immediately quit her job to care for her child. She chose to struggle on one salary rather than seeing her child abused. Parents and caretakers need to know then as the body develops, the eye-hand coordination, walking, lifting, and other such skills form. One should not expect the child to function beyond his/her stage of development.

As children continue to move through the early stages of development, they have a **high level of energy.** The energy level in some children can be so high that that child could be mislabeled as hyperactive. A note of caution to parents is that, instead of assigning a negative label, find an outlet for that growing child to use the energy. Children at this stage have a great need for movement, and therefore adequate space and time must be provided for release. Many communities now have parks with age-appropriate play areas. Those who lack space at home should utilize these play areas where children can find a wholesome outlet for the energy they have.

Another noticeable trait at this stage of development is **emotional insecurity.** Children are emotionally insecure as well as being immature in the early years of development. Parents must understand the source of such instability - is just a part of their natural development or something else such as bullying, being molested by others- and use the opportunity to guide their children carefully. Here are some suggestions offered to parents to help them identify insecurity and immaturity in their children:

1. A trusting relationship with adults and reliance on them to make decisions for them.
2. A willingness to please adults. In other words, they are compliant because they do not want to hurt that adult in any way.
3. There is a fear of the unfamiliar- the unknown. Children are most comfortable with familiar territory.
4. They crave attention from everyone and express in their actions, the desire to be loved by everyone.
5. They have a deep need for affirmation from adults and anyone who can give it. Thus, when a parent says, "good job" or "that's great," the children are happy.
6. They express a shyness that does not readily give expressions about feelings.
7. They do not like to get many questions, although they ask lots of questions.

Parents should know that because of the immaturity and emotional insecurity expressed at this stage, they need to be extra cautious with their children. Sexual predators prey upon children because they understand their vulnerability at this stage of development. The trust that children have in adults can be detrimental because many adults betray that trust and violate these children instead.

That our developing children have a **practical approach** to life is not clearly understood by many parents. Children at this level have a very concrete approach to life. And parents can enjoy this in their children without labeling them as "little liars" as we sometimes hear. If children can see it, if they can feel it, then it is real. We often talk about how concrete children are in their approach to life. They have not yet developed the ability to think abstractly, and therefore, everything is literal for them. They must be able to feel it or see it before they can accept it as authentic. In other words, they are very visual in their orientation. As such, they make no connection with the past. Events that occurred in the past have minimal impact on how they operate.

That is what is so precious about children in this stage, for they will not necessarily connect things done to them in the past with today.

In the early childhood development stage, children begin to acquire fundamental skills such as number concept, reading, and writing. These skills are none existent at birth and are undeveloped in the majority of children up to age five. We have seen and heard many parents being overly concerned that their four-year-old is not reading or their five-year-old is not counting. Very often, such parental concerns put these little ones under so much pressure to achieve. In our roles as educators, we have had to correct many individuals about putting undue burdens on their children to read, write, and do mathematics. Children at this level develop skills at a different pace and will acquire such skills when they are developmentally ready. Yes, some four years can read and recognize numbers, but this is not true of every child who is four years old. Our firstborn, at four years of age, was reading at the third-grade level. However, his younger siblings did not function at that level when they were his age. He was different from his siblings, and we did not expect them to attain the same level at four years old. But many parents pressure children to overachieve at an early age, and the result is early burnout. And many times, the child/children do not achieve their true potential later. A word of caution, therefore, is to allow children to develop at a healthy pace. You'll be surprised to find that your child who did not begin to read at four years old, when he/she is eight, might attain the same level as the other eight-year-old that started reading at four. In other words, if there are no setbacks, children will get to where they need to be at the appropriate time.

The above discussion is not to dissuade parents from providing a rich environment for their children, but to suggest that in the competitive culture, more damage is being done to children than we might care to admit. Children who are exposed to books (not forced) at an early age develop a high level of interest in reading. At this stage, many children gravitate toward books if given early

> **In the competitive culture, more damage is being done to children than we might care to admit.**

exposure. Children who acquire these skills early have a sense of pride in showing off their skills. We have numerous experiences as we visit with our grandchildren, our nieces, nephews, and children of friends -ages three to five. We recall with delight, the declarations of each demonstrating his/her ability to read. Some might only be reading pictures while others are decoding words, but we took note of the smiles on those faces as they displayed their abilities.

Sometimes we marvel at the development process. For while children are learning we wonder how is such possible because of the observable characteristic of short attention span. Children move from one activity to the next like a butterfly flitting from flower to flower. In ten minutes, they might run through several activities because of the **inability to sustain attention.** We have witnessed parents scolding their children because they expect them to sit for an extended period without moving, and we laugh because, in some circumstances, even us adults cannot keep still. Many parents and adults become annoyed when they take a child to places such as concerts, weddings, and other sites where limited movement is necessary.

> **In our contemporary technological culture, many children are struggling with sustained attention span.**

Have you ever watched the disgusted response of some adults when a child makes a sound or moves in the pews at church or any other such places? We have seen it and continue to hear some adults telling parents to take the child outside so that there be no disturbance in the audience. Some parents become embarrassed and blame the child. Some parents go as far as telling their child/ren how much they are "spoiling" their (the parents'") day. This kind of response from parents results from not understanding the stages of development fully. Parents and other adults must realize that the lack of sustained attention is also a part of the growth process of this stage. However, if the behavior continues as the child gets older, there might well be other challenges that parents must address. When we were bringing up our children, on many occasions, we had to sit close to an exit, in the absence of a parenting room, where we could make a hasty retreat so our children could move a bit. We encourage parents not to vent their frustrations by spanking the child and demand that they sit still and pay attention. Now, whenever we see the feud between parents and children, we ask to take the children for a walk. Whenever we do this, we talk with the children and give them space to move around for a while. But we also use it as an occasion to give parents time to regain their composure. Besides, we model what they can do to help children who want to move. Very often, after removing a child, we can return them to their parents without a struggle. We are not suggesting that we were perfect parents because we, too, had our moments of lapse before we realized that our children have limited attention on certain occasions.

Alongside their short attention span, it is also noticeable in how children can be **easily agitated.** We have heard many times, parents complaining that their children are becoming agitated by wanting to move readily from one thing to the next. But some parents do not realize that somehow, they are encouraging the behavior longer than it should last. Modern-day parents have found a new way to keep their little ones quiet without proper parental attention. Advancements in technology impact their children in positive and negative ways. Things on the screen move quickly. Children at an early age can flip from one screen to the next and are not learning that they need to wait; that they need sustained attention to somethings that are crucial for development. Parents need to be careful about the use of the television, iPhones, iPods, iPads, and other forms of audio and visuals, as babysitting tools. Very early children might believe that everything must move rapidly as the screen. But children, as they mature, might become excited as they begin to learn that the real world is not moving as fast as the gadgets. Or when the gadget is taken away, children become agitated, and some to the point of temper tantrums. To quiet the child or keep from being embarrassed, some parents give back the gadget. And have also seen children throwing tantrums because parents are not moving fast enough to give them what they want. Some parents become frustrated that they opt to leave the scene or become abusive to the child. Yes, because of the stage development where the children are, they become easily agitated- unable to sit still for long periods; they need to move. Parents need to allow children to move and not use substitutes for keeping them quiet.

We have briefly alluded above one way in which misguided uses technology impact children. Although there is a full chapter dedicated to technology and its full impact on children and their development, we mention here another caution to parents. Because children at this stage have **no sense of is real or unreal** of what is fact or fiction, parents must be careful in how they use the technology with small children. While this is a part of early development, unstructured use of technology can have negative impacts on children in how they identify fact from fiction. Children interpret what they see on the screen as authentic because they have no sense of what is fact from fiction. Many imitate what they see and may even develop violent habits or seek to replicate dangerous stunts. There are numerous kids cartoon stunts that children think is real and will attempt to test them if left without proper guidance. Several years ago, the cartoon characters Batman and Robin, brought excitement to many children as they saw them flying in the air. The reports were that several children (between the ages of five to seven) took towels or anything which they thought looked like a cape and went flying through windows to their death. Parents must exercise controls over what children see so that what is a healthy development will not create challenges for them and their children.

An extension of what is real or unreal is **imagination.** Many children might develop imaginary friends and even have difficulty separating from them later in life. The child's interaction might amuse many parents with these imaginary friends. But while it brings moments of laughter, parents must ensure that children are not overly fixated - stuck in this stage. As they develop beyond the early years, begin to help them to understand what is factual, and what fiction is, what is real and what is imaginative.

Self-centeredness or egocentrism is yet another issue that accompanies this stage of development. Children tend to focus more on themselves and less on others. That they are possessive often show up in the expression- "mine" Everything is theirs and no one else. Some parents might become frightened and complain about how possessive their son or daughter is. However, the good news is that it is quite natural at this stage. Unaware adults also call egocentrism "selfishness." Children at this do not understand what it means to work with others, and when parents or adults see that they label children as selfish. Again, this is natural for this stage of development. The danger, however, is when these tendencies persist long into the other stages. Alert parents need to observe these traits and carefully guide child/ren through the process without breaking the will. Encourage children to share in simple things, and don't forget that example is the most influential teacher.

Have you ever heard the term "inquiring minds want to know"? Well, this phrase is a clear description of our children during this phase of their development. They want to know not because they are searching for knowledge, but they are just **curious.**

> **Learning takes place by questioning, so don't be afraid of the curious questions that your developing child might ask. Try to give attention to them and answer them.**

They exhibit a natural inquisitiveness or curiosity. They ask many questions - Who? What? Why? When? How? Their questions coming in rapid succession can be quite disgusting for many adults who do not understand the driver behind the questions. We are fascinated each time we come in contact with these little questioners. As the flurry of questions come at us, we often chuckle and wonder what is next. One day our three-year-old niece came to visit us at our church. As she sat, the inquisition began, and in as much as I (June) enjoyed the questioning, I must admit that it was a bit tiring. "Where is my uncle?" I told her he was sitting on the platform. She looked and saw him but was not satisfied, and so the next question, "Why is he there?" The response that he had to speak was not satisfactory either because she immediately asked, "but why?" After several more questions and explanations, she seemed somewhat satisfied. Many parents or adults would probably try to shut her up by saying "be quiet" or "you ask too many questions," or you are too nosey" or "you are too inquisitive." Our niece had the opportunity to ask several questions, tiring as they were. But because we understood that being curious (note not "busy body or nosey as many parents like to say) was a part of the development process and that she needed to understand the world around her. Curiosity leads them to explore because they want to know how things work, what is the composition of some things, and why some things are the way they are. Children ask numerous questions as part of their learning process. Parents should not seek to shut them up but instead, encourage them to explore.

Curiosity, when handled in the right way, is a tremendous learning tool for children as they develop. When children are curious about something, they will ask questions, and that is legitimate. However, some parents might become weary because of the numerous problems that children at the stage might be facing. As the questions come, parents must make sure that they give the correct responses at age-appropriate levels. For example, many children want to know where babies come from, and many parents find creative ways of misguiding them. Quite frequently, many parents find creative ways- fictional stories such as the stork brings the baby. Such a myth is perpetuated when we see books with pictures of storks flying in the air with a bundle in its beak. The bundle shows a baby in it. When we were growing up, we were told that the airplane brought the baby. Of course, children today might not believe this story because many have the opportunity to fly in a plain. Many parents might not tell mythical stories, but instead, they go to the extreme side in giving too much information about conception for which the child is not ready. Think of a simple and honest response and prepare for the next question, for it will come. So, parents, read and be equipped with an answer when the question of how the baby got in mommy's stomach. Parents are ready because this is the stage that they ask many questions on a variety of subject matters. Some questions might even take you by surprise. You might not be able to answer immediately if you don't have the correct answer, but also promise to respond another day. Parents, read, prepare, be ready, for the question will come again, and do not give fictional answers.

Aside from being overly curious, children are **adventurous**. Because many attitudes go hand in hand or emanate from one another, no one should be surprised that curiosity and adventure are connected. These two are inseparable in the sense that curiosity pushes one to explore. An adventurous spirit has a strong desire to know. Always wanting to find new things, wanting to know what something is like, wanting to know what is it made of and how it works. Of course, these are adult interpretations, but children want to know what's in the box because of the spirit of adventure and a natural curiosity. Remember, at all times, that this is a part of the learning process, and how we respond to the child is the difference in ensuring healthy development.

Developing children are active and like to participate in numerous activities. We might argue that because children at this stage are curious and adventurous such would heighten their activity level. They like to **participate** in what others are doing. They always want to be a part of activity because they are confident that they can do it. They believe that they can do many things. Parents who understand this kind of development will make every effort to include them in various activities. When parents are in the kitchen, young children want to help with the dishes; they want to cook, or they want to set the table. Or when parents are out in the garden planting flowers or working on the car, young children want to help. Parents should find safe ways in which they might include these children because when they grow older, that same willingness might not be there. Again, we must emphasize the need for safety. Many children have been hurt in trying to participate in the activities that parents do, sometimes unknown to parents. There are numerous horror stories we could share, but that is not the intent here.

Children at this stage live in a world of wonder. Many individuals discount their ability to manipulate adults. They like to push the boundaries to see what is allowed or not allowed. Many adults are not as alert as they should be and, therefore, become enablers. They justify the behavior under the pretext that the child does not understand. If you are around children, watch when they want something. They might throw a tantrum until parents give in, but note that they will stop when reinforcement of negative behavior goes unrewarded. Why do you suppose babies cry and then stop when picked up? Notice that the longer it takes for the child to be picked up, the more intense the cry. But note also that when the baby senses that there is no reinforcement, that mode of attention-getting ceases. We are not suggesting that a baby should be allowed to cry continuously, but parents need to ascertain why the baby is crying. Is it just for attention (which he/she needs at times)? Or is the child sick or hungry? Many parents make the fatal mistake in giving in or saying, "Well, he or she will grow it out." Yes, this stage passes, but if children learn that they can get what they want through manipulation, there is the possibility that they will become fixed in their ways. Such attitudes might become deeply rooted and, in later years, be a source of challenge for many parents.

A final fact about children in the early years of development is that they have limited social skills, so they might easily offend others, or not interact with others correctly because they are not aware of the protocol- the social cues of relationship. These skills, of course, develop to their fullest with careful guidance. It is at this early stage that we must teach, through modeling, the correct ways of interacting with others. Teach them to say "please," "excuse me," "thank you." Children do not develop these in a vacuum; they model what adults do, so parents must exercise caution in how they act and speak in the hearing of their children. If children see the right models in the proper context, and they are not developing age-appropriate social skills, parents should take this as a cue that something is wrong. They might need the evaluation of professionals to determine the level of the challenge since inept social skills might be an accompanying characteristic of some disability.

To encapsulate what we have stated about this developmental stage, we say for reinforcement that parents must take careful note of what is happening in the lives of their children and guide them through in healthy ways. It is easy, when growing children, to overlook the importance of parental observation and carefulness in training. We have raised three sons, and we are not sure that we saw all that we are now observing in two of our nieces and seven grandchildren. After watching them, we wish that we had another chance at making an impact. Parents, you have a once in a lifetime chance to monitor your children. Make it count by careful observation of the stages and use what you glean to guide and nurture the healthy development of your children. In other words, be involved in the lives of your children. Have limits and structures in place for your children. Let them know that you love them unconditionally.

Later childhood (6-8) years: Later childhood is the most exciting stage of development. For the child/ren following a normal path of development, this age grouping ranges from the first grade through the third grade. Later childhood is the period of transitions. Education is more formalized and moves children toward independence. This move toward independence can be a traumatic period if parents and other support personnel misunderstand their roles in supporting and guiding children. It is crucial for all who work with this age group to have explicit knowledge of the physical, emotional, intellectual, and social development of children. If they must participate effectively in the lives of children, deeper understandings of how children move through the developmental stages is not a choice but a necessity.

Karen DeBord calls the development of 6-8-year-olds, the "outward journeys." These journeys can be (significant) steps in the lives of 6-8-year-olds. Socially, it is a venture out from the security of the caregiver into the world of friends, peers, and other individuals. Physically, they move into the world of games and schools, and finally, cognitively when they begin to enter into the adult world of communication, abstract ideas, and logic.[7]

While many individuals might categorize these stages differently, the traits manifested are indeed journeys for both parents and children.

---

[7] Karen DeBord cited in an article titled, "An Individual in Transition: Between Family and School, Childhood and Preadolescence, Dependence and Self-reliance." h://www.music.edu/fm_ruralclerkship/projects/04r01 37pedsdmcurr2a.pdf

And they can be frustrating as children begin to experience changes internally and externally.

A noticeable feature of later childhood is continuing **rapid physical development**, which parents and other adults cannot miss. The increase in height and weight, the loss of baby teeth, and the growth of permanent ones are phenomenal. These are indicators that the child is maturing. The awkwardness that was evident in earlier years has disappeared, and children are now more active and have control over their gross motor skills, and to a lesser degree, their fine motor skills. Controls over the larger muscles are evident in their ability to run and jump without frequent falls, as well as throwing a ball with more accuracy.

We have several moments of laughter with our children as we often reminisce about the growth of our grandchildren. One, in particular, has had so many falls, with each taking heavy tolls on her body. The stitches here and there and scars were the telltales. Even though we knew that she would develop, were anxious, for we hated to hear her screams and see the bruised she sustained. As she bypassed that stage, we noted her calmness as she gained control over her gross motor skills. The good news for all is that as children get closer to eight, the eye muscles, hand coordination are more developed. Children can use a pair of scissors to cut straighter lines. They also have better control over the pencil or pen as they write, paint, color pictures, and follow patterns. They can complete tasks that demand manual dexterity with minimum challenges. Parents should note these developments carefully and provide regulated activities in which their children can be engaged since, at this stage, there is a higher activity level and also the desire to be involved.

Another noticeable area of growth is social development. As children at this age mature, they begin to become **independent** of parents, and a move to build **friendships**. They are more aware of those around them, that is, those with whom they must interact daily. It is the beginning of a new kind of learning - how to be friends with their peers. However, friendships are usually with the same sex. We know that in this day and age, many parents become paranoid if they sense close interaction of children of the same gender, but this closeness is developmental. Parents can be helpful in monitoring and giving positive feedback. Parents should provide guidance, provide structure and support in their children's activities. Children at this stage of development might even talk about several best friends, and parents might call the idea ludicrous, forgetting how they were as they were growing up. But the idea is not ridiculous for they do have several best friends at times. And as they form these friendships, they develop a sense of appreciation for the opinions of their peers. But while there is a closeness with friends, children still have close connections to their families. Parents, no need to worry yet; you have not lost your child/ren.

Even though children at this stage are moving to build friendships, it is quite noticeable that there is still an intense preoccupation with the self. There is a spirit of competitiveness in which the self- means more than friendship. It is quite an experience to watch these children as they become **Self-absorbed**. One only has to watch them when they are playing games, exceptionally competitive sports, and note how the self is projected. Most children in this age group hate to be losers, and so some might even revert to being a two-year-old throwing a tantrum. The following story is just one example that demonstrates the importance of winning as opposed to losing. A group of six-year-olds and seven-year-olds children were engaged in a math time table race, and when one student recognized that he would not be the winner, he grabbed the worksheet of his friend, ripped it to shreds, and then threw a temper tantrum that frightened everyone. Amidst the screams, he blurted out, "I am supposed to win. He is supposed to make me win." Those present noted the bossiness and the level of control he tried to exert to win. He felt that he was the only talented player there, and no one else mattered. We have seen similar attitudes with the age group, especially in activities which involve competition. Children participate in activities, but the interest of the group or team is not a priority. In the child's mind, team participation is individualistic - I am supposed to win. We could well interpret the unspoken sentiments as: "It is my game. I am going to win despite the others."

Can an observer understand the group chemistry when a group of 6-8-year-olds is involved in a team activity in which each sees himself/herself as the winner? The short story related above is typical of the attitude of many in this age group. One can sympathize with this attitude as no one wants to be called a loser. However, no matter how good this kind of reasoning seems, the view of self-centeredness should not be encouraged. Even though it is clear that such characteristic is developmental, all those who work with these age groups should be careful as they guide children through the stage.

Recognizing the lasting impact that selfishness and self-centeredness can have on children as they grow, we encourage parents and other adults who work with this age group to be careful with the activities they select and, most of all, give proper guidance. Activities such as games should focus more on team effort rather than individual achievement. Avoid activities that involve competition for competition often increases the desire to win. A child might become so passionate about winning that the activity, instead of being fun turns into an argument. Children must learn the inclusive language of "We," "Us," instead of "Me" and "I." This concept of inclusiveness is vital. If the pattern of self-centeredness is allowed to continue into the teen and adult years, the negative consequences might be enormous.

Another phase of development that parents and teachers need to watch closely is **emotional development.** It is at this stage that children are learning to manage their emotions. Their emotions can run wild, ranging from sadness and being insecure to feeling safe and confident and wanting to see everything go right. Children think that parents and other adults have set rules which they should follow. Therefore, if they see something that they perceive as unfair, as not honest, or telling the truth, they call for fairness and "rat out their friends, and at times unwittingly, even their parents. For example, a mother went to church, although she was not feeling very well. The usher shook her hand at the door and asked, "how are you today?" The mother, with a smile, replied, " I'm very well; thank you." Almost immediately, her seven-year-old daughter turned to her mom and said, " I thought you said that you had a backache." Her daughter knew that Mom always insisted on telling the truth, and now she wasn't. Some parents would punish the daughter while others might call her a tattletale or talebearer. That is not the case. At this stage of development, children are not vindictive nor willful; all they are seeking is honesty. In other words, the talk of playing by the rules that parents set because everything must be fair. Fairness for this age group is to be kind to each other. "A new study suggests that children as young as six have advanced ideas about fairness and are willing to pay a personal price to intervene in what they believe are unfair situations."[8]

While children at this stage call for fairness, they also expect punishment to accompany any violation. **Punishment** is necessary for any infraction - real or perceived. Interestingly, the call for punishment might even be at the expense of friends and friendships. The concern of the child/ren is to see that there is a consequence for an infraction. That is why they report to adults and expect that they will exact the revenge because the act was "naughty." Sometimes one wonders if these children are locked into a punishment mode. No, they are not; it is just a developmental phase that should pass.

Alongside the need to see fairness, children in this stage are **fragile**. They have intense fears about failures, and that's why there is such a focus on winning. Additionally, their egos are fragile, and they become hurt quickly. They cannot handle criticisms of themselves. That is why parents and adults must help them understand that criticism can be a learning tool. While parents seek to help children learn how to deal with criticism, many times, they are guilty of comparing their children to other children and thereby hurt and destroy their child.

Children are impressionable, and parents should not forget that. Parents should always be mindful that their words and actions impact the lives of their children positively or negatively. Sadly, parents affect

---

[8]   https://psychcentral.com/news/2014/08/19/even-6-year-olds-have-advanced-ideas-about-fairness/73790.html

their children, especially in negative ways, unknowingly. In our many seminars on parenting, we have encountered numerous individuals who still hurt because of thoughtless comparisons their parents made while they were at an impressionable age. We recall in one of our workshops, one woman about thirty years old telling that when she was about six years old, her mother told her that her younger sister was smarter than she was. "That statement from my mother has paralyzed me and thwarted my academic growth," the young woman recalled tearfully. She bought into the criticism, and each time she tried, she failed, and then her only comment- "Mother was right." There are many mothers and other adults, who unwittingly, plant seeds of discouragement in children. To such parents and adults, we say, "cease the unfair comparison and instead help children with self-esteem – build them up, affirm them so that they can develop to see themselves as good as anyone else, achieving their true potentials."

As we ponder our growing, we recall how often some adults would say, "children must be seen and not heard." Sure enough, many of you might have been called "Curious Katie," or told " you are too nosey" or "you are too curious," if you asked questions about what something is or why something is the way it is. Some parents believe that 6-8-year-olds during this stage of development should not be asking questions - they should not exhibit any form of curiosity. What these individuals do not understand is that **curiosity** is still part of development and learning as it was in the earlier stage of development. Hence, it is at this level, only to a higher degree. The questions children ask at this level are more serious. There is a desire to know how things work and the reason behind them. They want to understand the workings of nature, why things are the way they are, and the way people are. Their desire to understand is not aimless and meaningless. All they want is to acquire knowledge. One of our relatives tells this story. He and his brother kept looking at the clock on the wall and wanted to know how it worked. Instead of asking their parents, who probably could not explain either, they decided to explore on their own. One night while everyone was asleep, they took the clock down and pulled it apart, trying to find out about the sound. They successfully pulled it apart but could not put it back together. Children just want to know, but the undiscerning parent might see this as a destructive behavior rather than a desire to learn. Parents who allow their children to ask questions without labeling them will have a significant impact on their children's development by channeling curiosity into teachable moments.

Whether it is pulling apart a clock, a toy, or another item, children are also learning to do things on their own. They are beginning to become independent of parents by trying to seek answers on their own. Parents can use this opportunity to talk with their children because they are open to talking. While children are learning about **independence,** they are still very much connected to their parents and want that closeness with them. Talking with them is one meaningful way to maintain closeness. Engage them in a discussion that encourages positive thinking. Engage them in problem-solving talks, which open their minds to cause and effect. Make things with them and discuss why some things will or will not work when put together in a certain way. Parents need to use the opportunity not only to engage their children in discussions but also to listen to them. Children are open to trying new things, free to gain new experiences, as well as expanding themselves.

As children move toward the next stage of development, many new skills emerge, and others mature. Their ability to group things, sequences things, grasp a pencil correctly, their ability to write or draw, understand number concepts, and read increases with each year. They are by no means competent in these areas at the beginning, but as they get closer to age eight, they become more confident, self-assured, and responsible. Parents need to provide healthy environments where these skills can be encouraged and developed, thereby preparing the child for a bright future.

Pre-adolescence (Tween years) stage development is quite different from the preceding stages and demands even more care on the part of parents as they seek to influence their children. Many parents believe that once their children have reached the ages of 9-12, they can relax because "they have passed the worst," as some like to say. In one sense, it might well be, but in another sense, the worst is still ahead. Some educators call this stage the "**Pre-adolescence or Tween Years**"[9] And rightly so. If one knows anything about this age group, they can genuinely attest to the appropriateness of this title. Children at this stage begin to get what was lacking in the first two stages. Now they enter into a subtle period of growth. Their physical, mental, and social dimensions experience much development. Besides, this stage marks the beginning of thought and ideas about their career paths. These developments move them toward understanding the world around them and how they should interact with it. The child/ren desire more independence from parents and instead more connections with their peers. While many parents might be happy to see the growth and development of their child/ren, others might be frustrated and confused by the new events they are seeing. They feel that the child who, a year or so ago, was open to discussions with them is now becoming secretive, self-assured, and exhibiting profound confidence in their newfound skills. Moreover, they are expressing interest in the opposite sex.

Because many parents are protective, the thought of losing their child/ren to maturity can cause them to strangle the child/ren's development. On the other hand, there are those parents who tend to be lax. They rejoice at the growing independence of their child/ren and all the other developments they are seeing and treat their children as adults before they are ready for such. This attitude can have devastating results, as well as the lives of their preadolescents.

Lack of knowledge on the part of parents can be detrimental in the long run. To work with them effectively, parents need to be proactive rather than becoming frustrated and discouraged. Many parents are frightened when they sense their sons or daughters asserting their independence. The children who once sought parental approval for almost everything, who depended on them, the ones they trusted so much, the ones who valued their opinions, are changing. We have heard

---

[9]   childmind.org cf. https://www.ahaparenting.com/ages-stages/tweens.

many parents bemoaning that fact and in as much as they want to see their children grow up for various reasons; they are not ready for what is coming. A parent should understand that the health of their children depends on them. These years of new development can be frustrating for many of these children as well, because of what is happening to them. But these years are also exciting because they can explore and expand their knowledge. The list below shows some things that impact children at this level of development.

1. These years are periods of rapid changes physically. It is the beginning of puberty when children of both genders experience a myriad of bodily changes. There are changes in height, weight, strength - and especially boys; the bodies begin to assume adult features. The menstrual cycle for many girls begins around this stage. This time can be frustrating for many parents who, many times, are not sure how to instruct their children about the changes they are occurring. Children experiencing these changes are often confused and concerned. Puberty is a time of uncertainty, especially where parents are not knowledgeable about how to handle what's happening, and children don't know how to deal with the new changes spurred by the hormones.
2. As children grapple with the hormonal changes, there are increases in their cognitive development. They exhibit a willingness to learn new things. Their creative energies begin to blossom, and they take on the challenge of creating and building things. They are also more prone to find ways to explore new ideas and form attachments to different ideologies. As high levels of interest and creativity emerge, parents and adults should encourage these developments and provide the means where these developing skills can be honed.
3. While children continue to mature and go through the different stages of development, there are marked differences. For example, whereas children in the earlier stages of development have a short attention span, this stage displays a more sustained

attention span. They are developing more focused attention on what they do. Many develop a love for books and spend extended periods reading. The emerging skills of earlier years are now more substantial, and children become more confident in their abilities.

Parents and other individuals who work with this age group should be excited about sustained attention. Children are now able to take on tasks that demand a longer attention span. They are also able to handle more complex tasks. Also, they are now able to perform many activities independently. This new development should provide some relief as parents, and other adults need not hover over the pre-adolescents -middle-agers - perform some tasks.

4. These years also mark the development of the capacity to memorize crucial facts. However, with the availability of so much technology, we see more and more children relying on it than on the innate abilities which they have. Nonetheless, this age group is at one of the most fertile stages of their lives. As such, parents, teachers, other adults, must encourage them to use their memories to the fullest extent possible. Encourage them to memorize Bible passages, poems, songs, number facts, and other information to enrich their lives as they continue to develop. It is also the right time to encourage the proper attitude towards the pursuit of various tasks.

Even though preteens are now adjusting to the changes occurring in their bodies, they still exhibit behaviors that many parents might consider troubling. Some parents are still not ready for the **differences in moods** they are witnessing in their child/children. Often preteens become somewhat testy by beginning to talk back to adults to exert independence. Parents, on the other hand, seek to exercise authority to allow the child/ren to know that they are still in charge. This administration of authority, of course, sets up the conflict and might push children away from their parents. It is at this point that our children are very vulnerable and begin to gravitate toward gangs or exhibit other kinds of rebellious behaviors. What is most confusing to many adults about this stage of development is that while their children might demonstrate their need for independence, they also exhibit much fear, frustration, and doubt. These emotions can potentially mushroom into rebellion if parents misinterpret and mishandled them. The fear, frustration, and doubt they exhibit are part of the effort to reconcile their inner world. However, the intensity of the emotions they express decreases as they mature and come closer to the end of this stage. The turmoil, the fears, the worrying become more subtle as children mature. Parents might then sense a calmness in their child/ren's demeanor even though there might be much passion about likes and dislikes.

Alongside the likes and dislikes that preteens display is a **Perfectionist** attitude - wanting to be perfect. If ever the child/ren sense failure, temper tantrums, anger, impatience, and much confusion might appear as in the very early stages. Parents, however, can make the difference by being patient, cautious, and loving in dealing with their son/daughter. In today's world, many become pre-occupied with sports. Such preoccupation consumes much of their time, to the dismay of many parents, who do recognize this as part of the developmental stages. Preoccupation with sports pushes preteens to develop interests in the rules of the game because they want to be good at what they do. It also enables them to gain an understanding of each other through play. Coming closer to the end of this stage of development, they become sports enthusiasts where they learn what it means to cooperate and compete. The spirit of competitiveness and cooperativeness are necessary for integrating and participating in all kinds of activities in which they have high interests.

While the spirit of **competitiveness** is essential in the developmental process, it can potentially create tension in the home through sibling rivalry. Siblings might even be competing for parental attention or develop the feeling that one is better than the other. Interestingly, many parents play into this type of competition by acknowledging the skills of one over the other. But parents should note that their role is to advocate for each child, knowing that each child is different -that each child develops at a different pace. Parents, instead of destroying your child/ren, build the esteem of each child. Help children to develop qualities that will enable them to have a healthy spirit of competition.

We have seen that there is an intense desire in our child/ren to do well what they desire – to be perfect. That is why when they are involved in competitive games, sports, etc., and they learn the rules of the game. Connected to the perfectionist attitude is the call for **justice** - what is fair. The call for fairness, in an earlier stage, is now heightened. As children mature, a stronger sense of justice emerges. They have a sense of what is right and wrong and preoccupied with what is fair. Many parents have heard these words, "it's not fair" when they have had to discipline their child in one form or another. Note that children do not necessarily equate fairness with what is right so that what seems right to a parent might be interpreted as not fair by the child. The child's insistence on what is appropriate should not be a deterrent to parents who must follow through on what is in the best interest of the child. Parents need to help children understand that what is right might not necessarily be fair.

Even though children are preoccupied with issues of fairness and justice, many times, the decisions they make are not made on sound judgment but rather on how one feels at a particular time. If you recall, this is called the feeling of years where emotions take precedence over sound judgment. While they seek justice, on the one hand, one must remember that their faculties are still not fully developed. Sound parental guidance is essential. When carried out with love and firmness rather than mean and hostile ways, children understand that parents are in charge and that rules are necessary for a cohesive family unit.

If one pays close attention to this age group, they realize that as children move toward adolescence, there is a gradual move toward **independence and freedom.** In all the postures they take, there is the call for freedom and independence. Such a shift broadens their view of life and enables them to identify who they are clearly. Children now begin to sharpen their abilities to give expressions to their thoughts and feelings. Even though children might express the desire for independence by their words and actions, they still need adult support. While parents should not hover over their children twenty-four-seven, they should not be lax in their responsibilities and assume that these children have attained the level of maturity to make crucial decisions on their own. Parents and other adults must stay close enough, not to strangle growth, and yet not too far to allow them to fall. Give them space but be at a safe distance where children feel that they are getting the freedom for which they seek but, at the same time, appreciating parental guidance.

A final note is that even though our children want their freedom, their independence, they expect parents to be **Consistent.** Our children love consistency. Although parents see signs of maturity in their children, many do not understand that even though children might be unhappy with a parental decision, they still expect parents to be consistent. Even at a young age, children are capable of capitalizing on any form of inconsistency they note in their parents. Parents must note that if something is wrong or right once, it should be that way every time it occurs in that context. Children can easily manipulate the inconsistencies they see in their parents and get their directions.

When parents understand the nuances in the developmental stages, they will have the ability and moral suasion to guide their children through the process. As parent-child relationships become stronger, they will see healthier children who can interact positively with the world around them.

Here are some things parents should understand about their developing children:

- They like the dramatic, and they are willing to participate in sports, plays, skits, and anything that utilizes drama.
- They are more tolerant and accept others willingly.
- They are more sociable as they begin to build stronger bonds and friendships.
- They like to socialize, but they are not necessarily concerned about who their friend is and who sits next to them.

- Their friends easily influence them. Peer pressure has much influence on how they act. Peer's acceptance is high on their list of important things.

Teen years are challenging (13-15): The most challenging years, according to some individuals, are those from thirteen through fifteen years. For some, it is the ending of elementary school and the beginning of middle school. For others closer to fifteen, it might be the end of middle school and the beginning of high school. These years are probably the most challenging period in the life of a child. Whenever we hear parents complain about their children in this stage, we seek to assure them then help them to understand that it is difficult for their children as well. It's as if they are caught in midstream somewhere; they are no longer our little children, and they are not young adults as yet. It is no wonder that some individuals call it the years. They are just trying to find who they are – crafting as it were, an identity. Children, during this period, enter the time of serious thought processes. Even though they are thoughtful, it is nonetheless a period of turbulence. The turbulent years bring numerous changes that cat teens toward adulthood. There are still changes occurring rapidly that impact their emotions, bodies, and minds.

Additionally, the parental expectations, the pressure to succeed in school, peer pressure, and the desire to belong are all factors with which this age group must grapple and cope effectively. These are indeed trying years for parents and children. In alluding to the seriousness of this period, one author says," The biggest danger for tweens is losing the connection to parents while struggling to find their place and connect in their peer world. The biggest danger for parents is trying to parent through power instead of through relationship, thus eroding their bond and losing their influence on their child as she moves into the teen years."[10] Although this quote references the "Tween" years, we believe

---

[10] https://www.ahaparenting.com/ages-stages/tweens

that it is also relevant here. Anyone who has to deal with teens at this stage knows the care that is necessary for working with teens.

Many times, as children struggle through these periods, parents are not sure how to deal with them. One individual suggests that It is a lot like parenting a toddler in some ways. The developmental stage is all about moving toward independence, not always gracefully or responsibly.[11] Yes, all adults pass through the changing and turbulent years of growing up, and while some things never change, others do. As life becomes more sophisticated and complicated, the more difficult it becomes for the youth growing up in this age. Hence the need for parents to be more proactive than reactive.

It's about hormones - they wreak havoc. Hormonal changes bring drastic changes to the body than in late childhood. Maturity is more dramatic and impacts the bodies of developing teens in multiple ways. Often many feel very stressed and frightened by the gravity of the changes occurring but opt not to express their feelings to their parents. While there are struggles with communicating with parents, hormones have significant effects on the emotions. At one moment, there is joy and excitement. And at another moment, there are sudden bouts of sadness and depression. It is almost a roller coaster ride for the youth with numerous ups and downs, highs and lows. These youngsters express their frustrations of developmental changes in many ways. The rapid changes might be overwhelming and might even manifest itself in some, as temper flares. Oft times, the onlooker might suggest that the youngster is out of control and just needs a "strong hand." This assumption might be correct in some instances, but many times the child is unaware of the source of the feelings and might be frightened about what is happening to him or her. Parents who understand, are knowledgeable about what's happening with their child/ren, and are patient with them, can influence healthy development at this time.

---

[11] https://www.ahaparenting.com/ages-stages/teens

The most dramatic impact of hormones on development at this stage is in the physical makeup of the child. Their limbs become longer, weight gains, acnes appear mainly on the face, and body hairs appear in different parts of the body. Long limbs might cause the child to be clumsy, awkward feel out of place and uncomfortable. The new physical features can potentially cause some teens to struggle with adjustment problems. In some cases, it can even lead to a feeling of being inferior. The mind also is impacted significantly by puberty. The child's sense of reasoning is now developing, and therefore, the ability to evaluate situations more clearly.

Have you ever suffered from a broken limb? Does that limb feel like the other unbroken? We have had broken limbs and understand how clumsy it can be. Well, think about youngsters with long limbs, weight gain and other changes which they have never experienced before. Are these teens frightened about the changes? Are the changes in them challenging? Many adults seem to forget those phases in their experiences. We have heard many parents berating their youngsters when they break things or when liquids spill or things fall to the ground. There seem to be no understanding of what these youngsters are experiencing. Some parents are even reluctant to provide their teens with suitable clothing to facilitate the changes in body shape, size, and other noticeable features. Yet they expect their teens to behave as if nothing is happening to them.

Are there **expectations** for developing teen? Surely society, parents, school, and others have their hopes for this age group. And quite often our expectations manage to make the development more complicated for these. Many of the expectations are explicit, but there are many unstated expectations. We expect that youngsters should act independently, that they should think abstractly, and behave maturely. In essence, we tell them to "act like adults." But the demands are overwhelming. They are complicated because there is no clarity of expectations. As a result of the mixed messages we send, many teens might behave in inappropriate and negative ways. Parents and other stakeholders must have realistic expectations - expectations that are doable and reachable for the youth.

Growing up for our children is not only a roller coaster ride, but it is also filled with many **contradictions.** Aside from the expectations of society, home, and school, teens have their agenda. They want to integrate into their peer group. They want to be a part of the group to feel a sense of belonging. They want to fit in and find ways of fitting into that group. No youth wants to be an outsider. They will fit in at all costs, whether by the use of clothing, hairstyles, gang involvement, involvement in sports, music, and or risky behaviors. In seeking to fit in, the youth is saying that he/ she is becoming more **independent** and less dependent on family structures, which traditionally gave support. And yet, while there is the deep need to fit in, they still expect parental support. They do expect parents to understand their desires and affirm them.

The attitude of teens often sends mixed messages to those parents who are unaware of what's happening in the lives of teens. How can parents know when their child is seeking to declare his/her independence? Whenever children are establishing their **independence**, they try to challenge parental authority. They are ready to talk back and even shout at parents over what could be considered straight forward requests. Many also become defiant and refuse to comply or cooperate with parents in carrying forward simple activities. In many instances, there is a high level of disrespect for the authority of the parents.

Here are some noticeable traits that might concern parents during this period of development:

- Unpredictability - not being sure of what next to expect
- Grumpiness
- Demanding
- Selfish
- Moodiness or temperamental
- Becoming easily upset

Despite the negatives that one can find in this age group, there are many positive aspects which are also present. However, many adults are so disturbed by the negative side of growing up that they tend to overlook the positives. When children begin to challenge parental authority or tarnish the parenting image, parents might become inflexible and exacerbate the situation. At the onset of what might be considered a challenge to parental authority, many parents begin to ask, "who is this new person we are seeing?" Some even question their parenting skills by asking, "What wrong have we done?" Be assured that it might be nothing wrong that you have done. It's only a new phase of development. As difficult as it might seem, parents should understand that their children are struggling too. If parents do not understand this stage of development or try to educate themselves as to the manifestations, they run the risk of helping to destroy their children. Some parents might be culpable for other inappropriate behaviors that the child/ren might exhibit but are not. Some parents might be frightened because the older son or daughter was not like that. One word of caution – if you have not learned it yet- each child is different; love that child for the variety he/she brings to your life.

As Christian parents God expects us to be in charge of our child/ren's life despite the developmental changes. We have a responsibility to find ways of relating to them so that they can develop in healthy ways. Now, are parents ready to accept the multitudinous challenges, emotions, and attitudes they encounter in their teens? How well can they handle some of the following that they might see in their children?

- Defiance
- Negativity – "NO" means "no" gives the rationale for the response
- Feelings of being separate and unique
- Conflicting emotions that bring frustration
- Awkward body growth
- Incomplete thought patterns and emotions that run the spectrum –confident and competent – tears, tantrums dependence

- Giving more prominence and credence to the opinions of their peers than their parents.
- They are making crucial decisions and choices based on the suggestions and opinions of peers rather than their parents.

If parents make use of all the resources and materials available, they will be able to build at least a working relationship with their children.

The Latter Teens Years 16-19 is the time which many anticipate, while many parents dread it. Teens are looking forward to graduating from high school and going to college while parents are worried about their child having to leave home or the additional expenses of college in a few years. Teens see themselves not as minors anymore but moving rapidly toward adulthood. Parents might see them moving toward adulthood but still not fully matured, so in a sense, they are still teens.

Yes, these late teen years are more challenging for both ones for both teens and parents. Some teens feel that they have arrived and cannot wait to get out on their own. On the other hand, parents sense that they are losing hold on that dear child they held in their arms not too long ago. They are afraid to let go thinking that they must hold on. For many parents, especially mothers, there could be a feeling of let-down. It is the kind of feeling one might get when a trusted boss for whom they've worked for 38 years just fired you without explanation. There can is much hurt, pain, anger, and even resentment because of the tireless efforts put into ensuring the growth of the business. For some parents, the feeling might not be as extreme but certainly sets the stage for struggles, confrontations, heartaches and heartbreaks, and a host of challenges and disagreements.

As children grow, they will always want to separate from their parents. They want to be independent. But many parents have serious challenges when their children are exhibiting high levels of independence. They hold onto them and not ready to accept that the babe born yesterday is now in the late teen years and prepared for college or in college. Parents must **learn how to let go**. Allow your teen to develop. Build a relationship of trust with them and act as mentors and models. It is undeniable that these later years are indeed difficult ones for both teens and parents. Teens feel that they have arrived, and parents' sense that they are losing hold on their children.

Often, parents want to hold on to their children as long as they can. They believe that they have to cater to every need of their teen. Many times, we substitute materials things for real genuine love. If, as parents, we would ask teens what they need most, likely we would be pleasantly surprised to find that what we think teens want is not the case. In as much as many teens will lead parents to believe that they are independent and do not need them, deep down, if pushed to the truth, teens will confess their need for parental guidance.

Several years ago, just after the Columbine massacre, the famous talk show host, Oprah Winfrey aired a program featuring teens and their parents. Many parents received a shocker from their teens' responses. Whereas many parents saw themselves working to the death to supply the material needs of their teen son or daughter, the teens had other ideas. The teens reiterated to the shocked parents that their demands were not necessarily the material things that they were working hard to give them, but rather the time spent with their family. It was not just time, but they wanted attention from their parents so that they could feel special. They also wanted to hear the words from their parents, "I love you." Not only do they want the feeling of being loved, but more so hearing parents say those words. Such words, for the teens, are crucial to their well-being and development.

America has had to learn a few sad lessons from the rash of school killings, which made the headlines from 1999 until the present. Teens from affluent homes went on shooting rampage in schools and some communities, killing several teachers, students, and anyone else in their path. Such students were not deprived of material things but indeed of love. While parents were out, their teens were in the confines of their rooms, strategizing how to destroy others. They had money, they had cars, but they needed parental guidance through the trouble-filled years. Having grown three sons, now watching four-teen grandchildren grow, and besides, taught middle schoolers, high schoolers, and college, for over forty years, we have had the unique opportunity of interacting with thousands of teens. We attest to the fact that teens crave quality time from parents, teachers, pastors, coaches, and anyone willing to share time with them even though they are asserting their independence.

Teens certainly need adult guidance and input as they begin to move rapidly toward adulthood. The late teen years is a continuation of the early teen years with violent episodes still impacting their lives. They are still confused because of the physical and emotional changes they are experiencing. At the same time, they face **pressures** from several fronts. On the one hand, they must deal with peer pressures that demand that they fit in and, at the same time, must participate in teen activities.

On the other hand, parents are demanding high academic performance; teachers are expecting class involvement and task completed on time and efficiently. At the same time, many participate in sports or other extra-curricular activities, and in some cases, holding a job. The pressures brought on often impact some teens negatively.

While the pressures are impacting teens, and while they might be demanding their independence, the **uncertainties – the unknowns** are many. They are maturing but have not attained adulthood. They are still seeking an identity of their own. Thus, it is often a difficult period. Teens think that they are independent and want to be independent, but at the same time, they are dependent on parents for sustenance. Teens, however, despite their lack of knowledge of the unknown, want to declare independence. If it means disassociating themselves from parental values, they will make clear who they are becoming. An article from The Center for Parenting Education notes, "One very effective way that **teens separate themselves from their parents is by rejecting the parents' values.** If teens have not been allowed to voice an opposing view all along, they may rebel more strongly in the adolescent years as a way of decisively differentiating themselves from their parents."[12] They might sometimes engage in strange ways and even dangerous behaviors. Some might become involved with drugs, connecting with gangs, tattooing their bodies in every imaginable place, and dropping out of school. Others, however, might seek to show their detachment from parental values by the way they dress, friends they hang out with and aligning with cliques that share their values. They may also experiment with new values, ideas, and anything that they think will define who they are. This effort at transformation may be uncomfortable for parents, but the move away from parental norms and values are but few of the teenage phenomenon. Although teens might not know the path ahead, many will defy parental wisdom and rush forward because their friends are doing it.

Despite the turbulence and the negatives that adults tend to see in the later teen years, parents need to remain hopeful because there are bright moments as teens mature. Teens do not **stay** encased in their battles against parental norms and values, but as they get older, they are beginning **to accept the changes** taking place in their bodies. The period of rapid growth slows as they into early adulthood. By age, 14-15 girls tend to reach their maximum height while boys grow until they are about sixteen. The slowing of growth marks the transition from childhood into adulthood. The body is preparing itself for the move toward adulthood. Boys tend to gain muscles while girls gain fat. The physical contours of the body are quite evident, especially in. Some girls might be excited about what they see in the mirror, while some are rather shy. Boys experience a drop in the voice, which can be a source of frustration for them. We have worked closely with our youth choirs and note the frustration and disappointments of some young men as they were not able to sing some of the songs sang earlier. There was one young man in particular, who had a rich first tenor. One

---

[12] https://centerforparentingeducation.org/library-of-articles/indulgence-values/values-matter-using-your-values-to-raise-caring-responsible-resilient-children-what

night as he went to choir and opened his mouth to sing the lead for a specific song, a raspy tone came out instead of the pitch to which he was accustomed. Some of the young ladies laughed, but fortunately, we were there and quickly explained what happened. The director wisely allowed him to sing in the range where he was comfortable. Yes, it can be uncomfortable as those who are unaware of developmental stages.

As changes in youngsters continue, and they begin to accept their physical changes, they begin to expand their social outreach. The bodies start to take on adult proportions, and so the **attraction to the opposite sex** is highly essential. Teens begin to build relationships and develop the skills that will sustain such relationships. Teens will further develop those skills as the need for bonding in groups become evident while at the same time, they will relate closer to some in the groups than others. They become more selective in their relationships. They seek to spend more time with some and not with others. Some parents become frightened as their teens want to spend more time with a specific person and present themselves as a couple. Social development, however, is not just about dating; teens also wish to have an education and jobs as part of their development. These are important for developing independence as they become more detached from the traditional groups of which they were a part before the teen years.

As teens begin to understand and accept the changes in their bodies, as they realize that their bodies have taken on adult proportions, they begin to become **emotionally detached from their parents.** Instead of being happy about the developments in the lives of their children, many parents feel a sense of rejection. But teens want an identity of their own and therefore begin to detach emotionally from their parents to do so. They want independence. They want their own identity and not their parents". This period of transition is a rather unsettling one for teens, and so, parents should not feel that they have lost a son or a daughter, but also consider the turmoil in the mind of their child/ren. Lack of understanding on the part of parents can heighten the emotional chaos and tensions as teens seek greater independence while at the same time, desire the protection of the home. They respect their parents and others and want to be seen as responsible.

Alongside of transitioning toward adulthood, teens begin to have **their dreams** they have about what or where they want to be in life. They set goals that they want to achieve and strive to meet them. Many parents need to be mindful of their teens' thoughts and feelings. Teens seem to set their intellectual goals based on what they see as their priority and what they will need for life. Many might refuse to accept suggestions from adults, even though their life goals might be unrealistic at times. Parents might feel a sense of rejection and hurt when teens dismiss the goals that they have for them. The teens want to function according to what they believe are their needs.

We have seen many teens as they enter college, focus on what parents want them to do and not what they had chosen to do in the first place. Often, they complete college and are unfulfilled because they fulfilled parent's dreams and not theirs. They might even work in the field of study but never happy until they turn to the goal, they had set earlier on in their teen years. As parents, we all have big dreams for our children and want to see them succeed. Many times, the professional choices we have for our children are unrealistic and not in line with the child's abilities and personality. Yet many parents continue to force their dreams on their children even to the point of threatening to dispossess them or withdraw financial support.

> **As parents, we must understand that our teens are not the little children of yesteryear - playing with toys and seeing everything in the concrete. They are maturing and moving toward adulthood.**

Many a parent seeks to fulfill their unmet dreams in their children. Some will go to extremes in pressuring their children to do what they want them to do, at the risk of losing a son or a daughter. Some parents are professionals and have the dream for their children to be like them. The challenge is that both parents have different careers, but each parent begins to make their pitch for their profession to the teen. Where ever this happens, teens can be confused and overwhelmed. The tragedy might be that the child feels caught between parents and finally does nothing with his or her life. We are not suggesting that parents should become uninvolved with the career goals of their children. Teens do need our careful guidance, but a parent should be cautious not to impose their wills on their children. Parents who are aware of the needs of their teens and their developmental stages will understand their children's need for independence. The child/ren's quest to be independent is not about the rejection of parental dreams and values. We've all been there; but how soon do we forget.

As teens progress in their development, they must learn to set their goals for the future and begin to prepare themselves to take on those roles. Parents, on the other hand, must understand that our teens are no longer little children playing with toys and seeing everything in the concrete. Instead, they are developing into intelligent beings who can participate in intellectually stimulating conversations with a clear understanding of the abstract. Their conversations demonstrate the development of strong cognitive abilities and mastery of the subtleties of communication. In effect, our teens are getting ready to take on adult qualities. Parents should be excited instead of being frustrated about their child's/children's attitudes. Work with your child/children instead, and help them to fulfill their dreams and aspirations.

Conclusion

There are several kinds of parents who impact their child/ren's development in different ways. Some involve themselves in their child/ren's life from birth and will continue to guide. At the same time, they recognize that their teens are becoming thinkers and need less adult guidance. Parents who treat teens with respect, learn that teens are individuals who need their space to develop. Then there are those parents who, tragically, are too lax or permissive and give teens no guidance at all. They allow them to live anyhow and do whatever they want. There are no limits, and no structures in place to ensure a successful transition to adulthood. There are those parents who seek to influence their children when it's too late. They try to "lock the gates after the horse has been let out" and then might blame the children, blame the school system or any other they can find to blame, or might even spend the rest of their lives lamenting what happened to their child/ren. There are also those parents who want to hold a firm hand; they are rigid, overprotective, and controlling. Such parents seek to monitor the entire life of the teen. The teen has no freedom to state his/ her views about life and where he/she would like to go. This sort of parental rigidity leads to rebellion and conflict after conflict. In effect, a son or daughter might become angry and bitter, and desires to sever connections with the home at the earliest chance. Many a son or daughter becomes involved in gang relationships and membership where they feel loved accepted and respected. Others move toward a life of promiscuity where they think that that is a true expression of independence and individuality.

Parental permissiveness and rigidity are two extremes that are dangerous when dealing with teens. Parents must respect the development of their teens. Parents must appreciate their sons'/daughters' ideas. Parents should learn to listen to their sons and daughters and use these moments to create healthy dialog. Parents, PLEASE! Always seek to keep the lines of communication open with your children.

Parents who take the time to understand who their children are, and where their children are, will receive many surprises by the choices their children make. Many times, children turn to the profession of their parents without cajoling or fighting. The fact is that most often, teens follow the model they have seen; if parents are patient, their teens do well. The result will be teens and parents who are happy and having the uttermost respect for one another.

Many persons might wonder about the relevance of this discussion in our present context. To clarify, we argue that if parents misunderstand the changes that occur in their children's lives, they, along with their children, will be frustrated and destroyed.

Parents who are unaware of where their children are, often make unrealistic demands on them. From our observations and discussion and being parents of grown children, we can talk about the harm that we have seen when parents try to parent through ignorance. One experience we have had to deal with is of a parent who always whipped her child because the child's development was not where she thought the child should be. The parent sought to measure what should have happened to her child based on what she thought was the norm for a child at that age. We tried to reason with that mother by helping her know that the child was on target and would develop the necessary skills at the appropriate time. Today, that child is at the highest level of the educational ladder, but of course, she retains vestiges of anger from the whippings received for not developing with her peers. Many hours of counseling and intervention have helped somehow, but the emotional scars are still evident. We have seen other children of the ilk just identified, they, of course, are not so blessed with the resources to extricate themselves.

In effect, "To be forewarned is to be forearmed." As youngsters seek to find themselves and take ownership of their lives, we might be helpful to them by looking at what took place at the various stages of their lives.

QUESTIONS FOR REFLECTION

1. What do you understand by the question, "Do you know where your children are?"
2. How does the question, "Do you know where your children are?" affect parental advocacy?
3. Concerning parental advocacy, what do you think of the suggestion, "To be forewarned is to be forearmed"?

4. How beneficial is the knowledge of developmental stages to any parent?
5. How can this knowledge aide in the structuring and restructuring of environments, targeting children at their levels of functioning?
6. In what ways will the knowledge of the development through stages help parents in guiding children to develop values that last?
7. Can parents use the information in their role as advocates for their children?

CHAPTER III

Do You Know Who Your Children Are?

Four teenagers sitting in an office were given a copy of the chart below and were asked to write a word or a sentence that properly described who they were. It was quite fascinating watching them. After they had gazed at the chart for quite a while, they seemed jittery and frustrated. They were soon asking for word definitions, but it was clear that they were not so much concerned about word definitions, but worried about writing down whom they thought they were. Did they know or did they not know? Maybe they did not know, for growing up is a time of self-discovery, it is time of finding out who one is.

Personality	Often when we think of personalities we think of the choleric, sanguine, melancholic, and phlegmatic. Myers Briggs Personality Type Indicator test identifies at least 16 types but some persons think there are more • ISTJ - The Duty Fulfillers • ESTJ - The Guardians • ISFJ - The Nurturers • ESFJ - The Caregivers • ISTP - The Mechanics • ESTP - The Doers • ESFP - The Performers • ISFP - The Artists • ENTJ - The Executives • INTJ - The Scientists • ENTP - The Visionaries • INTP - The Thinkers • ENFJ - The Givers • INFJ - The Protectors • ENFP - The Inspirers • INFP - The Idealists Other ways that we describe personalities suggest that they are: Energetic, jittery, fiery, organized, disorganized, patient, kind, distrustful, distractive, Exuberant, listless, moody, affectionate, caring, talkative, quiet, self-centered, and so forth.
Attitude	Playful, rebellious, docile, sloppy,
Character	Honest, dishonest, hardworking, thoughtful, hopeful, graceful
Behavior	Active, hyperactive, acceptable, unacceptable, normal, abnormal, rational, irrational
Uniqueness	Birthmark, special gifts, talents, capacities, creative, singing, not afraid of loneliness

Habits	Good, bad, controlled or uncontrolled, health habits, sexual habits – controlled or promiscuous, internet - controlled or junkie,
Strengths	Intelligent, Commonsensical, Caring, loving, forgiving
Weaknesses	Addictions, risky behaviors, attentive, hyperactive, easily bored, laidback, trusting, suspicious, nervous, morose, vengeful
Anxieties	Personality anxieties, the contexts of anxiety - school, church, home, or peer relationships. The timing of the anxiety, the impact of the anxieties.
Commitments	To family and friends, studying, sports, respect, survival, confidence

While children and youngsters are struggling to define who they are, they are also concerned whether or not their parents know them as they are maturing. In several of our workshops we have attempted to find out what children think of their parents' knowledge of them. These children have expressed such concerns and frustrations as follows:

- I wish my parents knew that I am the kind of person who wishes to achieve higher things in life.
- I wish my mother knew how much I love her.
- I wish my parents knew what kind of relationship I had with the Lord.
- I wish my parents knew what kind of relationship I had with my friends.
- I wish my parents knew that I need their attention more.
- I just wish my parents would know how scared I am of growing up.
- I wish my parents knew that I prefer their attention instead of all the things they buy me.
- I wish my parents could really know how much I want to leave home and be on my own.
- I wish that my parents would say no to me sometimes.
- Ii wish my parents didn't spoil me so much.

- I wish my parents could understand that I am not a child anymore.
- I wish I could tell my parents how afraid I am to leave home.
- I wish my parents knew how hard it is to make friends.
- I wish my parents would try to understand how I think sometimes.
- I wish my parents would stop me when I get out of line sometimes.
- I wish my parents would spend more time with me and just talk to me.
- I wish my mother would listen so I could tell her how I feel.
- I wish my parents would stop treating me as a baby and treat me according to my age.

Even though all of the above suggest the lack of parental awareness, one might get the feeling that many parents do not really know if the children's perceptions of what they wished their parents really know of them, is correct. If one should take the chart above and ask parents "Do you [really] know who your children are?" one might find the reaction quite interesting.

Who children are

Most parents might have a general understanding of the attitudes of children, namely, their:

- **Simplicity:** Children lack complexity, they do not know a lot about deception, and they "play by the rules."
- **Loyalty:** Even after children have been hurt, they easily forgive and seek to reconcile their relationship. As adults we pout, become angry and seek to destroy each other for reasons we cannot explain.
- **Dependence:** Children depend on anyone around them to manipulate their environment.

- **Trust:** Except they are coached otherwise, children tend to trust those who are around them. This, as you know, opens the path to abuse.
- **Adaptability:** Because of their vulnerability, and dependency, children always adapt easily. Sometimes they wish to fight back, but because they do not have the tools to fight, they quickly resign themselves to new situations.
- **Teachableness:** Children are teachable; they are ready to learn adult behavior. They imitate adults in language, culture and actions. Just as it is easy for them to learn, so it is for them to unlearn and relearn.
- **Un-beguiled love:** Children are very open to relationships - they are receptive to love. If they are not guided to positive love, they quickly accept substitutes.
- **Vulnerability:** On a general basis child are vulnerable and even more vulnerable when they have been abused. They can easily give themselves to adults with whom they feel affirmed and thus be destroyed.
- **Innocence:** Children are naïve or innocent. They often do not think of the evils that can happen to them. They are not usually afraid of anything until they are taught fear. They like to explore life and are often led into difficulties that more experienced adult will seek to avoid.
- **Honesty:** Children are generally honest; they often do not think of the long-term consequence of their actions. They are not able to do the kind of analysis that make adults deceptive. Children see facts and they speak of them as they see them. They speak in terms of black and white. Adults will see facts and deny them. When a child comes to church as says to a pastor or another adult "Did you know that Mommy and Daddy are not sleeping in the same bed?" is demonstrative of the depth of concern and honesty the child has. Although the parents can deny that as much as possible, but we have to accept the facts the child gives, of course without betraying the child's trust. Judges,

counselors and others know all too well, that in the majority of cases, a young child's story is honest.
- **Humility:** Children are not filled with the prejudices of adults; they learn much of their pride and prejudice from adults. They are not as pretentious as adults. They are willing to submit themselves to the authorities around them.
- **Receptivity:** Children are like sponges - they soak up everything.
- **Obedience:** Children are obedient, they understand authority and power wherever it is in place and easily responds to it.
- **Creativity:** Children are creative. Their minds can see art in life and they like to experiment with things, to make something of it.
- **Friendliness:** Children are friendly. We have seen them interacting with other kids and note how quickly they can form friendships. They don't care about each other's color or complexion. They don't care whether they speak the same language. Except they are taught prejudice by their parents who sometimes call them aside, they will reach out quickly to others that they meet.
- **Religiosity:** Children have something about them that seems to be natively religious. Their response to God is often quite simple but serious. Dr. Robert Coles studied children of many world cultures and found that there is a depth of belief in most children.
- **Courage:** Generally, children are courageous. They are bold. Their fears are mostly developed from the adults with whom they mix. Children will take risks; we see them in sports how flexible they can be. They are not fearful of experimenting and experiencing new things.

Even though some might consider the above as mere theoretical notions, we suggest that they are helpful and should allow us to know that our children need our support, our protection, training and whatever else is needed for their development and ultimate survival.

Deeper knowledge

The work of parents as advocates for their children demands deep and personal understanding of who our children are. In acquiring such understanding, parents must look at both the constructive and unconstructive perceptive of whom our children are by answering the following questions. Are our children:

- Decisive or indecisive?
- Honest or deceptive?
- Respectful or rebellious?
- Disciplined or risky in behaviors?
- Controlled or strange in general relationships?
- Normal or addictive in personality and practices?
- Energetic or lax in conduct?
- Likeable or unlikeable in character?
- Tolerant or intolerant in attitudes?
- Prejudiced and arrogant?
- Capable or incapable?
- Able or disabled - Affected by any challenge such as Attention deficit disorder (ADD), Attention deficit and hyperactivity disorder (ADHD), Specific learning disability (SLD) Autism, Dyslexia, specific learning disability?

Being careful with identification

While we should know who our children are, we need to be careful that we are not too quick to label them or project ourselves upon them.

Labeling and Stereotyping: The world likes to affix labels and stereotypes on others. Many people are unconscious about the stereotypes and labels others place on them. At varied times in a culture, the climate seems open stereotypes but stereotypes can damage an individual emotionally. In our contemporary it seems that labeling makes life easier. Yes, it is easier if it's done on clothing, foods and other inanimate things. Labels are harmful when affixed to people. Labelling people is demeaning, it is not helpful, it is annoying. Labels tend to stick and children live up to the best and worst expectations.

Some time ago, a mother asked if she should test her children to know their IQ. We asked what was the motivation. Her children were doing well in school; they were way above their peers and getting enrichment classes. She just wanted to know their IQ to tell her friends how brilliant her children were. Many parents use the IQ to label their children. If we have two children in a family and both are tested and one receives a high score and another a low score, the tendency is to focus on the one with the higher score as if the score really tells the ability. We have heard parents based on IQ scores, determine what profession and what school each child will attend. The truth is that the test might tell more about the child's test taking strategy rather than the ability.

Projection and self-serving biases: Often enough the labels we attach to our children are mere projections of our self-service biases. We do not know them or care to know them, but we put upon them images that we like or dislike. We project upon our children our adequacies and inadequacies, our strengths and shortcomings, our good and bad behaviors. What we project on our children, we help to create confusing picture of them.

Effective knowledge

Gaining effective knowledge of who our children are does not come by chance. It is a process which can be quite demanding, for it needs focused attention from very early. Parents need then, to explore and use some of the following approaches to build a broad knowledge base about their children.

Careful observation: As soon as children are born the alert parent will begin to observe them, - how many fingers they have, how many toes, what is their personality like and so on. The changes that they make in their daily development should also be observed with carefulness. If a parent is two distant or detached from their child/ren, they will not know. This is why parents should not pass off the care of their children to others because they will miss out on the uniqueness of those children. They might miss the first step, the first word and so much more. The most careful observer of any child ought to be the parents.

Dialogue: Aside from careful observation, nothing else can teach a parent about a child more than a healthy dialogue. Dialogue demands speaking with a child and listening to the him/her. Dialogue demands honesty and openness.

Giving time to relationship: Personal knowledge demands time to be open. Even children need time to build trust, for a healthy relationship is foundational to trust. When children trust their parents, they tend to be more open. On the other hand, parents should express trust in their children as well. A solid relationship of trust needs time on both sides.

Counseling services: Parents today do not have to struggle on their own to train their children. There are parenting counselors, school counselors, psychological counselors, social work counselors, pastoral counselors and many other kinds of counselors who can be of service in clarifying and sharing their understanding of who our children are. While these services are available, some parents' culture determines the extent to which they will or will not accept such support services. This kind of cultural bias create challenges and hinders many parents from getting the help they desperately need in order to support their children in an effective manner.

Understanding the total demand

Yes, to gain full knowledge concerning our children puts upon us a total demand. For those who might question why all the fuss about knowing who our children are, the answer is quite simple: "Once a parent, always a parent until death do parents and children part. Understanding our children is a lifelong process. Conscientious parents are always observing their children and seeking to bring out the best in them. The more they observe, the more they see and understand in spite of age. Parents who are seeking for understanding will always have insights.

When parents begin to gain insights into the individuals their child/children is/are becoming or might become, they have the opportunity to give guidance. If one senses that there are tendencies that might be negative, they can explore possibilities for correction. Parents can know where they need to invest more time and energy to effect change. Very often, some parents see tendencies but are clueless about what's happening while others might choose to ignore on the premise that time will correct it. For example, a child who throws temper tantrums for everything should not be allowed to persist with such attitude for time will not change it. Parents must act early before such an attitude becomes engrained in the child. On the other hand, parents might see very positive attitudes and, in some cases, overpower their children or do not affirm the child in order to strengthen what they are seeing. We get from our children what we put in. In other words, it takes time and effort to really understand who our children are. It takes thorough knowledge and understanding to know when to pull back or become engaged.

The Bible gives several examples of parents who knew from very early who their children were. Mary and Joseph are models of profound respectability. On the basis of divine revelation, they knew that Jesus was the Son of God. Of course, such revelation is possible to all parents who are submissive to God. Because Mary and Joseph sensed who Jesus was, they recognized their duty to spend countless hours training and guiding Him. Many persons have falsely assumed that because Jesus was the son of God that he grew up on his own. However, before he reached the age of accountability his life was guided by his earthly parents who had to discern who he was.

Another parent that the Bible tells who knew his children well was Jacob. In Genesis 49 he spoke prophetically about the character of each of his twelve sons without apology. As one reads the history of the tribes of Israel, one senses that Jacob's predictions came true. The obvious reality is that he had great intimacy with each of his sons. And while it is true that he had many more years to relate to them and exhibit control over them than parents do today, it should never be felt that parents today should have any less knowledge of who their children are.

In fact, what Marshall Fritz argues in his article on parenting, "Restoring Parental Responsibility for Education" [13] is an issue that we need to focus on in all aspects of our children's lives. We are to know them and take responsibility for health, clothing and the contexts of safety and security in which they live. We are not to "hand off" our responsibilities for knowing and training to schools, governmental agencies and churches. A great promoter of parental responsibility from more than a century ago says it this way:

> Parents, you carry responsibilities that no one can bear for you. As long as you live, you are accountable to God to keep His way… Parents who make the word of God their guide, and who realize how much their children depend upon them for the characters they form, will set an example that it will be safe for their children to follow.
>
> Fathers and mothers are responsible for the health, the constitution, the development of the character of their children. No one else should be left to see to this work. In becoming the parents of children, it devolves upon you to co-operate with the Lord in educating them in sound principles.
>
> How sad it is that many parents have cast off their God-given responsibility to their children, and are willing that strangers should bear it for them! They are willing

---

[13] Marshall Fritz, "Restoring Parental Responsibility for Education," *The Freeman: Ideas on Liberty* - July 1996, Vol. 46 No. 7, http://www.fee.org/publications/the-freeman/article.asp?aid=3868

that others should labor for their children and relieve them of all burdens in the matter.[14]

The lessons that we should take from this is that if we are to be good advocates for our children, we need to know who they are. We have an awesome responsibility and while we might not be able to correct flaws as when our children were younger, we still can make an impact through prayer, through dialog and through the depth of relationships we maintain with them.

QUESTIONS FOR REFLECTION

1. What do you understand by the question, "Do you know who your children are"?
2. What are some of the challenges parents might face when they do not know who their children are?
3. What are some of the benefits in helping our children to find out who they are?

---

[14] Ellen White (1952), Adventist *Home*, Hagerstown, MD: Review and Herald Publishing Association, 187

CHAPTER IV

How To Parent In A Digital Age

Living in an era of advancing technology

Technology has revolutionized our world and has just about overwhelmed us. The Millennial and the Z generations live in a digital world. They are "the digital generation." Although the generations might use the social platforms in different ways, with the Z Generation opting to use fewer platforms than the Millennial Generation, yet both generations are mostly digital. "Despite Global Web Index data showing that Generation Z spends longer time most days on social media than the Millennials (nearly 3 hours, vs. 2 hours 39 mins),"[15] yet they are both wholly digitally oriented."

In effect, the digital generations live on their smartphones, I pads, and computers, engaging in text messaging, writing and reading blogs, file sharing, photo swaps, Facebooking, Tweeting, Instagram messaging, Snapchatting, YouTubing, emailing, and doing other things that are

---

[15] https://wearesocial.com/blog/2018/03/three-differences-gen-z-millennials-use-social-media

digitally based. They own iPad, computers, smart televisions, play stations, and a host of other gadgets and platforms that are changing their world at the fastest pace in the history of any generation.

The December 2019 AARP Bulletin referenced what was suggested in the 1983 movie War Games. The young Matthew Broderick hacked into his school's computer to change a grade, has been brought into real life. A computer in the Downingtown Area School District, in Pennsylvania, was hacked to find out students' home-addresses with the intent of winning a large-scale water-gun fight. Sounds like a joke, but as the saying, attributed to someone who was run over by a car, goes, "what is a joke to you, is death to me."

The fact of interest for our present discussion, of course, is the impact that the digito-techno culture has, not only on society in general but also upon our children and their parents. It is especially troublesome for some parents, whose ability to parent effectively might not be what it should. In an article in *Psychology Today*, Diana Graber says:

> Parenting is tough, the pay is horrible, and you basically get one shot at doing it right. And that was before some genius invented the smartphone. That little go-everywhere, always-connected device makes raising kids even more challenging.
>
> While parenting is not for sissies, consider what it must be like to be a teen today. Your young brain is all wired and ready to test boundaries, connect with peers, and make poor decisions without care for long-term consequences—and you've got that very same smartphone in your possession. It almost seems unfair. Any kid who can survive modern adolescence without

suffering a digital mishap should win an Olympic medal.[16]

The digito-techno culture is profoundly pervasive in homes, at work, in schools, at the shopping centers, in hospitals, prisons, government offices, the military, media centers, entertainment industries, grocery stores, restaurants, gyms, airports, laundromats, zoos, libraries, nature preservation centers, churches, and everywhere. And what is more, parents and children, cannot get away from it. While at one time, one had to visit a theatre to see a movie or use a TV or a DVD or DVR player, today you get a video by downloading it on Netflix or a smartphone or other smart device.

Power, Possibilities, and Challenges for Families, as for Society

If a person were to go live in a cave, the digital world could still reach such a person, so instead of being overly horrified about its rapid development or seek to hide away, there is an enormous need to learn how to live in the new culture.

In effect, it is always important to understand that each new technology brings power, possibilities, and challenges. Let me date myself by sharing that, in my time growing up, I went to school with a **slate**. When bullies provoked some children, the children broke their slates and used a piece of it to chop at the ones who annoyed them. When we started to use the lead pencil to write in notebooks, some

---

[16] https://www.psychologytoday.com/us/blog/raising-humans-in-digital-world/201904/parenting-in-digital-age-what-experts-are-saying

children used the sharpened pencil to stab the ones with whom they had a conflict. Today students use social platforms to bully those they consider enemies. They post demeaning pictures or the fights in which they engage, just to humiliate the others. Does it mean that the slate, the pencil, the writing tablet, or the new digital platforms did not or do not have positive value?

The positive potentials are enormous, but while each new technology has its power and possibilities, it also offers challenges. At the time when social media was just beginning its explosion, an article written by Dr. Nicholas Carr, in the *Atlantic Monthly*, asked: "Is Google Making Us Stupid?" He was not just interested in Google, of course, but all media that function in the way that Google does. His concern was how new media affects the mind, how memory was being transformed, how attention to in-depth reading was being altered, and how life was being reprogrammed. He argued that while the web had become a "godsent," thus making research and information flow much more accessible; yet, it was chipping away at the capacity for concentration and contemplation. It seemed, to him, that the neural circuits in the brain, the part of the brain used for reading were negatively affected. Even much more extensive, he felt that there were notable changes in people's personal lives, such as changes in their personality, in a way that inevitability people begin "to take on the qualities of those technologies." In the area of language, the metaphors that people use to explain themselves to others are changing. People have changed how they communicate and how they make ethical decisions.[17]

In 2013 Dr. James Paul Gee followed with the same observation, in a preface to his book, *The Anti-Education Era: Creating Smarter Students Through Digital Learning*. Here is a brief quote of what he had to say:

---

[17] See Nicholas Carr, "Is Google Making Us Stupid?" *Atlantic Monthly*, (July/August 2008), 56-63 for a comprehensive view of the impact of web technologies on personal lives and society.

> I want to warn that digital tools are no salvation. They can make things worse just as quickly as they can make things better. They are great tools with which to become dumber just as they are great tools with which to become smarter. It all depends on how they are used. And key to their good use is subordinated to ways of connecting humans for rich learning and that they serve as tools humans learners own and operate and do not simply serve. Video games and social media will not make us smarter by themselves any more than books have.[18]

Gee also points to the impact on literacy by stating that the digito-tech culture has created "gaps" in literacy and other forms of learning. It is also creating different kinds of class structures. His conclusive point is that while the contemporary world thinks that we are smarter than other generations of humanity, instead of being smart, we are as dumb, and not any smarter than the generations behind us. That is, while our intelligence has led us to create a highly complex, fast-changing world, at the same time, we have made the world profoundly dumber and riskier.[19]

Many social scientists are very conflicted with the ongoing discussion as to whether the digital generation is being "dumbed down." The fact that the digital generation can find information quicker than generations of the past makes it possible that they do not filter or ask critical questions. Only a few will ask ethical questions about footnoting

---

[18] James Paul Gee (2013), The Anti-Education Era: Creating Smarter Students Through Digital Learning, New York: St. Martins Publishers. P. XIII.

[19] Ibid. The point of the whole book is that substantial changes had had profound unintended consequences. At the moment of revising this book, the stock markets over the world are reeling – dropping thousands of points in a single day. As is made clear, through the modern media, "If they sneeze in China, we catch a cold in the US," and the world over.

their research as in generations past. They rarely take time to make distinctions between truth and falsehood (fake news) as some other generations.

The digito-tech culture and contemporary and future concerns

Do we think that Carr, Gee, and others who are raising questions as to whether the digito-technological world is making us stupid, trivializing reality? We should not think so. The assessments they make should challenge us to think about the implications of the media with which we are so fascinated. They help us make the point that the systems that we have created for knowledge expansion and communication are outpacing our capacities to adjust. Or put another way, we might say, while we are facing new frontiers of power, we are also opening "demons in pandora's box,"- demons that are very challenging to be controlled. We might enjoy the freedoms, but we need to be concerned about our personal lives and values and that of our children.

Parents, teachers and all persons who bear responsibility in our homes, in our families or in public organizations are concerned with where the digito-tech culture is taking us. A look at the transformations from the Industrial Revolution can be instructive, for while these transformations brought development in education, personal freedoms, financial gains, and labor-saving convenience, numerous challenges resulted. Some of the ripple effects of the revolution were unhealthy working conditions, the breakdown of family structures, and the profound destruction of our ecological order.

Only a minuscule number of humanity understood the harmful effects of industrialization until it was too late. And today, it seems to be the same. But it is more challenging than many social scientists are expressing. Our digital world is way beyond our understanding. Robert Louis Stevenson is credited to say, "To travel hopefully is a better thing than to arrive."

Between parents and children

In March 2018, Dr. Alan E. Kazdin and Amber J. Rieff shared an article to help parents in their struggles with the enormous challenges facing parents. Such challenges are how parents monitor, oversee, and control the media that their children and adolescents are using. And here is what they said parents need to accept today:

- That the world of today includes all sorts of new technology. We can run from them, but we cannot hide from them. The terrorist leaders have come to find this out.
- That there is a vast range of activities and resources that one can do with these devices.
- That children and adolescents have a social world at their fingertips to connect with friends, relatives, strangers, predators, and others.
- That young people rely heavily on these applications as a primary means for interpersonal contact with others.
- That adolescents spend nearly 9 hours per day using screen-based media, 3 hours on their phones, 45 minutes of television and send/receive 30-100 texts on average in just one day. On a typical day, children spend at least 2 hours in front of screens on weekdays and twice that number weekends;
- That everything one might want on a screen seems available 24/7, and that includes the last things parents might want their children to see on the screen.
- That it is easy to download and purchase sought-after items that are otherwise unattainable or illegal.

- That one cannot take the apparent strategy of eliminating all technology from the child's or adolescent's environment. Education and school work at all levels rely on technology, and increasingly online "books" and reading materials, podcasts, little movies, and animation are all part of the young child's daily work and require access to technology.
- That over 50% of children over the age of 4 have their own television, and even more own tablets or other mobile devices.
- That 92% of one-year-olds have used a mobile device and children ages 3-4 can begin using these devices without the help of a parent or adult.
- That with children becoming increasingly familiar with, and having access to technology, we are not completely surprised to learn in the news that a 9-month old accidentally rented a car online.[20]

In effect, while parents need to embrace the new technologies, at the same time, they must understand the significance of being vigilant to save their children from self-destruction. The challenges each new technology brings to parents and children are just being discovered. In 2008 Peggy O'Crowley wrote in the *"Star Ledger,"* a newspaper in New Jersey that "Too much cell phone use by adults can lead to problems for kids." Today her conclusion is being verified. She pointed out that mothers, fathers, and other caregivers were compromising the safety of their children at playgrounds, community swimming pools, and in supermarkets by their constant talking on the phone and texting. She also pointed to the fact that the communication gaps between parents and children were widening.

Further, while parents are on their cell phones for an extensive amount of time, language exchange between them and their children

---

[20] https://alankazdin.com/challenges-of-the-internet-and-social-media-for-parents/

became very limited. Since interaction and stimulation are most important for children to learn to speak, many children are becoming more delayed at the beginning of their language development. The same observation can be made with the interaction between one child and another. We noticed it, when our grandchild or grand-nephews and nieces come to our home, or when we visit them, that they are on digital platforms or playing games on their phones or tablets, that they seem very isolated. We note the same isolation not only at home but also in church and social gatherings.

Uncontrolled use of gadgets can cause both parents and children to become overwhelmed, and often tension builds up in the family as is demonstrated in the following story. An anxious mother invited her pastor to her home to speak to her seven years old son. The pastor became overwhelmed, too as tried to help. The pastor shared this story with us later as we were discussing the challenges of parenting in a technological age. The mother felt her son had lost total respect for her commands. When she needed her son to attend to any chore, he would always be yelling from his room, "Just a minute Mom," and would forget to come. Upon his visit to the house, the pastor requested to speak first with her son in private. The pastor asked the boy to tell him about the problem he and his mother had. The little boy responded, "Pastor, I do not have a problem; my mother has a problem." Upon hearing the response, the pastor called in his mother. When the mother entered and seated herself, the pastor continued. "Your son said that he didn't have a problem, but that you have the problem." The pastor wanting to have more information, asked of the mother, "Tell me, what toys and media equipment does your son have in his room?" The little boy interrupted with, "Pastor, I have a TV, a play station, a computer, and a cell phone." Then the pastor said, "I can now see why there is a problem." The boy did not notice the change in the pastor's comment, but insisted, "No Pastor, I do not have a problem; my mother has a problem." Then the boy added without much thought, "A man got to do what he got to do." The pastor was so startled that he said a few words about respect, but felt the case demanded a counselor's attention. After recommending the name of a counselor to the mother, left feeling nothing but pity and sorrow. As the pastor drove off, the thought that consumed his mind was that the boy was right. The boy's mother had a big problem. Of course, the boy also had a problem. The world of new technology had caught up with them.

The above scenario might seem extreme, but it speaks to the situation in many homes. While the new technologies are now parenting children, parents have numerous concerns. They are asking several questions such as, what must I do? Where can I find help? What should be my most significant concern in the digital area of life? Where is the balance between children's use of the new media, and where and how to apply controls?

Parenting effectively in the age of digital media

Most parents who are dealing with the challenges presented by the new media have suggested that they are unaware of the depth of the challenges they are facing. They do not know how to create the kind of balance that would bring sanity to their environment. Here is a suggestive list of challenges collected from parents in our workshops, and our "How to" list.

The challenges

- Communication distancing between themselves and their children
- Communication separation between one person and others
- The possibility of tech addiction
- The invasion of privacy
- Anonymity – you do not know who is behind that which is written
- Information overload
- Compromised safety
- The impact of constant noise on the brain

- The development of impatient attitudes for anything that demands waiting
- Loss of boundaries in ethical behavior
- Mental and physical health risks
- Increasing violent behaviors
- Values erosion
- Extended boundaries to control
- The development of disrespect
- The destruction of truth and reality - Not everything on social media is true[21]

Managing the challenges

Having **identified** the challenges and **acknowledged** them, parents need to learn to **manage them**, so that there will always be positive outcomes in their behaviors and that of their children. No matter what new technology or media comes along, they will still create challenges. Parents need to establish some ground rules about how they are going to help their children face the challenges.

General rules

Here are some general rules that we have both presented over the years in our Legacy Seminars and what we have collected from parenting an educator, Dr. Kazdin, quoted earlier:

- Keep up with [some of] the rapidly changing digito-technology. It is hard to understand them all, but even if it means learning to learn from our children, learn something about them.

---

[21] e. We recommend that you read the book *Social Media and the Value of Truth*, edited by Berrin Beasley and Michell R. Haney, New York: Lexington Books, 2013

- Do not approach the new technology with a negative – fighting mind. Understand that technology is both liberating and enslaving.
- Speak to your children to understand the technology they are using and what it means to them. Understand what it should mean to you[22]
- Have some together time on the computer (tablet or smartphone) to help establish this is not just a solitary activity.[23]
- If you are blocking certain types of content, assume your child is likely to be skilled at getting around them, if not at home, then throughout the day at school.[24]
- Limit screen time.[25] Studies have shown that those who spend uninterrupted time on digital screens soon become addicted.
- Usually, explaining the challenges with a particular media, is not enough. "Parents might adopt the view that if they just inform the child of the dangers and reach some verbal understanding that will help. Certainly, explain things to the child. That has immense benefits well beyond this topic. Yet, explaining is not usually an effective method for changing behavior; that is, what one does. Explain, but more is needed."[26] We recommend making lists and hold the child to accountability.
- Decide when and how you are going to introduce your child to each technology (For example, ask how and when you will introduce and allow your child to own cell phone?)[27]
- Try to understand the personal costs of varied technologies such as those creating headaches, eye strains, muscle fatigue, muscular/skeletal injury, and back pain, etc.

---

[22] as a parent.
https://alankazdin.com/challenges-of-the-internet-and-social-media-for-parents/
[23] https://alankazdin.com/challenges-of-the-internet-and-social-media-for-parents/
[24] https://alankazdin.com/challenges-of-the-internet-and-social-media-for-parents/
[25] https://alankazdin.com/challenges-of-the-internet-and-social-media-for-parents/
[26] https://alankazdin.com/challenges-of-the-internet-and-social-media-for-parents/
[27] https://alankazdin.com/challenges-of-the-internet-and-social-media-for-parents/

- Help your children understand the economic cost associated with the media.
- Use a time management chart to help your child manage the media.

Some Internet rules

- Do not allow your child/ren who are not of a responsible age to go on the internet without supervision.
- Be definite about the purposes for which they want to be on the net.
- Have filtering systems on the internet.
- Let younger children using the system for school work to do so in open space.
- Educate as to the kind of information that they share (No privileged information should be shared).
- All rules of safety must be observed – Let your child be aware that once they on the internet, someone might be looking over their shoulders. (PWOMS - Parents watching over my shoulders), POS – Parent over shoulder) The sites they visit are to be secured.
- Make clear that not all that appears on the net is factual or truthful (Everything must be carefully thought about before it is accepted).
- Never share passwords with anyone, apart from (your) parents.
- When they use the net for research, give the appropriate credit.
- Be careful of anonymous postings.
- Limit screen time – Decide on how much time they use per internet session.
- Be a proactive parent and monitor what is sent and received over the internet.
- Make sure that no bullying messages are sent or accepted.

Some Television rules

- Establish when, where, and how the television will be used.
- Decide what kinds of filters you will use on the TVs.
- Be unambiguous about the times that TVs are turned on and turned off.
- Be clear that TVs will not be children's bedrooms.
- Be definite that TV and study time are never in competition.

Video game rules

- Discuss with your child/ren the kinds of games they are playing and the impact they can have on their lives.
- Establish how much time your child can spend on video games.
- Determine the times when your child/ren is/are allowed to play.
- Set limits on where games can be played.
- If your child/ren is/are prone to aggressive behavior or anxiety, be careful that the content of the video games or other material will not make things worse. For example, anxiety and fears, common in early childhood, can be made worse by watching trauma or events that depict terroristic acts, violence, death, and dying in detail.[28] Immodest sexual suggestions can degrade the mind and encourage harmful practices.

Cell phone rules

- Decide at what age you wish for the child to begin the use of the cell phone.
- Establish clear rules for how your child will use cell phones.
- Make clear that text messaging is to be thoughtful and polite.

---

[28] https://alankazdin.com/challenges-of-the-internet-and-social-media-for-parents/

- Do not allow the cell phone to be in younger children's bedrooms late at night.
- Make clear the cell phone camera can be misused – no picture is to be taken and passed along that is intrusive.
- Work by a budget and try to avoid cost overruns.
- Watch the amount of screen time your child uses.

Understanding the language and acronyms of social media

Learning the language used on social media is most significant. When children use the media, they find ways of communicating, using acronyms, and emojis that their parents sometimes do not understand. No one should be dogmatic by saying, "I have learned the language" since it shifts with such rapidity. But parents can ask their children what the acronyms and emojis mean. Here are some examples of acronyms:

Acronyms	Meanings
CYA	See Ya
JK	Just kidding
TTYL	Talk to you later
DGMW	Don't get me wrong
LMK	Let me know
IDK	I don't know
GTG	Got to go
ILY	I love you
ASL or a/s/l	Age/Sex/Location
ILY or ILU	I love you
AMA	Ask me anything

If you are having trouble understanding the language, check out one of the Dictionaries about Acronyms of Social Media Dictionary, and the emojipedia.

Model the behavior you want your child to reflect.

The best way to teach rules of behavior or is to model that behavior. There should not be any incongruence between what is said and what is done. For example, ask yourself:

- How do I use my telephone at a dinner table, in church, or any other space where others are around me? Is your behavior respectful?
- Do I text while I am having a conversation or in family time?
- Do I text while I am driving?
- Do I just plop myself before a Television and forget my duties, and expect my child/ren to exercise discipline about their work?
- What kind of language do I use on the internet?
- How much time do I spend on the digito-systems named?
- What identity do I portray online?

The point is that we must model what we teach. If, as a parent, I expect a child to exhibit positive behaviors, then I must practice positive behaviors.

The purpose of making digito-tech rules

The whole purpose of having technology rules is to make sure that the fundamental values for a good life are not compromised. In this vein, we must ask ourselves:

- How balanced is our children's exposure to all technologies with which they are in contact; are the technologies controlling them, or can they control the technologies?
- How are the technologies contributing to their physical, mental, emotional, social, intellectual, personal spiritual development?
- How are the technologies affecting their attitudes of respect?

- Are the children finding time to develop their thoughts and emotions from caring, competent sources?
- Are the children developing relationally as a result of the technology?
- Is there long-term radiation affecting the body as a result of the technologies which are being developed?
- Are the children being mesmerized by the technology?
- Does technology offer our children the opportunity for creativity and imagination?
- What is prepackaged information doing to our child/ren?
- How is the technology affecting the gratification and frustration quotient of our child/ren?
- How is technology impacting the moral and ethical development of our child/ren?
- What is the impact of technology on the close, loving relationships with responsible adults?

These simple questions are not intended to suppress the value of any newly developed technology or the courage to use the same, but they are intended to offer some cautions so that the freedoms offered by the technology will not be abused and become the basis of self-destruction.

When parents are sensitive to the needs of their children, the children will most likely be able to grow into the kinds of individuals that the parents would wish them to be.

Parents need to learn, for example, that they are not only living in the present but that the present is the future. At one time, people waited for a long time to get to the future. Today, the future is the present. The five themes that James Canton identified in his book *The Extreme Future*[29] have been realized in our digito tech age:

---

[29] James Canton (2006), *The Extreme Future: The Top Trends That Will Reshape the World for the Next 5, 10, and 20 Years*, New York: Dutton Publishing, 4.

1. Speed – Rapid speed
2. Complexity – profound complexity
3. Risks – with possibilities and danger
4. Change – Swift changes
5. Surprise – Amazing surprises

The point is that no parent should live in ignorance, for there are numerous resources to help them with any digito-media frustrations. Here are a few that parents can explore:

>www.safekids.com/guidelines-for-parents/ (from Safe Kids—an organization devoted to child Internet safety).

>www.aap.org/en-us/about-the-aap/aap-press-room/Pages/Children-And-Media-Tips-For-Parents.aspx and http://pediatrics.aappublications.org/content/pediatrics/138/5/e20162593.full.pdf (from the American Academy of Pediatrics which is devoted to the health of children).

>https://journals.lww.com/practicalpsychiatry/Abstract/2013/05000/Psychiatrists_Use_of_Electronic_Communication_and.11.aspx

>https://childmind.org/article/media-guidelines-for-kids-of-all-ages/

QUESTIONS FOR REFLECTION

1. What strategies might you as a parent use to get quickly acquainted with the changing digital and social technologies so that you can give positive guidance to your child/ren?

2. What are the most appropriate ways to introduce your children to new technologies without losing parental control?
3. How is the present technology affecting your child's thinking, performance, and behavior?
4. What do you know about the new (digital) media?
5. How fearful are you of the new media?
6. Have you attended a workshop to sharpen your understanding of the new media?
7. Do you know how to identify what is factual from falsehood, on the new media?

CHAPTER V

Parenting In A Culture Of Violence

Our children and violence.

It is being said that are more than seventy wars being fought around the world these days. In one day, a BBC film crew was taking pictures for more than sixteen of them. One of the crews interviewed a child soldier in Somalia highlighting the fact that in many places, it was not uncommon for children to be included as fighters. The fourteen-year-old who was  interviewed was brandishing a gun. He told the crew that he had to protect himself from the many gangs that were around him. Both of his parents were already killed by the gangs. Within four days of giving his interview he was killed.

We often hear that our children are the future of society. All of this is being recited glibly. However, a look at the mounting violence our children are facing tells a different reality. The multiple reports on children, youth and violence are profoundly upsetting. For example, in the United States of America:

- A 2009 DOJ study showed that more than 60 % of children surveyed were exposed to violence within the past year either directly or indirectly. And as has been made clear, children exposed to violence, whether as victims or witnesses, are often affected by long-term physical, psychological, and emotional harm. Children exposed to violence are also at a higher risk of engaging in criminal behavior later in life and becoming part of a cycle of violence.
- 60 % of children who are exposed to violence, crime, or abuse, are exposed in their homes, schools and communities.
- 40 % of American children are direct victims of two or more violent acts, and one in ten are victims of violence five or more times.
- Almost one in ten American children has seen one family member assaulting another family member, and more than 25% are exposed to family violence during their life. [30]
- In 2007, 5,764 young people ages 10 to 24 were murdered--an average of 16 each day. Of these victims, 84 percent were killed with firearms.
- For young people ages 10-24, homicide is the second leading cause of death in America.
- In 2008, more than 656,000 young people ages 10 to 24 were treated in hospital emergency departments for injuries due to violence.
- Among 10 to 24-year-olds, homicide is the leading cause of death for African Americans, the second leading cause of death for Hispanics, and the third leading cause of death for American Indians, Alaskan Natives, and Asian/Pacific Islanders[31]

---

[30] https://www.justice.gov/archives/defendingchildhood/facts-about-children-and-violence.
[31] https://www.childrenssafetynetwork.org/injury-topics/youth-violence-prevention

Parental Advocacy

- Between 2016 and 2018, eight multiple-victim shootings claimed the lives of 31 children at primary, middle and high schools in the United States, according to the U.S. Centers for Disease Control and Prevention report.[32]
- The total number of deaths and death rate among persons aged 10–19 years declined between 1999 and 2013 but then increased between 2013 and 2016.
- For children and adolescents aged 10–14 years, the injury death rate increased 11% from the recent low in 2012 (6.4) to 2016 (7.1).
- For adolescents aged 15–19 years, the injury death rate increased 19% from the recent low in 2013 (32.8) to 2016 (39.0).
- After a brief period of decline (1999–2001), suicide and homicide increase between 2001 and 2007, homicide rates declined by 35% between 2007 (5.7) and 2014 (3.7) before increasing 27%, to 4.7 in 2016. The suicide rate for persons aged 10–19 years declined by 15% between 1999 and 2007 and then increased by 56% between 2007 and 2016. As a result of the suicide and homicide trends, suicide replaced homicide as the second leading intent of injury death among those aged 10–19 years in 2011, with the number of deaths due to suicide exceeding homicide. In 2016, suicides numbered 2,553, while homicides numbered 1,963.[33]

What is stated above is that before many children reach adulthood, they have confronted so much violence that they may fear getting up from bed each morning. From the violent video games to domestic abuse, to the blood and gore on television, violence continues to take its toll on our children. Individuals who work in the human and social service fields are daily confronted with children in despair because they

---

[32] https://www.upi.com/Health_News/2019/01/24/Data-confirms-school-shootings-have-become-more-deadly-in-recent-years/9191548366647/
[33] https://www.cdc.gov/nchs/data/nvsr/nvsr67/nvsr67_04.pdf

have been raised on violence. Because of violence our children, at their earliest ages, are being stripped of their innocence. Therefore, researchers are becoming increasingly interested in the effects of violence on parents and children today. Let us note some areas of concern.

Video Games violence

The most prominent train of outrageous school violence in America was noted on April 20, 1999, when Eric Harris and Dylan Klebold launched an assault on Columbine High School in Littleton, Colorado. By the time they were stopped, they had murdered 13 persons and wounded 23. Although it has never been told exactly what caused the teens to attack their own classmates and teachers, a number of factors have been isolated including violent video games. The two youngsters "enjoyed" playing the bloody, video game Doom, a game licensed by the U.S. military to train soldiers to kill with effectiveness. The Simon Wiesenthal Center, which tracks internet hate groups, found a copy of Harris' web site with a version of Doom that he had custom-made. In his version there were two shooters, each with extra weapons and unlimited ammunition, and the other people in the game could not fight back. For a class project the two youngsters made a videotape that was similar to their custom-made version of Doom. In the video, they dressed in trench coats, carried guns, and killed school athletes. They acted out their videotaped performance in real life less than a year later.

While the researchers have not been dogmatic about the effects of video games on violence, most insist that since the 1970s with the introduction of the Atari game called Pong, a simplified version of ping pong, the relationship between parents and their children had begun to break down. Disrespect and disregard were on the increase, and today we are reaping the heritage of the seeds sown. More and more people are questioning whether our children should be playing violent games.

Television violence and other public media

Another area of investigation with regards to children and violence has to do with what is presented on Television and other public media. While efforts have been made to monitor some of the violence on such media, there are still subtle ways in which the producers are getting around regulations and still expose children to a lot of violence. It is said that "these days, just about every time you turn on the TV, you're met with a barrage of violent images including explosions, suicide bombings, and war casualties. And that's just the news! Many popular television shows -- even those in the so-called "family" time slot of 7-8:30 p.m. -- also feature much more violence than shows aired in this time slot, just a few years ago."[34]

Since children copy what they see and hear, it takes much vigilance to control the amount of violence that gets to them through the media.

Sports violence

When one hockey player intentionally breaks another's rib, or baseball, basketball, football players fights, violence is accepted as normal by our children. Many researchers are convinced that the media occupies a paradoxical position. That is, while it helps us enjoy sports it also exposes our children to violence as normative to sports. It glamorizes players, often the most controversial and aggressive ones. Its commentaries are laced with descriptions of combat, linking excitement with violent action. The exposure given to sports violence by the media has caused many children to think that violence in sports is normative.

---

[34] https://www.webmd.com/parenting/features/tv-violence-cause-child-anxiety-aggressive-behavior#1

Music violence

A great amount of violence perpetrated against children, as we have it today, has been traceable to music violence. While some scientists have argued that one cannot establish a strict cause and effect, yet, it has been noted that since the last three decades of the twentieth century and the opening decade of the twenty-first century, some music lyrics have become increasingly explicit -- particularly with reference to drugs, sex, and violence. Heavy metal and rap lyrics have elicited the greatest concern, as they poison the environment in which some adolescents increasingly are confronted with pregnancy, drug use, Acquired Immunodeficiency Syndrome (AIDS) and other sexually transmitted diseases, injuries, homicide and suicide.[35] Only a blind person will scoff at the evidence, what is of interest is that a lot more complaints are being heard today concerning this kind of violence than a few years ago.

Violence in the home

Parents should be the most positive role models for their children and should advocate nonviolence to the fullest. However, there are many instances when the greatest perpetrators of violence before children are from parents. Many innocent children are subjected to "in-home" violence. The following is a brief summarization, taken from the handbook of Battered Women's Resources, Inc. located in Fitchburg, Massachusetts.

> Children are the other victims of domestic violence. Spousal assault is cyclical. This means that it is behavior learned in one generation and taught to the next.

---

[35] Frank Palumba, (Nov 6, 1997), http://www.aap.org/advocacy/washing/t1106.htm, "Testimony on the social impact of music violence before the senate subcommittee on oversight of government management, restructuring and the District of Columbia."

Children who witness violence in their homes, such as hitting, slapping, etc., learn that violence is a "natural" way to communicate and solve problems. As adults, they are more likely to be involved in domestic violence either as a batterer or a victim.

Children from violent homes have experienced a great deal of fear. This fear manifests in a variety of ways, including violently acting out behavior, role reversal or involvement in parental struggle and withdrawal and passivity. Not all children will have these feelings and manner of coping, but many children will.

The violent home is an unpredictable, scary place to a small person who cannot possibly know when or how bad the next outbreak will be. The resulting vulnerability and lack of control felt by these children often manifests in a tough exterior or aggressive, violent behavior. On one hand, many children find themselves intensely involved in their parent's struggle. Frequently, the child will assume the responsibility of trying to stop or prevent the violence from occurring. Because of this intense involvement, these children often have trouble separating their own identity from that of their parents, thus, the child often assumes a caretaker role with siblings.

On the other hand, the child witnessing violence in the home and identifying with the victim displays passive, withdrawn behavior. Home is not a place of healthy relationship and security, but a place of unpredictable danger. The passive child has extreme difficulty asserting his/her needs and copes with the violence by withdrawal and isolation. The danger in this behavior is that the child, upon reaching adulthood still assumes a victim role in interpersonal relationships and may find it difficult to form healthy, intimate relationships: thus, the cycle continues.[36]

Bullying

Bullying is called the unwanted, aggressive behavior among school children. It is the effort of one child or a group of children to terrorize, tyrannize, torment, browbeat, or intimidate another child or group of children. It not only takes place in face to face encounter, but in our contemporary frame it perpetrated on the multiple platforms of social media. It persist most dangerously on cyber media platforms because the possibility of anonymity.

And it is a tragedy that in the same way that children and some adults stand by and watch bullying in school yards, there are adults who standby when children are being bullied on the cyber platforms. The do not challenge their children not to participate in bullying or help their children to understand what bullying is. Many only realize that there is bullying when someone gets injured, or, and, commits suicide.

In effect, we need to make youngsters aware of the possible causes of bullying. The most common are:

- Cultural prejudices that are easily picked up by children. The feeling of being "better than."
- Lack of acceptance for people who are differently abled.
- Race and ethnicity – such as the historical perceptions between black and white.
- Class differences – such as divides between the rich and poor.

---

[36] *Handbook of Battered Women's Resources*, Inc. located in Fitchburg, Massachusetts.

- Social polarization – The pervasiveness of "in group" and "out group" such as when there is a focus on people as aliens and foreigners.

Whatever the reasons, bullying is never excusable. We need to secure our children from participating in it or be abused by it.

The gangster family

Many children who have tough lives at home, and are robbed of affection and affirmation, and they become enamored and join gang families. They find in these gang families companionship and support. They get involved so that they can feel that they belong to someone and somewhere.

Of course, even youngsters from stable homes can get caught up with gangs. Their curious desires and peer pressure, drive them to think that the life on the other side is better. In fact, Gangster Rap has normalized gang behavior and inspired many youngsters to leave their homes and join gangs.

The points being made are that gangs are pervasive and that they prey on children wherever they can find them. They will recruit whoever they can. Therefore, parental advocates need to take seriously the fact that these gangs exist and protect their children away from them.

Physically abusive family

Physical abuse might be one of the areas that has the greatest effect on violence among children. Here are some disturbing figures as taken from the MacLean's magazine on sexual and physical abuse of children in Ontario, Canada. The study conducted by researchers at Hamilton's McMaster University and the Clarke Institute of Psychiatry in Toronto, was based on nearly 10,000 interviews done in 1990-1991 with subject's aged 15 and up. It found that almost one-third of males experienced physical abuse as children while 12.8 percent of females reported being subjected to some form of sexual abuse. The survey identified natural fathers as the most frequent physical abusers of boys, while sexual predators outside the family perpetrated abuse more frequently.[37]

Yes, physical abuse continues to be a major source of childhood injury. Although government laws, particularly in the northwestern metropolitan nations of the United States, Canada and Europe, have lessened incidents of physical violence and neglect of children, yet angry parents find clever ways of perpetuating these kinds of violence. Children with burnt body parts, broken limbs and bruises are still showing up in schools. Children who are left without care are found by social workers on a daily basis. And no one can deny the prevailing phenomenon of sexual violence. We have spoken of the latter in another discussion and will not linger on it here, but it should be noted that sexual abuse might be the most conceited from of physical violence that many of our children encounter.

The verbally abusive family

In speaking to children from violent families we not only note those who are physically abused, but those who are verbally abused. Many children have been so put down with words that they have not been able to think of themselves as persons. The Bible says, "And you fathers, do not provoke your children to wrath, but bring them up in the nurture and admonition of the Lord." (cf. Eph 6:4; Col 3:21).

Here are a few put down words and phrases which cut to the core

"You are stupid."
"You can't learn"

---

[37] http://scholar.google.com/scholar?complete=1&hl=en&q=author:%22Estes%22+intitle:%22THE+SEXUAL+EXPLOITATION+OF+CHILDREN+A+Working+Guide+to+...%22+&um=1&ie=UTF-8&oi=scholar, (MacLean, 110:29 (July 21, 1997) 15.

"You are worthless and no good"
"You idiot"
"You dummy"
"You are lazy"
"You have no sense"

There are also some parents and adults who use "Swear words" to their children. Many times, we have witnessed parents using swear words as means of correcting their children. And the biggest irony we have seen is that whenever children repeat these words to parents or other adults they are punished and considered disgraceful.

We list here a few don'ts for parents

- Don't label your children.
- Don't publicly embarrass them.
- Don't make value judgments.
- Don't say "Shut up."
- Don't say, "You are dumb."
- Don't say, "You never make sense."
- Don't say, "You always do that."
- Don't say, "Do it because I say so."

The point being made is that verbal abuse has detrimental consequences on children. The scars and wounds might just in childhood but throughout the lifespan. Social scientists have identified some effects of verbal abuse as:

> Low self-esteem, depression, withdrawal, severe anxiety, fearfulness, failure to mature, aggression, emotional instability, sleep disturbances, physical complaints with no medical basis, inappropriate behavior for age or development, overly passive/compliant, suicidal, extreme dependence, stealing, underachievement, inability to trust, feelings of shame and guilt, frequent crying, etc. self-blame/self-depreciation, overly passive/compliant other forms of abuse present or suspected

The drug abuse family

A daunting challenge for our time is substance abuse. It is estimated that more than eight million children younger than age 18 live with at least one adult who has a substance use disorder (SUD) that is a rate of more than one in 10 children. The majority of these children are younger than age 5 (U.S. Department of Health and Human Services [USDHHS], 2010). The studies of families with SUDs reveal patterns that significantly influence child development and the likelihood that a child will struggle with emotional, behavioral, or substance use problems.[38] Opioids are the drugs that are most being spoken about, however there are many other substances being listed these days for abuse. Many household items such as fabric protectors, whippets (small canisters of nitrous oxide that propel whipped cream), vegetable cooking spray, liquid correction fluid, halon fire extinguishers, gasoline and propane fuels, spray paint, hair spray, markers, Windex, WD-40, are all suspects. Children who engage with these substances do a lot of harm to themselves and often enough destroy innocent lives.

Sometimes it is easier to tell children about using some kinds of drugs, but it might be more difficult especially when the drugs of choice are items used around the home for carrying forward a task. It was very painful listening to Steve Harvey's son, in a tribute to celebration of Steve's birthday. He thought it was cool when his Father Steve smoked the first cigar with him. As parents we need to think seriously about what we offer our children. We must be careful about what we have around our homes. Here are some questions parents must ponder as they purchase items that have the potential to be destructive if used inappropriately.

1. How can parents alert their children to the inherent dangers of these chemicals, especially those used around the home?

---

[38] https://www.ncbi.nlm.nih.gov/pmc/articles/PMC3725219/

2. How can they teach about the inherent dangers, especially when others are doing it?
3. When should parents begin to tell their children about responsible use of those things that are necessary?

Gun violence

It would be very hard to conclude a discussion on violence without taking into account the most insidious form of known violence affecting our children today. Between 2009 and 2018, at least 177 of America's schools experienced a shooting. It used to be argued that the shootings were targeted to school yard scuffle in in poor communities, however it is now being the tragedies are as diverse as the nation, that since Sandy Hook in 2009 the shouting are taking place on a mass scale. There is no standard definition for what qualifies as a school shooting in the US. Nor is there a universally accepted database. So, no one knows the fullest number of shootings, but it is noted that school shootings are increasing, and no type of community is spared. In 2018 it was reported by one source that since 2000, there have been **school shootings** in 43 of the 50 states. I have researched and found that it is now 45 out of 50 states. (The exceptions being: Alaska, Idaho, Kansas, Maine, New Hampshire, North Dakota, and Wyoming.)[39]

When teachers in schools are being asked to arm themselves and children have to be constantly given active shooter drills, there are reasons to show our concern. What needs to be said about the fears of our child and the guns in our homes and the possibilities of children buying guns are themes that must be in daily conversation. Children need to understand that those who "live by the gun will die by the gun". In other words, when we practice violent behaviors toward others, it comes back full circle. Many parents need to understand what they are introducing

---

[39] Cf. https://www.google.com/search?client=safari&rls=en&q=list+of+school+shootings+2010+2020&ie=UTF-8&oe=UTF-8.

to their children when they give toy guns to them, or other kinds of toy weaponry or let them play video games that includes shooting. We watch with dismay sometimes when these children seek to simulate the actions of gunmen as they take aim at their peers and even adults. And what is most disturbing is that many adults find these actions amusing. Parents need to be more perceptive and think about what their children are learning now and the possible consequences in the future.

Violence in religion

Another area that we least expect to speak of in our survey of the violence that many parents have passed on to their children is the area of religion. And yet it has been our finding that in many Christian homes, children complain that the rule-based religion of their parents has felt abusive to them. Abusive religion is not just the demonic religion about which we hear of parents starving their children and so on, but it can also be found in the homes of those of us who are training our children to be perfect. Many parents seek to use the Bible as a whip to train their children. An overemphasis is just as destructive as neglecting to guide in religious principles. Sometimes we want our children to be so perfect that we overdo it and thus fail to show them the way of forgiveness, love, and redemption. When a child fails the best way to teach them about God is to teach them forgiveness.

Abortion violence

One of the most tragic acts of violence against children occurs at the level of unborn children. Approximately1.2 million children (so called fetuses) are aborted each year. Many who do abortions are children who become pregnant and are encouraged by their parents or other adults, to have abortions. The reality is that when the act of abortion is treated as benign, the conscience is eroded and the displacement of the abortion violence is extended to some other person or place.

Violence on the self

The greatest form of violence is that which turns on the self. Suicidal tendencies, alcoholism, drug abuse, anorexia and bulimia are all ways in which teens seek to hurt themselves. Sometimes parents are at a loss as to how their child acquired such tendency.

The cycle of violence

Violent parents produce violent children. Violent children make for violent adults. Violent spouses are often from children who grew up in the context of violence. Social scientists speak of regressive characteristics and chronic relational identity, and such is truest in the cycle of violence.

Taking responsibility for exposing our children to violence

Whether our children are exposed to violence through the video games we produce, or the media we create, or in the sports we play, or in our homes, parents need to take more responsibility for the life of violence into which they are introduced. A well-behaved child is not the result of luck. If we want to have well-behaved, well-adjusted children, we need to understand how to protect them against what is sometimes called innocent violence. In effect, children are people too! They have feelings just like we do --- they want to learn to cooperate, and they want to do well in life. But they will not do well until we do well with them.

Parents need to help to create positive environments in which their children must grow. The impact of parental activity should not just be confined to the home for while they might be able to keep them safe at home, there are challenges in society. Parents must become activists to safeguard the innocence of their children. For too long many parents accept TV violence, music

> **Parents are to keep in mind that "An ounce of prevention is better than a pound of cure"**

violence, violent spouses, sports violence and all other forms of violence without being proactive. Parents do not perpetuate a cycle of violence for generations to come by sitting by and accepting what is happening as a given. Parents must reject a culture of violence for any form of violence whether seen or being subjected to for it can have adverse effects on the wellbeing of children.

Parents need to start by ensuring that relationship in the home is not predicated on violent behaviors.

- Define the standards that govern the home. Have rules that are simple and fair. Allow children to help construct some rules regarding violence in the home.
- Be consistent when rules are made. Be gentle with them but understand that the quality of being gentle does not mean that anything goes. Be firm but do it in love for both are not incongruous. Inconsistency creates problems.
- Keep violent movies, music etc. out of the home. Help children to understand the consequences of watching violent activities, of imbibing a violent culture, of feasting on a steady diet of violence via the media.
- Discourage violent behaviors, such as rash speech, angry blow-ups, and fights in the home. Encourage healthy dialogs and problem-solving sessions to settle disputes. And remember to affirm children when they settle disagreements without violence or rage.
- Ensure that children are supervised at all times by individuals.
- Love and affirm your children. Do not encourage violent behaviors under the guise of teaching the child to learn to protect him or herself. We know of many parents who see nothing wrong in teaching, especially their sons, to learn to fight. The chances are that that child will grow up into manhood believing he has to fight for everything. The truth is that he might become an abusive and violent spouse and parent because of a poor judgment call of a parent. Yes, your

child might be called a coward for not responding violently to situations. Know that it is a "big person" a "smart person" who can respond with calm and decency in face of aggression and violence.

- Parents be models for your children. Live honorably before them and show, by example, how differences can be settled peacefully. Avoid spousal violence in the home. Children are often terrified when they witness spousal abuse. Instead model appropriate ways of behaving. Children learn by imitating so that if they sense violence in the home the foundation is laid for a cycle of violence. The old adage "do as I say and not as I do" will not suffice

QUESTIONS FOR REFLECTION

1. How would you compare the culture of violence that we are facing today with that of your generation?
2. Make a list of some of the ways in which adults are exposing children to violence in the home?
3. What are some steps that parents can take to protect their children from violence?

CHAPTER VI

Parenting and The Sexualization of Our Children

The sexualization of our children

This chapter is intended to state that in as much as many social scientists recognize that definite efforts are being made to sexualize our culture, competing perspectives about sexuality and sexualization have become very challenging to the efforts of many parents to deal with the critical sexual questions confronting their children. Many parents note, for example, that:

- They are not very comfortable when discussing some of the most sensitive aspects of sexuality with their children.
- Others argue that while the advent of the internet has enhanced information about sex and sexuality, they find that its negative influence has impacted their children, adolescents, and youth in ways that they are challenged with how best to bring controls.
- Still, others say that while the development of sexuality education in the school system has offered better understanding for children and families, the insistence on a school-based curriculum for LGBT education is creating a challenge

Parental Advocacy

for those with differing values, beliefs of gender-based relationships, etc.[40]
- Because of the criminal culture of sexual molestation, harassment and abuse, parents are also confronting greater and greater need to be more aware and cautious about how their children are involved with anyone or anything that raises questions of sexuality.

It was tough for us to accept the report as the news media and the talk radio hosts gave it in one of the countries that we visited on one of our vacations. We heard that 10 men "trained" a twelve-year-old girl to be promiscuous. Of the first five men who were arrested, four were eighteen years old and one twenty-four. At the time of the report, the other five men were still on the loose. Our prayer was that the other men would be caught and duly punished. No question that we were angry. And while we were angry, we kept wondering how would the life of this little girl be transformed even if the men were caught. In the discussions of the talk radio, one social worker stated that sometimes when girls are thus sexually abused, it forms the basis for the promiscuous lives that they lead for years to come. From all we know, the consequence of sexual abuse is more than making a person promiscuous.

On our return from vacation, we were listening to the morning news and were struck by reports of sexual crimes perpetrated against

---

[40] See, O. S. Hawkins (1993, *Moral Earthquakes and Secret Faults: Protecting Yourself from Moral Lapses that Lead to Major Disasters*, Nashville, TN.: Broadman and Holman. Cf. Sol Gordon PhD. & Judith Gordon, MSW (1983), *Raising a Child Conservatively in a Sexually Permissive World*, New York: Simon and Schuster. Josh Mc Dowell (1987), Teens Speak Out: "What I Wish My Parents Knew About my Sexuality?" San Bernardino: CA, Here is Life Publishers, INC. See especially chapter 7 of the book that focuses on Sex Education. McDowell states that he appreciates the fact that sexuality education clears up a lot of misunderstandings that society and parents sometimes perpetuate, but the sexuality education sometimes, also, encourages experimentation.

children. The news report told of a father who was arrested because he spent years forging an incestuous relationship with his daughter. In a few days, the news reported quite a few teachers who were fired from schools across America because they had molested their students. Because we were preparing to write this chapter on parenting and the sexualization of children, we went back to reflect on the scandals many churches were facing concerning sexual offenses against children. One diocese of the Roman Catholic Church offered eighty-five million dollars to over five hundred victims who claimed to have been molested or assaulted when they were children by several priests. We know that the Roman Catholic church is paying a hefty price today for the years of abuse by its priests.

At one of our pastors' convocations, we spent more than a whole day trying to understand the demand for background checks for all volunteer workers who have to be in contact with children in the churches. While speaking of its collateral, unintended consequences, we affirmed its necessity, because of the pervasiveness of sexual offenses taking place against children across all organizations within our modern world. At the end of the meeting, we pondered what we had heard and prayed earnestly that our seven grandchildren, our nieces, and other relatives be spared from such sexual experiences.

While preparing to address a church board meeting on background checks, we were even more sensitized to the sexual plight of children when we listened to news reports stating that fifteen men were arrested in Orange County, New Jersey, for pedophilia. These men came from different states to engage their sexual appetites with minors. What they did not know was that they were part of a sting set up by the FBI. They were arrested, but anyone who understands the culture of the times should be more aware that while some persons are caught with such public evil, there are multitudes of cases that have not been reported.

As we were writing this chapter, another breaking story hit the airwaves. The body of a twelve-year-old girl was found in a shallow grave near her home in Maine. It was reported earlier by her uncle that she asked to go to a convenience store and that she had not been seen since. The shocking news was that the uncle abducted her to become a part of a sex ring. The full truth might never come to the fore, but what we know is that the uncle was a registered sex offender.

Yes, the news has exposed the plight of children concerning inappropriate sexual experiences. But there is more to the sexualization of children than what is being reported in the news media.

Sexualization and education

Sexualization education has become quite challenging in our contemporary frame. What used to be thought of as parental responsibility has now been farmed out to teachers in the schools. The decision to strip parents of their parental responsibility to transmit values and educate their children is a fundamental flaw that is inconsistent with natural and moral laws. All parents have the fundamental right to teach their offspring by precept and example. When that right is taken away, it raises questions on broader issues, such as:

> How does abstinence-based education fit into particular school curricula? What approach is taken to safe sex-based education?

> How is the LGBTQ school-based programs and policies, inserted in the curriculum affecting your child/ren's participation?

> Are the ideas being taught in a way that your child/ren have a wholesome conception of human sexuality?

> How are questions of sexual choices and decisions being framed?

In facing these questions, one public school sexuality education teacher who became profoundly disgusted with the sexualization curriculum was overheard to say:

> Times have changed considerably. I've been involved in public school sex education for over twenty years, yet, I am amazed at the significant numbers of children who express sexualized behaviors at younger and younger ages. As a whole, they seem to be genuinely more interested in sex, as if their curiosity about sex has been ratcheted up several notches. For parents, the days of postponing any discussion about intimate sex with their kids until they become teenagers are long gone. Today, if you haven't discussed the biological, psychological, and moral implications of sexual relations with your kids, by the time they've entered middle school, the implications might be unsettling.

Commercial sexualization and exploitation of children

Even if one thinks one's own child is sheltered from what one might think is inappropriate sexualization, it is hard to hide when one considers what has been happening to the children through the commercial sexualization through the distribution of toys and the media. For example:

1. The production of gender-neutral toys is on the rise. These dolls come in a range of skin tones (though uniform body size), each having two different hairstyle options—short and long—and arrive in cheerful pastel-green-and-yellow packaging with a variety of clothing: jeans, skirts, tank tops, shorts, and so on. Mattel launched the first line of dolls in what the company touts as a move toward inclusivity. The company, by this move,

recognizes that gender comes in more than two options. The dolls have been welcomed by some as finally providing some recognition, even a sense of validation. However, they have been excoriated by others as signs of social decay.[41]

2. The contemporary media promotes sexualization of all sorts. In fact, the most dominant form of child abuse is sexual abuse, which is driven by the media. This includes the advertising that takes place on the television and the sexual exploitation that is taking place through social media. The most insidious daily occurrence affecting the lives of tens of thousands of children in the United States and tens of millions of children worldwide is through social media. Because of the supposed anonymity on the internet and social media, this is where the well-organized networks of traffickers in child and adult sex are plying their trade. Patterns of child sexual exploitation appear to be fueled by, (1) The use of "survival sex" by runaway and thrown-away children to provide for their subsistence needs. (2) The presence of preexisting adult prostitution markets in communities where large numbers of street youth are concentrated. (3) prior history of child sexual abuse and child sexual assault. (4) Poverty, (5) The presence of large numbers of unattached and transient males in local communities—including military personnel, truckers, and conventioneers, among others. (6) For some girls, membership in gangs. (7) Promotion of child prostitution by parents, older siblings, and boyfriends; (8) Recruitment of children as "sex workers" by organized crime units, and increasingly; (9) Illegal trafficking of children for sexual purposes both within and to the United States from developing countries located in Asia, Africa, Central, South America, and Central and Eastern Europe.

---

[41] (Taken from *a post as part of Outward, Slate's home for coverage of LGBTQ life, thought, and culture. https://slate.com/business/2019/11/mattel-gender-neutral-dolls-are-about-sales.html*).

Sexualization and advocacy

The simple point being made is that our children are living in the most sex-saturated society of any epoch in human history. We must educate our children on how to be safe in the choices and decisions that they are making regarding their sexual protection. We speak first to parents. It must be clear that parents are the primary sexuality educators of their children. Next in line are teachers, then mentors, and others who are in power positions and are serious about their duty to protect children. Even in this context, it is right to understand that, "It takes a village to rear a child." And as such, we ask all those in the positions we name, how are we helping our children to make positive and effective sexual choices and decisions? How are we helping them with sexual advocacy?

The rest of the discussion is to simply outline some critical strategies that parents, and those who are in power positions, can find appropriate tools for sexual advocacy. Not to know how to use the tools that are available to us in these areas is to be "going up fools' hill." It means we are leaving our children in the positions that they are most vulnerable. The words of Jesus are quite applicable here when He said:

> But whoever causes one of these little ones who believe in Me to sin, it would be better for him if a millstone were hung around his neck, and he were drowned in the depth of the sea. (Matthew 18:6 NKJV).

If Jesus seemed harsh, he needed to be, for when it comes to dealing with children, they are the most vulnerable of the human species. If parents are not taking responsibility, society will. But what children need is not the public order to give them their examples as much as they need those who are closest to them, namely their parents whose religion and values they are expected to pattern.[42]

---

[42] (See Sol Gordon PhD. & Judith Gordon, MSW (1983), *Raising a Child Conservatively in a Sexually Permissive World*, New York: Simon and Schuster. p. 91).

Music Videos, MTV, the Social Media, and Sexualization

In order to illustrate the state of vulnerability, we that music videos, MTV, and social media have opened a large door of freedom to sexualization. One researcher notes that between 20% and 50% of videos that are shown for teens contain sexual content, depicting intercourse and oral sex.[43] Other studies have linked video viewing to sexual attitudes with the following findings. (1) Teens who watch thirteen hours of MTV per week were more likely to approve of premarital sex than those who watched a show without sexual content; (2) those children who were exposed to degrading music videos were more likely to initiate sex than those who did not view those videos. Those who had greater exposure were more likely to assert that it is acceptable that women are sexual objects, while men are more sex-driven pursuers of women; (3) girls who watch more than thirteen hours of rap music videos per week were more likely to have multiple sex partners and also more likely to have STD.[44]

Today children are not spending as much watching television as in the past, but this does not mean that they are not intensely sexualized, for the internet and social media have given them, if not more, explicit exposure to sexual content than ever. In a 2019 blog written under the title "Internet is a Favorite Place for Predators to Lure Kids," Christiana Mink has the following evidence-based research:

> In 2018, 95% of teens reported they owned or had access to a smartphone, according to a Pew Research Center survey. A 2016 report from Common Sense Media found that teens average at least nine hours a day of screen time, excluding texting and time spent

---

[43] Larry Rosen (2007), *Me, My Space and I: Parenting the Net Generation*: Manhattan, New York: St. Martins Publishing Group, p. 140.p. 128

[44] *Ibid.*, p. 128.

at school or for homework. About 45% of the teens reported they were always online. Generation Z, people born in the early 2000s, average 17 hours a day using a device, according to marketing research from ReFuel.

"The devices bring the whole world into our kids' rooms," said Andi. She said it's hard to keep kids safe because access to the Internet is so easy.

One in five American adolescents, 13-19, self-reported that they have sent or posted fully or semi-nude photos of themselves online.

"Children (usually it's girls) as young as 11, 12 or 13 years old are sending inappropriate pictures to boys who they consider a boyfriend," said Kleiber. "Those girls later find that those pictures are used against them."

He said the boys will demand more pics or sexual activity, or they'll share the pictures publicly.[45]

How much are parents aware and concerned about their child/ren as sexual targets? This is a question for much reflection. In fact, we like to encourage parents to find as many resources as they can for guidance in a world that is as complex as the present, with the rise of the new technologies that seem to insert sex into everything.[46]

---

[45] (See, Chrisinna Mink, September 22, 2019) https://www.modbee.com/living/health-fitness/article234930282.html,

[46] See, Jeanne Elium and Don Elium (1999), *Raising A Teenager: Parents and the Nurturing of a Responsible Teen*, Berkeley, CA. Celestial Arts, for a full discussion on how the media we name above impact the understanding of sexuality among children and teenagers.

Being aware of sexualization

In the days when people were more conservative in talking about sex or sexualization, a seminary professor tried to help those who were struggling with public sexual discussions, by arguing out loud that "God Invented Sex." While we need to be thankful today that our sexual discussion needs not to be a subject of embarrassment, we need to think critically that the pretense concerning the popularity of sex education in our contemporary culture has not been denigrated to flippancy. While public discourse continues, many youngsters are still confessing their lack of understanding of the psychology and spirituality of sex. Children are taught the anatomical, economic, and sociopolitical functions of sex, but not of the aspects that impact their lives at its depths. The approaches many teachers and counselors use, conflict with the values that many parents hold. As a result, children are left in confusion. So, we say that parents need to learn how to teach concerning love and sex, for parents are their children's best teachers. Depending on social organizations such as schools to teach their children about sex is not good enough. Parents must fill their roles and not afraid to be open with their children. In fact, every parent needs to be able to make clear that sexuality is not just an act, it had to do with a person's:

- Identity: Who we person are - how we see ourselves.
- Relationships: Our interactions with each other
- Individuality: Uniqueness of personhood
- Generativity: Reproductive functioning
- Expressiveness: Emotional and psychological involvement

Moreover, in a value-laden context, it is also to be clearly understood:

- That sexuality is a definition of gender.
- That sexuality is also an act with profound life consequences.

- That sexual attraction is natural.
- That sexual emotion can be controlled.
- That sexual love carries responsibility.
- That the expression of sexual desire and passion have their proper place.
- That marriage is the place for the fulfillment of sexual expressions.
- That sexual relations are most beneficial in a long-term relationship.
- That some forms of sexual practices being adopted today are unnatural to healthy human life.
- That it is a contradiction that sexual purity is just for a few holy persons.
- That sexual abstinence is possible for any person.
- That the Bible teaches principles that undergird healthy sex.
- That there are profound relations between sex and one's spirit.
- That boys like girls need to/can be sexually pure.
- That there are profound benefits in virginity.
- That there is profound significance between sex and commitment.
- That reckless sex leads to regret and self-recrimination.
- That sexual activity in the wrong contexts will ruin marriage.
- That sexual activity in the wrong contexts can corrupt the character and debase a person.
- That sexual activity in the wrong contexts allows people to feel betrayed.
- That sexual activity in the wrong contexts leads to fear of long-term commitment.
- That sexual activity in the wrong contexts leads to distrustful and destroyed relationships.
- That sexual activity in the wrong contexts leads to a life of guilt.
- That sexual activity in the wrong contexts leads to rage.
- That sexual activity is related to early pregnancies.
- That sexual activity leads to sexually transmissible diseases.
- That sexual harassment is not acceptable.

- That parents need to teach the value of respecting sexual boundaries.
- That respect for one's body should be taught.
- That one ought not to be touched in inappropriate ways.
- That one ought not to accept the use of words with unsolicited sexual overtones.

Parents must help their children understand that sex places people's destinies in their hands. Through sex, we stamp our own values upon ourselves. With our sexuality, we set the value, and cannot expect to be sold for more. In other words, parents need to help their children to understand the interconnection between sexuality and the deepest part of their being - spirituality. This connection used to be the case in past generations, but in our culture of secularization, we have broken away from the root of our being. We picked up an old book, in a Thrift Store, by Sol Gordon, Ph.D., and Judith Gordon, MSW, titled *Raising a Child Conservatively in a Sexually Permissive World. As we skimmed it through, we were amazed at its relevance for today. Its* focus was on how parents in our contemporary times might respond to children facing a diversity of sexual values. While we do not endorse every suggestion, and we are not seeking to review its contents here, we use it to make one point - that instead of hiding from the reality that is confronting our children on sexuality, we need to learn how to negotiate at all levels that we might have the best outcome for them.[47]

Susan Calahan, a contributor to the book Family Life Education, Principles and Practices for Effective Outreach, states:

> Historically, sexuality education has been a lightning rod for controversy fueled by passion-filled debate surrounding many questions, the most basic of which

---

[47] Sol Gordon PhD. & Judith Gordon, MSW (1983), *Raising a Child Conservatively in a Sexually Permissive World*, New York: Simon and Schuster.

is, should it be taught at all, followed by what should be taught, at what age should it be taught, where it should be taught, who should teach it, and does it work? . . .[48]

Both the Gordons and Suzan Calahan remind us that since we are living in a culture where sexual activity is as pervasive among children, we must be engaged in the most comprehensive form of education. Since, according to the report, more than 60 percent of children being sexually active by the time they finish high school, we cannot wait until our children are older before we begin to give them the appropriate guidance and protection.

Actions for Sexual Preservation and Protection

Challenge any culture that seeks to make normal the sexual obsessions of the day. Parents should not forget that children can move quickly from one obsession to another. Their obsessions usually start with what they see on television, in movies, in magazines, what they hear or see in the music of the day, their interactions with the internet, what they receive or share on their smartphones, or the kinds of toys with which they play. Parents should also be mindful to address their own sexual mistakes with their children, so that they do not normalize unscrupulous behaviors.

1. **Talk about sexual obsessions that often set up the basis for accommodating uncanny behaviors such as the following:**

    - Sexual exploitation - e.g. One-night stands, hooking up with undisciplined friends and strangers

---

[48] Stephen F. Duncan and H. Wallace Goddard (2011), *Family Life Education: Principles and Practices for Effective Outreach*, chapter 11, Susus Calahan, "Sexuality Education," Thousand Oaks, CA.: Sage Publications, Inc. p. 211.

- Cybersex – sexting - e.g. Sharing or receiving sexually explicit pictures of one self with others
- Pornography – viewing sexually explicit images
- Homosexuality
- Bisexuality – One of us overheard a young girl at school telling her friend, about her overnight escapade, that her boyfriend was breaking her in both ways.
- Premeditated masturbation – that is, pre-planning a desired time, location, and length of time in which the fantasy of sexual activity should occur.
- Et cetera, Et cetera

2. **Talk about how friends and mates might impact sexual choices and decisions**

   - Talk about what kinds of sexual attitudes and actions should be expected from friends.
   - Encourage your children to find positive friends.
   - Guide your children in the formation of friendships with the opposite sex, particularly as they approach puberty.
   - Make sure that friends are not breaking the rules by lying, cheating, stealing, or practicing activities that can bring sexual hurt to one another.

3. **Talk about how relationships can be built without sexual involvement.**

   - Relationships do not to be sexual.
   - It is vital to know boundary violations.
   - There are ways to give non-sexual hugs, handshakes, and touches.
   - Avoid sexually inappropriate words.
   - Learn how to ask questions concerning sexuality in positive ways.
   - Seek age-appropriate information.
   - Give age-appropriate information.

- Use appropriate language to speak things sexually.
- Talk about puberty and sexual transitions.
- Be clear on the possibility of confusion regarding:

Growth spurts
Menstruation
Ejaculation
Voice changes
Body hair
The role of the oil and sweat glands
Sexual anxiety
The function of sexual intercourse
Sexual interest
Self-esteem
Role confusion
Gender identity
Refusal skills – How to say no
Safe places to be
Safe games to play
Reliable friends to be with

4. **Talk about the significance of safe sexual environments for children.**

- Make sure that all persons who are in constant contact with your children in public spaces are not sexual predators.
- Be very careful about who is serving as your baby sitter – Is it a person who understands sexual boundaries?
- If your children go to sleep-overs, make sure that they are appropriately supervised.
- The safety of the daycare – always check to see that it is safe.
- When you take your child/ren to the mall, make sure that they are not left in a vulnerable situation.

Parental Advocacy

- If you have to leave your child/ren with relatives, make sure that they are safe.
- In blended families, children are sometimes open to sexual abuse.
- If you are an immigrant and leaves a child in another country, you need to understand the risks you are taking.
- If you have a child with disabilities, you need to know that such a child can be more sexually vulnerable.
- Teach your child from early to recognize their own danger and what to do.
- Let children understand that they should not be keeping any secret for anyone and that you, the parent/s are their prime confidants.

5. Talk about the struggles that are common to all of us.

A poem signed RAK that was taken from an Internet site some time ago, shows the struggle against what a Jehovah's Witness called the abuses of her community. Its pathos is profoundly striking, as it makes transparent the pain of abuse caused by complexities of our hypersexualized culture, and the lack of compassion hearts in dealing with such pain.

> No more smiles and no more laughter
> No more handprints on the door
> No more "happily ever afters"
> The children's hour is no more
> Suspended in a lifeless haze
> There will be NO more sunny days
> No fairy tales, no birthday cards
> No picking flowers in the yard
> No Easter Bunny No Saint Nick
> Kill these things and kill them quick!
> And with those joys in this bleak world

Dies the spirit of a little girl
She did not cry, or scream, or wince
She did not fight in self-defense
But stripped of all her innocence
She gives her folks a tiny glimpse—
A glimmer of the nasty truth
Of how we're losing lots of youth
No more televisions shows
Or missing school because it snows
No more picnics on the lawn
These childish things are dead and gone
A grown-up figure takes their place
With hands on hips and scowl on face
These adults don't love, and they don't care
They cannot trust. They fail to share.
They are not true. They are not kind.
Crippled are their hearts and minds
And as their souls fade out to black
The children are NOT coming back! - RAK

In effect, our children are facing a culture of hyper-sexualization and abuse, and we need to make sure that parents are prepared to deal with the issues that they need to confront. What we have argued is that parents are never to forget:

- That their greatest responsibility is to love their children.
- That many children who get involved in inappropriate sexual encounters at the earliest stages of life are looking for someone to love them.
- That positive role-modeling in sexual matters will provide a pattern for our children.
- That high respect needs to be taught for the use of the body.
- That questions concerning sexual issues are to be answered in an age-appropriate manner.

- That children are to be taught how to wait before becoming involved in sexual activities so that they can have better opportunities for meeting the future.
- To learn how to work with media that seeks to lead children into sexual abuse.
- When it is appropriate, use sexual assault advocacy counseling programs.
- To check family advocacy and sexual response hotlines, and work with sexual health programs that focus on STDs, especially HIV/AIDS.

Contraception or abstention

It might seem a contradiction to put contraception and abstention as an alternative or complementary choice regarding sexuality education. But the complexity that parents are facing today makes it incumbent that we do so. As Dr. Calahan has pointed out, children are becoming, at a younger age, more sexually active, and increasingly getting involved in risky sexual behaviors. They are also getting the unintended consequences of early teen pregnancy, sexually transmissible diseases, with other related issues. Parents and other sexuality educators must think about what choices they make available to children. While some educational programs only focus on abstention, and others on contraception, the question to be resolved is how to achieve balance. What Dr. Calahan notes is that sexuality education that encourages abstention shows that such might be the best and safest choice for teens. In any case, if it is established that youngsters are sexually active, it is best to let them understand that instead of pregnancy or STDs, that the alternative is contraception. The argument is that contraception for children is to be a last resort. If there is a child that is unwilling to follow the path of abstention, then the child should be told of the alternative.[49]

Talking with children about birth control at an early age is a responsible approach that parents should take. As soon as there is an inkling, that your child is having a crush on someone or dating, have the discussion. Research has debunked the popular myth that talking about birth control is encouraging your child to have sex. Instead, the research shows that parents who discuss birth control with their children before the child becomes sexually active have avoided a lot of challenges for themselves and their children.[50]

Conclusion

The sexual wellbeing of our children has to be a primary value for all of us. This is most significant because what happens to a child sexually, impacts their entire lives. In our work in family, marriage, and parenting educators, we have seen the consequences and the tragedy of the over-sexualization of children today. Many come into adulthood with hurts that may never heal. Some have chosen sexual lifestyles that they think might take them away from those who have hurt them. Some become promiscuous because of childhood initiation. Others enter marriage and remain sexually frigid, still trying to deal with their hurts. We need not say more but revert to our opening goal - that we trust that as you have gone through the chapter, you sense the need for sexual advocacy, for any child who might come into your purview.

---

[49] Stephen F. Duncan and H. Wallace Goddard (2011), *Family Life Education: Principles and Practices for Effective Outreach*, chapter 11, Susus Calahan, "Sexuality Education," Thousand Oaks, CA.: Sage Publications, Inc. p.p. 214-219.

[50] Larry Rosen (2007), Me, My Space and I: **Parenting the Net Generation: Manhattan, New York: St. Martins Publishing Group,** p. 140.

Children are vulnerable. They are naïve. They cannot protect themselves in the ways that adults do. They, therefore, need the protection of their parents and of all into whose care they are given. Adults much learn what it means to advocate for them, especially in sexual matters.

QUESTIONS FOR REFLECTION

1. What do you think is best for you to do as a parent to build a positive culture of communication with you and your child/ren about sexuality education today?
2. What might you do as a parent to counter the negative culture of sexualization today?
3. How can a parent balance between trust and protection as they try to help their children positive sexual development?
4. At what age do you think it best to begin communicating with your child/ren about their sexuality?
5. Should you, as a parent, address the cultural confusion concerning questions of homosexuality? Explain your response.
6. How can a parent build into their child a biblical worldview of gender and sexuality without sounding legalistic or repressive?
7. What are some things that you need to tell your children about intimate relationships?
8. What is the baseline for sex education that you wish to make known to your children?
9. What are some ways in which you think it is essential for parents to speak to their children concerning sexual urges?
10. How can we help our children to resist peer pressure that says, "Everybody is doing it?
11. How can you help your children to understand the consequences of inappropriate sexual encounters?

CHAPTER VII

Parenting In A Culture Of Uprootedness

Uprootedness

I met him on a visit to the hospital. He was there to support his brother who was quite sick. The doctors were having a lot of difficulty diagnosing the brother's problem, and this made him more anxious than he had been, or so it seemed. His mother became quite anxious about how he was responding and voice her disapproval of his disrespectful when I (Robert) tried to speak with him and he would not respond. I watched and waited patiently for a moment until I could get his attention, and it did just when I was  about to leave the room. I was standing close to him and I touched him on his shoulder and asked, "Would you take me to the nearest elevator?" He agreed and as soon as I walked out of his mother's presence, I asked what was going on, what was making him so cold and angry. He paused then responded, "I am glad you asked me. I am sure my mother does not understand it all. I love her because she is very kind to me, but there are some things I cannot tell her, for I do not want to hurt her. We do not talk about school much, for it has become a sore subject. I do not have a lot of time to study, for I have to work to help the family. I also do not like the school that I am attending, but my mother is not able to help me get to the one I want to go. This is why I do not want to talk about it." Then I said, "tell me, where is your father?" And he responded coldly that, he and his siblings were separated from their father. He was only eight years old and they have never seen him again because they migrated to another country. My final question, "Do you miss him?" was met with a shrug of the shoulder and a casual response, "not anymore." His reaction was not frightening for it seem to be the story of many children.

Barrel kids

Another form of cultural up rootedness which many individuals do not even countenance is what is termed "Barrel Kids" This phenomenon is typical and finds resonances in families all across the world. The idea of "Barrel kids" has particular reference to children whose parents leave them behind to travel to such places like the United States, Canada, England and France.[51] to make a living. The view is that many "kids" have been left behind, supposedly at home, with relatives and friends while parents travel to the above-named countries. The parents who migrate send back barrels (once or twice per year) with a variety of little goodies for the children left behind. While the parents are caught up in the throes of economic improvement for the family, the children are caught up in feelings of loneliness, anger, anxiety, fear, abandonment and sadness for while they appreciate the barrel, it does not fill the void left by the absence of parents.

---

[51] On Sunday, June 08, 2008, in *The Sunday Observer*, one of the Jamaican News Papers, staff reporter Taneisha Lewis, has given some very powerful insights on Barrel kids from the perspective of the Caribbean.

Staff reporter Taneisha Lewis, who writes for the *Jamaican Observer* newspaper notes that Dr Audrey Pottinger, a consultant from the University of the West Indies, observes that Barrel Kids are often so angry that they sometimes become suicidal. Dr. Pottinger also states that the kids need grief counseling just like children who suffer the death of their loved ones. They develop the migration mentality, just waiting to see when their parents will take them. Often some are exposed to sexual abuse, while others engage in prostitution. Others become poor academic performers; develop low self-esteem, and depression.

While the children might look forward to the goodies that they receive from their parents, they remain in a state of anxiety and confusion. Even with the best of surrogate support, Barrel Kids face challenges that other children often do not face. For example, after a number of years when the Barrel Kids migrate to live with their parents, the realities of their parent's lives begin to become apparent to them. Many thought that their parents were living luxurious lives only to find them living in poverty. The reality that their parents were in a struggle comes to the fore. Add to that the grim reality of the feeling of estrangement between parents and children and one can begin to understand the tremendous challenges in that household. The parents, on the one hand, cannot believe that little Judy or Johnny has grown so much. On the other hand, the children are surprised that parents are surprised.

The biggest surprise, however, is that the shocked parents least expected that their little baby, now grown up into a teenager, could challenge their authority. But the child is angry and confused and almost in a "lock down" mode for Mom and Dad have not been around and therefore have no right to be giving them orders let alone dealing out punishment. Feelings such as these open the door for widening communication gaps. And if these gaps are not regulated, they will potentially develop into open conflict and rebellion. Yes "cultural uprootedness" is one of the greatest parenting dilemmas of the day, and those who recognize it as a negative phenomenon must step up to become effective child advocates.

Cultural uprootedness

When people are removed out of the situations in which they have developed most of their life's experiences, that is cultural uprootedness. According to Samovar and Porter, culture refers to the cumulative deposit of knowledge, experience, beliefs, values, attitudes, meanings, hierarchies, religion, notions of time, roles, spatial relations, concepts of the universe, and material objects and possessions acquired by a group of people in the course of generations through individual and group striving.[52]

Through cultures:

- Our modes are determined
- Our traditions are maintained.
- Our assumptions are made.
- Our perspectives are directed.
- Our paradigms are sustained.
- Our relationships are built.
- Our problems are resolved.

One of the earliest scientists of culture who came to the above determinations was Clyde Kluckhohn, who argued that:

- culture is the total way of life of a people;
- culture is the social legacy the individual acquires from his group.
- culture is a way of thinking, feeling, and believing.
- culture is an abstraction from behavior.
- culture is storehouse of pooled learning.
- culture is a set of standardized orientations to recurrent problems.
- culture is learned behavior.
- culture is a mechanism for the normative regulation of behavior.

---

[52] Larry A. Samovar and Richard E. Porter, *Intercultural Communication: A Reader*, 7th ed. (Belmont, CA: Wadsworth Publishing Company, 1994).

- culture is a set of techniques for adjusting both to the external environment and to other people.
- culture is a precipitate of history,"
- culture is a behavioral map, sieve, or matrix.[53]

So, what happens when the problem of cultural uprootedness affects a person? The simple answer is that conflicts arise, attention and performance are affected, motivations change and identity crisis increases or is exacerbated

Cultural shifts and parenting

Apart from the general cultural contexts in which people were born, one might think of the shifts in the cultures of family structures that directly or indirectly impact children. For instance, a child might be born in a two-parent family and becomes a child in a one parent family and so on. There are a variety of family types that might impact a person in a person's life time. These family types can be considered cultural types.

> *The two parent (family)* is a biblical paradigm of parents, that has been presented from the genesis of humanity. It is pretty rare in a large part of our societies today. Maybe in some parts of the world it is still considered the ideal parental type, but it is not as pervasive as it once had been.

> *The single parent (family)* type is a common phenomenon in a large part of the world of the day and is considered almost cyclical within families. As teen pregnancy and divorce increase, this parent type increases exponentially.

---

[53] Though many scientists have contended that Kluckhohn placed too much emphasis on culture and not enough attention to inherited tendencies, yet no one has disputed the profound effect of culture.

The extended-parent (family) type is gradually losing its place in society. Its absence is noticeable in the lives of many children who had that kind of support but have been drawn away from it. Many have now been drawn into a life of crime, abuse, and parental neglect.

The step-parent or blended (family) type is becoming more and more prevalent especially with the high divorce rates. This type occurs when one or both partners bring children from previous relationships to form a family. Such a configuration has its challenges for it brings certain stresses and strains on child/ren and parents that sometimes can be destructive for both. However, this kind of parenting is better than none at all.

The kinship-parent (family) type has to do with relatives who take on the care of their kinship children. Relative caregivers such as grandparents, aunts, uncles, cousins and siblings who provide kinship are often challenged by the task of parenting.

The nuclear-parents (family) type is one, which declares its independence from family and everyone else. It mirrors the individualism, which is an integral part of Western culture. This type has had devastating results on the lives of children especially when both parents must work and there is no additional family support available for the children. We connect this type with uprootedness mainly because it presents a paradox - parents are present but absent.

The divorced-parents (family) type has been swelling the single parent category and also step-parent family type. In many instances, this family type has led to many angry and maladjusted children. But it is necessary for people to admit to the realities of this type. Many children caught in this family type harbor extreme anger as they often become pawns of parents. Often, they are caught in the middle of two individuals they love. As these children are tossed from one parent to the next, and as parents move from one place to the, the children have to cope with uprootedness.

The adoptive-parents (family) type is becoming a viable type, sometimes cause by death, divorce or the inability to have a child for reasons known or unknown. Adoptive parenting has proven beneficial to many children who otherwise, might have been societal pariahs. Even though it might not be the ideal, it has become a haven for many children in providing them with some amount of stability.

The foster-parents (family) type is a rapidly developing type. It is developing mainly because of dysfunctionality in the many family types. Interestingly, it has not succeeded in being very helpful to many children and youth because many individuals now see it as a business rather than a love for children in need.

The immigrant-parent (family) type is quite prevalent in urban areas, for as economic pressures face the world, people use every means to migrate to other parts of the world where they feel that personal economic conditions will be better. But immigrants face many challenges as they try to fit into their new culture. Often there is *culture shock*. That is, experiencing radical differences and anxieties because what they are experiencing in the new country is different from the world of stability from which they came. While children might make the transition quite readily, parents usually find it most difficult to adjust. And when the children begin to emulate the ways of the dominant culture, there are lots of family conflicts. Parents are prone to cling to, and demand behaviors consistent with the old culture, while children, feeling the need to belong, become a part of the new culture. In effect, it is important that parents and children who are faced with cultural uprootedness become aware of the differences and learn to deal with them. Such is important for family unity.

The alcoholic and drug addicted family is included as a family type because it is one in which children are fifty times more likely to practice the habits and behaviors of these families. The cycle in this type is often replicated but for the grace of God. Often enough, this or these family type(s) are so unstable, that there is always the daily threat of uprootedness.

The incest-family. We include this as a family type because these families produce cycles of human tragedy and maintain the deception of the tragedy. When a child in such a family type is being destroyed often the whole family enters into complicity. No one within the family will confront the reality and no one will advocate on behalf of the child. If the case comes to light, and there is advocacy on behalf of the child, it will mean that the child will have to be removed from the family environment. The abuse becomes a well-kept secret in the family for a few reasons: (1) Economic reasons - the perpetrator is the mainstay of the family (2) Keeping the family together (3) Family pride- the name of the family cannot be destroyed. While these might be valid reasons, little thought is given to the long-term impact on the child.

The question that one might be tempted to ask is how are these various parent/family types are connected to or contribute to uprootedness. In some instances, it might be easy to see but not as easy in other types. Very often the lives of children have been disrupted by various things happening in families. Some children are sent to live with relatives, some become wards of the state, and others acquire new parents, or might continue to live with dysfunctional family members who are always on the run. As such, these children are removed from friends in school, church, and other organizations. Some are removed from their parents and the ways of life practiced. They must adjust to new individuals with new norms and values which can be challenging for both the one receiving the care and the primary caregiver. These caregivers are now surrogate parents and need to understand the many challenges and pressures brought to bear. They are challenged in understanding the values, the norms, the language, and the various other issues connecting with the new additions.

There is another form of uprootedness, which one might argue does not fit the paradigm but one which should be brought to a high level of awareness. The rules of engagement and resolution might be different, but from a child's perspective, is indeed a form of uprootedness. The types we reference are the one in which children live with both parents and are relatively comfortable. However, these parents have jobs which require frequent relocations, as parents get promotions or their skills are needed in other locations. Very little attention is paid to the difficulties these children experience as they must leave friends each time and forced to make new ones. Children in this category might have difficulty building trust, getting into close relationships, connecting or bonding with anything or anyone, for soon they sense that the "nomadic "lifestyle cycle continues. We can relate to this for we heard the cries of our children for "friends" as we relocated from one place to another. Fortunately, we were able to create stability for a considerable period of time until they were grown. But one of us grew in a family where job promotions, sometimes every three years, necessitated relocations. Even though now an adult, the years of movement have left marks for there is still difficulty bonding with anyone outside of the family.

How parents can mediate culture in their children's development

The point of the foregoing discussion concerns the importance of recognizing cultural uprootedness as one of the most challenging issues for couples as they embark on their parenting journey. Even as parents move from one place to another or one stage to another they want to parent as they were parented in their old culture. They wish their children would like what they like, eat what they eat, appreciate the music they like and speak as they speak, but there are cultural, generational and other shifts that bring much tension between parents and their children. Here are some areas that are ready ingredients for conflict that one might need to think about as one deal with cultural uprootedness.

Communication and language.

One of the greatest areas of conflict that people have to deal with as they confront cultural uprootedness is communication. Edward T. Hall, a respected, world renowned anthropologist of the 20th Century, wrote several popular practical books on dealing with cross-cultural issues. He rightly notes that culture is communication, and communication is culture.[54] The point is that to communicate with youngsters, who move from one culture to another, is most difficult. In communication one should always remember that patience is the best virtue. Remember that one cannot communicate with another if one does not know the language of the other. Language, as Hall states, is not only what is

---

[54] See http://en.wikipedia.org/wiki/Edward_T._Hall

said but what is felt[55], not just words but gestures, not just gestures but even our stance, or what Hall calls "Proxemics," that is, space that people stand when they speak. So, a few suggestions for dealing with communication are necessary:

- Learn to the language of the other. How does such and such a person speak? Note the tone and accents. Note the meaning of words.
- Learn to listen. One learns by listening, just as babies learn by listening and observing. Listening does not only mean hearing but watching - noticing. As one listens one will find that meanings open up.
- Learn to overcome prejudices. Even a few words learned form a new language can open up a whole lot of worlds between peoples of different cultures. Learn to overcome the prejudice of accents. Just because a person speaks with a different accent does not mean the person is dumb. This observation is quite instructive to parents and to all others who are seeking to honestly deal with cross cultural issues with their children.

Discipline and punishment

How does one's view of discipline and punishment differ from one's parents or style from one culture to another? Many parents tend to discipline and punish in the way they were parented. In discipline, one thinks of how one instructs, trains or schools, guides or directs, and in punishment, one thinks of correcting, chastising, or challenging a child/person to good behavior. The concepts might be the same, but how such is practiced differ from culture to culture.

---

[55] Hall speaks of how other issues than speech is to be considered in his book *The Silent Language*.

- Thus, one who is transitioning needs to think of what compromises exists between the old culture and the new.
- One needs not think that discipline and punishment must be either or. They might need adjustments but there is no letting go of one or the other if one is to have a child/ren that is/are well managed and controlled.

Dress

How does your child/ren clothing from the old culture differ from the culture which they came? Children want to fit in, and dress is one way that they seek to do so. Dress is one way of defining their identity. They sometimes wear clothing that suggests resistance and rebellion. The question is must parents react when their children wear clothing that does not fit the parent's cultural mood? This can be a great test that allows parents to lose their patience. But it is most significant we teach our children about the importance of dressing appropriately. Let them understand that the way one dresses can affect their success or failure. The kind of acceptance that is received often depends on dress. First impression can be lasting. Dress might be superficial but it carries a great impact.

Relationship with friends

What kinds of challenges exist for people as they move from one place to another? What kinds of frustrations are felt when people do not feel like they fit in? What kinds of relationship struggles, challenges, and obstacles might be experienced between parents and their children because of their lives in a new culture? These are not questions to be treated lightly. Here are a few forthright questions that parents must assess carefully and answer. Are you as a parent effectively prepared to live in a multicultural world? Are you preparing your child/ren for a multicultural world? Are you prepared to accept when your child who is Mexican or Caucasian brings home a person who is of African or Indian extraction and vice versa? Even within peoples of the same race, or ethnic communities, there are differences in the conceptualization of relations, and there are differences in culture. There are particular norms for relations and friendships, and there are constraints and controls. With that being the case, every parent and every child should be trained to find ways of building linkages and face the frustrations of not feeling left out. Relationships are always possible if one is willing to work at them.

Time

Time is viewed in diverse ways in various cultures. For example, while in one culture the event supersedes the clock, in others the clock takes precedence over everything. If a parent from a culture that focuses on the event were asked by teacher from a culture that focuses on the clock to appear at a meeting, there might be moments of frustration. The parent might turn up a long time after the appointment and might be considered disrespectful or disinterested in his or her child. The differences in perceptions can create setbacks. It is therefore crucial for parents to work hard to understand the significance of time as they move from culture to culture. In fact, time management demands the understanding of time. Not to have a mutual conception of time might mean that one will never be an effective advocate.

Work

People from varied cultures of the world, have different views regarding work. In some cultures, work is of primary importance while in other cultures relationships are more important than work. This can be a major challenge as people move from culture to culture. For instance, where work takes precedents over relationships the stability of the family suffers. A further reality is affected by the philosophy of work as it relates to gender. In some cultures, Dad goes to work while Mom stays at home. When such parents move to cultures where economic pressures suggest that both parents work, Dad might insist upon finding two or three jobs just to keep the order of providing for the family; but in the family loses the attention of Dad and Mom becomes frustrated with this lack of attention. Another scenario is one in which Dad stays home as the primary caregiver while Mom goes to work and becomes the bread winner. However, Dad's friends might see him as abdicating his responsibility and ridicule him. Conflicts might arise in the family because Mom insists that in order to survive, she must work. The point is that struggles can be triggered because the status of the culturally uprooted work partner is compromised. In some instances, a person was a high professional in one place is now subjected to menial tasks because of licensure. We have seen how movement from one state to another here in the Unites States can compromise a professional's life.

Another issue that might be noted in regards to the culture of work is that of child work permits. Sometimes parents do not know:

- The proper age at which a child can be employed, even by their own parents
- What kinds of work are prohibited for children?
- What are the times of day that children are permitted to work?
- The number of hours that children are allowed to work in a day or a week
- Where to apply for a work permit when a child goes out to work
- What kinds of consents are required?
- What obligations employers have for the child who goes to work
- What options are available if the school work of a child who goes to work suffers
- What kinds of employers' liability insurance requirements are available in order for a child to be secured in the workplace?

The point of the outline above is to suggest that up-rootedness presents critical challenges for parents and their children in relation to work. Attention, also, needs to be given to proactive parenting, so that a child's life will not be compromised.

Authority and power

Conceptions of authority and power vary from culture to culture. That is no less with parental authority and power. In the western world, for example, where there is much emphasis on individual autonomy, choice, personal decision and freedom, quite often there is an assault on parental authority. Thus, frequent conflicts and disagreements occur between parents and children, especially with the adolescent. In the East, where parental authority is given strong endorsement there are fewer public conflicts and disagreements. Therefore, life can become very interesting for parents and children as East and West gets mixed.

In the latter frame many parents feel challenged by their children with regards to their understanding of authority and power. In fact, studies have shown that there are relationships between parental authority and academic achievement. When parents have greater authority in their children's lives, their children perform more highly, whereas children whose parents demonstrate little authority perform poorly.

There might be confusion as to what is meant by parental authority, whether one is referencing the authoritarian – controlling – domineering parent, over against the permissive parenting – with little or no boundaries, which are often the choices we make in our Western culture. What is being offered is the kind of authority which is understood as authoritative parenting, where the parents are responsive to the child's needs while at the same set clear limits and are consistent in enforcing them.[56] In the latter there is much love and respect shown to the child/ren, as is expected from the child to the parent.

When a family moves to any context where there is confusion on the question of authority there will be conflicts. A friend phoned us some time ago and asked, "When can both of you come to meet with parents in my community, because the children are *running all over* the parents?" The suggestion was that there was no clear understanding of

---

[56] Cf. https://www.parentingforbrain.com/authoritative-parenting/

authority and power between the parents and their children and how they could build healthy relationships.

The above reflects that in many contexts there is a critical need for parenting education.

Education

Maybe one of the areas that are most challenging when a family is dealing with cultural uprootedness is that of education. Children who move from one system of education to another suffer much instability. Even in the United States itself, many differences can be felt from state to state and for sure just between school districts. The differences are expressed because of the location and funding of each school district. However, a great difference that calls for our interest is that of the educational challenge that is brought to families who are in transition from one culture to another. We speak particularly of immigrant families, because we have noted such families in the throes of displacement and frustration of dealing with their new systems of education. The following examples suggest the levels of distractions that can be experienced:

- Parents have little conception of the demands of the educational system in their new domicile.
- Teachers are sometimes unaware of the educational frame from which the children are coming.
- Conflicts develop because the parents have language limitation to speak with the teacher.
- Anger is expressed because the teacher does not understand the accent of the student or the parents and vice versa.
- The children are misplaced in parts of the educational because they are dealt with as special needs which in many senses do not exist.

The point that is being made is that the parents who will act as the children's advocate need to take time to study and understand the new systems in which they find themselves so that they can help their children to adjust and participate most effectively in the education. If you are a parent or mentor reading this you will want to find the kind of help that can be effective as you seek to negotiate the system in which you are now placed. It is your child and no one has a greater interest in that child than you. Take time to make sure that those who teach your child/ren have an understanding of multicultural/cross-cultural education. Watch carefully and when you see that your child is being treated in a pejorative manner, call the teachers attention to it and if required go beyond the teacher. It is you job to protect your child and secure his/her best future.

Individuality and community

We have mentioned earlier that as part of the challenge of dealing with cultural uprootedness is the difference in views on individuality and community. In the West, for instance, the emphasis is on individuality, in the East the emphasis is on community. When a parent from the West moves from one community to another in the West, such a parent quickly finds ways to survive, while a parent from the East who has moved from their community to the West will find it challenging to survive. Of course, this distinction is false since it does assume that anyone can live without community. Whether from the West or East, all human beings must depend upon community. But the point here is to focus on the fact that when parents seek to advocate for their children, whether from East or West, they are not to make assumptions about one's understanding about "individuality" or "community." If they do, they might be frustrated. Every person is to be treated as individuals in community, for no one is an island; no one stands alone.

Cultural uprootedness and advocacy

The point of the foregoing discussion is to focus attention on the fact that one of the most significant challenges confronting parents today is that of cultural uprootedness. Families, as a whole, that are culturally displaced often need others to advocate for them. In the meanwhile, parents need to be aware that they must advocate on behalf of their children. It is very interesting how often the children of immigrants' families get in conflict with their parents. This is because the children feel alienated, often seething bitterness that they would wish to tell their parents. At one of our family reunions, we were discussing who had it better or worse - those of us who were left behind with some family members to supervise us, or our little sister who accompanied our parents to Canada. We thought our little sister had it so much better, but then it came out how she resented the fact that she had to leave here siblings behind. Her anger came out in her school work. She would fail subjects just to punish Mom and Dad, or so she thought. It was not until someone intervened that she was able to focus and change her direction. The left behinds recognized that being taken away from siblings also had its negatives. The point is that both groups suffered hurts.

Advocacy as prevention and advocacy as protection

The reality is that many children of uprooted families struggle with:

> *Identity* (and crisis) – They struggle with a sense of who they really are.
> *Intimacy* – They want to belong - it is no wonder that there are so many gangs. formed by children from uprooted families.
> *Safety and Security* – They feel the intensity of these two needs of humanity in a most intense manner and are anxious them to be provided.

This is why parents of uprooted families must learn advocacy as prevention and advocacy as protection.

As a means of advocacy parents need to:

- **Know the services that are available** in the community where they live. We have suggested a few of the kinds of such services in the appendix of this book.
- **Build up their network** connection with individuals and organizations that can be helpful to them.
- **Find mentors and couches** who will direct them to what is available for their aid.
- **Become more open with their children** to know what their struggles are, as they deal with their daily emotions.

The point is that advocacy is never easy. It takes time, education and personal sacrifice. But the end result is that it pays a great dividend when our children are saved from possible destruction.[57]

QUESTIONS FOR REFLECTION

1. What are the ways in which you would consider yourself a culturally uprooted person?
2. What are some challenges your family have faced as you have moved from one context to another?
3. What kinds of changes have you had to make on behalf of your children as you have moved from one place to another?

---

[57] Look at the hotline numbers in the appendix to see how you might find help.

CHAPTER VIII

Parenting Through A Pandemic

This reflection on the gravest pandemic to have hit our world in the last hundred years is directed to parents. It is important for parents because their world has turned topsy turvy. Some parents report that they are losing their minds by having their kids' home for so long and uncertain are very period as to what will happen next. It is not that parents hate their children, but because of the uncontrolled dislocations that have come upon them, with such haste. They have had no time to prepare for the eventuality. The unexpectedness and the chaos are just too much to take. Many parents have tried to find a balance, but as each family situation, resources, school, and work environment are different, so is the stress to find the right balance.

Two of my sisters drove all day from states far away so that they could help their children in providing temporary care for their grandchildren. In the one case, the nanny quit because she had to care for her children who were out of school and had no other caregiver available. In the other case, the parents are essential workers, and therefore not allowed the time at home to supervise their children. But how long can the grandparents be present? Even though they are grandparents, they still have tasks to which they must attend in their own homes.

What is difficult for couples is even more difficult for single parents. Even if they had been coping as single parents before, their regular schedules are now no more. I read a story of one single mother who, when the stay - at- home order was made, broke down in tears. The mother took off from work that afternoon, ate some brownies with her 5-year-old, but she kept wondering how she was going to get through three more months of working from home while taking care of her son on her own. She thought she had found a balance until her son went up to her while she was on a work call and whispered, "Mommy, I miss you." Right there, she felt deflated. Situations such as this are pushing parents everywhere to "try to adjust to the eerie new normal" of virtual classrooms. The inability to find child care is particularly daunting especially for single parents, struggling to navigate what they did not previously perceive.

It is harsh enough for homes that have not been hit directly by the virus. Just imagine the homes in which a child or a parent has the virus. Not only does one speak of social distancing in such situations, but the family is confronted with hospitalization, quarantining, and in some cases, death. People who have lived in war zones, and other places where diseases and extreme disasters have hit, understand displacements. They shared their bizarre stories, but without having similar experiences, it has been hard for the rest of the world to accept.

However, covid 19 has created a worldwide war zone and giving those of us who were unaware, a taste of what others have been experiencing.

I received a rather informative video that was shared on social media by a young doctor from New York City. He is not a specialist in psychiatry, but he used an interesting phrase that caught my attention. He spoke of the fundamental emotional challenge that many persons are facing as **Corona Induced Anxiety** (CIA). An interesting term indeed, because it is a reality that everyone in the family seems to be facing at this time. The fact is that families are facing a challenge such as we have never encountered, and we must face it "with fear and trembling". No one is exempt, neither parents or children.

Parental Advocacy

I have collected many insights about the pandemic that I consider essential reminders for parents, especially those with school-aged children. Here I share some of these practical suggestions:

1. **Keep a Schedule/Routine-**
   Routines help children to feel more in control. Schedules with intervals of playtime and learning time will help children deal with some of the anxiety and stress of being out of school and away from friends.

2. **Practice Social Distancing Activities**
   You can do activities such as going on walks, bike rides, garden work, and virtual hangouts with family and friends. If you choose to do a social distance activity outside, make sure you do it with your immediate family (those you live with) and keep a **6 feet** distance between you and others.

3. **Keep A Journal**
   Let children write down (or draw) how they are feeling. This is a fun activity and also a healthy way to help children express their feelings and emotions.

4. **Be Honest & Calm**
   Be honest with your children and let them know what's going on, in an age-appropriate way. Limit the amount of news they watch and remain calm with how your feeling. Children feed off of our emotions and may feel overwhelmed or unable to share how they feel if we express anxiety around them.

5. **Know About Available Resources**
   - Free Breakfast & Lunch for children in your County offices ($2 for adults). Eg. https://www.fcps.edu/news/coronavirus-update-food-resources
   - Emergency Needs (Clothing, Shelter, etc.) – Call
   - CDC's Disaster Distress Helpline- 1-800- 985-5990

- For Daily updates on COVID-19 text- FEMA
- For questions or concerns about the coronavirus call or visit the CDC.

6. **Follow the more general rules that are given daily by the experts. Sometimes they might seem quite trivial, but they are crucial for our survival.**

- Avoid large crowds.
- Observe the rules of social distancing.
- Wash hands (for 20 seconds at least).
- Use the right sanitizers to clean our hands often.
- Wear masks – the right kind of masks.
- Practice social distancing – keeping a least 6 feet from other persons in public spaces.
- Gather only in small groups (some places, no more than 5 or 10).
- Stay away from sugary diet and other things that will compromise our immune system.
- Get enough rest and sleep at night.
- Get some sunlight each day.
- Exercise daily in the fresh air for at least 30 minutes– keep the right distance
- Get tested if you feel your body has been compromised.
- Drink the adequate amount of fluids each day (between 6 to 8 eight once glasses)
- Self-quarantine (if you have been in contact with someone who has the virus or feels sick).
- Cover your mouth each time you cough
- Do not touch your eyes, nose, or mouth unless you have just washed your hands.
- If family or friends want to visit during this time, let them know they will have to wait until the worse stages of the virus have passed.

Parental Advocacy

- Use whatever herbs you can to build your immunity.
- Keep connected with family and friends.
- Check out the authenticity of all information.

The concerns discussed focuses on:

- **Preparation** – Although it is quite challenging to prepare for a pandemic as we have seen, yet we must always be prepared for a crisis. We will face many in life, small and great. One never knows when one will come.
- **Prevention** – Although there are no guarantees that one will never get a disease, one should do all that one can to make sure that they practice prevention.
- **Protection**:Home is supposed to be the best place of safety. Home is where children feel safe.
- **Production**: During this time, one must make the passing moments productive, rather than boring.
- **Practice** the right safety habits. Habits are never be easy to be changed. Thus, those who seek to teach new habits need to practice them as well. Show that they are essential. Watch for bad habits and try to break them.
- **Petition** the God of mercy to assist you. Prayer does not replace all of our needful interventions. But there is a general agreement among respected medical professionals that prayer has a profound impact on the healing process when one is ill or facing a crisis. Those who have faith, and are attuned to prayer, understand that "without human effort divine effort is vain." It might seem trite, but it is really true that "God helps those who help themselves."
- **Passion**: While I write, the Christian world is celebrating the season of the Passion and Resurrection of Jesus Christ – Easter. It was in such a time of suffering that Jesus prayed his garden prayer, called one of his greatest prayers for the church and the world (Matthew 26:36-56; Luke 22:39-46). While we think of

such a prayer, we can think of his many other prayers prayed for those who suffer. And we can think of the prayer he prayed for the mothers and children who went to him. On one occasion, as they came, the disciples sought to turn them away. But Jesus intervened and told the disciples, "Let the children come and do not stop them." "Then he placed his hands on the children and blessed them before he left the area where he was." (cf. Matthew 19:13-15).

My concluding point here is that we are in this time of crisis together, and we need to trust The Only One who can help us. We need to do all we can to secure our homes and children. But after that, leave all in the hand of the God who alone knows who we really are and what our needs are.

PART II

The Tools Of Advocacy

CHAPTER IX

Parenting as Advocacy

Children often struggle with so many challenges in this life that there needs to be the full realization that a major role of parenting is advocacy. Of course, many parents do not have a great theoretical or practical understanding as to how to be effective parents, much more being advocates. The mother and her friend in the picture who brought her son to counsel with me (DK) gratified my heart. She took time from all else that she was supposed to do that day because of her profound concerns for her son's future. This discussion and the immediate ones to follow will focus on the what and how of advocacy for parents. The point is that even though we have argued the limitations of many parents, we are persuaded that:

- Parents can be the most effective advocates for their children. Self-interest might be the first force that will drive them; however, that is not the only reason that they should be advocates.
- Parents know their children in a more profound way than anybody else. They have had years living with, observing, reacting to, understanding, and responding to their children. They have learned under what conditions their children cooperate or resist, initiate or follow, interact or withdraw, and when they are most eager to communicate.
- As parent speak on behalf of their children, they will find others, such as teachers and physicians, who can support them in advocating for their child/ren. Parents can consider these professionals their allies. They can use their influence to assist parents in receiving needed services and programs for their child/ren. For example, a family doctor could write a letter to the school board describing the magnitude of a child's anxiety concerning the child's language immersion program to speed up a placement in a program where the child will be taught in their first language.
- Despite the professional help that parents might seek along their advocacy journey, they are their child/ren's full-time advocates —the ones with the file, so to speak, on the ways to help the child/ren succeed socially and at school.
- As a parent, be aware that not all the professionals you consult will appreciate your openness. Some professionals may take the view that parents are too emotionally involved to be objective. However, it may be your very connectedness that helps you understand that your child is different from the child/ren's peers, and that spurs you to take action to get the child help.

As your child/ren's trusted confidante, you know what really worries them and how complex their problems really are. Likely you are the person who knows how much school failure terrifies your child/ren. They have probably asked you, "What's wrong with my brain?" Of course, you know that often it is not a problem with their brain, but with all the distractions that are impacting them. They do not have a clear sense of their life's goals, both short term and long term. They need to know what is to be done now in order for their future achievement.

What is Advocacy?

- Advocacy means challenging persons and changing conditions so people are treated and cared for in a just way.
- An advocate is a person who effectively speaks up for, acts in behalf of, or supports someone else.
- An extension of the definition makes the advocate one who seeks the redress of others, working for their protection, making sure that they might receive the best they can receive out of life.
- Because children are as vulnerable and dependent as they are, parents are to be seen as their first and greatest advocate.

Jesus: The World's Greatest Advocate

Jesus is called the quintessential advocate because he is the one who stands in place for all humanity. He "pleads" for humanity. He seeks to "protect" humanity. He "defends" humanity against any satanic attack. The Bible tells us, "If anyone should sin, we have **An Advocate** with the Father, Jesus Christ the righteous" (1 John 2:1). We can find one of the greatest moments in the work of Jesus as advocate when he stood up against his disciples and spoke to them when mothers brought their children to him to be blessed. The disciples drove the mothers and their children away, but Jesus said, "Don't stop them, let them come, for to such the kingdom of God belongs" (Mark 10:13; Matt. 19:13–15).

The Why of Parental Advocacy

Why is it so significant to be advocates on behalf of our children? Children are totally dependent on adults for survival. Children are filled with innocence. Although parents and psychologists today argue that children have personalities, feelings, intentions, and social abilities, yet they are also convinced that they are naive, incompetent, and vulnerable. No creature might be as vulnerable as children. In most cultures, children are not given adult responsibilities until they are between the ages of eighteen to twenty-one. When children are in their infancy, they are often thought to be little angels. Most persons who see them as babes will say, "Isn't s/he beautiful?" "Isn't s/he cute or cuddly?" It is a known fact that in most prison cultures, the one who is taken in because of some crime against a child will suffer great retribution. The prisoners will turn on such a one because s/he has done something evil to "an innocent child."

It is not just a question of perception; it is a reality that children are innocent and dependent. When we refer to them as infants, we mean that they are incapable of speech. When we refer to them as babes, we mean that they can barely babble. When we refer to them as toddlers, we mean that they are just beginning to learn how to walk, speak, touch things, develop social values, and have their will and way. As they walk and fall and seek to have their way within these stages of development, we say that they are emerging with their own identity, or that they are becoming self-aware and moral beings. But until now, we do not trust them with grown-up responsibilities, for they have not yet passed through the stages of early childhood, middle childhood, and later childhood or what is called in our Western culture adolescence. And even here, we still think of the innocence of children, for in adolescence, they must still learn the significance of freedom and the power of choice. Whatever the culture of adolescence and the definitions that are given to it, what is clear is that even at this stage, there is a realization that a child is naive, immature, inexperienced, and unsophisticated and can be preyed upon.

Stripped of Innocence

In effect, it is a tragic thing when adults in any society look upon children—who are to be the objects of their protection, nurture, and care—and attack, abuse, molest, violate, and force them into adulthood where they are "stripped of innocence." When we speak of the multiple negative conditions that children face in our world, we reference the unsolicited circumstances thrust on them.

1. *Children in war.* Children who are trained to hate their so-called enemies, like one Palestinian mother said, "I want my baby to suck the milk of hate from my breast." In war zones, children who see the death of their parents are filled with anger; often such children are forced into training as soldiers to participate in revenge. Children in gangs might be placed alongside children in war; adults bring children into gangs, teach them hate, and give them deadly weapons that are not even worthy for adults to use.
2. *Children in violence.* In situations of domestic violence, children are the most affected. When parents are violent, children are traumatized by such violence. Multiple studies also reveal that when children watch violence in the media, they are negatively affected by such violence.
3. *Children as pawns in divorce.* While divorce might benefit parents, children are rarely benefited by it. More often than not, they are caught between two feuding parents who are only thinking of themselves in the divorce. But the process of the divorce produces an excruciatingly painful life for the child/ren.
4. *Children in pornography.* At a time when child pornography is on the rise, especially with the Internet, greater attention needs to be given to curb children in pornography.
5. *Children in prostitution.* More and more children are being used as agents of prostitution. The economic benefits to parents and adults who bring children into such activities are often thought

to be of greater value than the value of the child/ren, for the child/ren are only as valuable as the money they can bring through prostitution.
6. *Children in drugs.* Children are often witness to the use and sale of drugs. Many times, children are used as drug traffickers because they cannot be put in jail as adults are.
7. *Children in incestuous relationships.* The incest is a growing problem for children. The conditions and moral codes in many families make incest possible. The issue of step-parenting exacerbates incest.
8. *Children as laborers.* One of the oldest problems for society is the use of children in the labor force. Children are often put to work in conditions that, at times, are not even suited for adults.
9. *Children as con artists.* Children are sometimes used as frontiers for adults. On a visit to a certain country, we noticed a mother with a baby in her arms and four small children standing near, standing in the hub of activity. She suddenly shrunk in the shadows, and as each unsuspecting individual came by, she sent them out into the busy streets as she pretended not to know them. We were horrified by what we saw since the eldest child could not have been more than about seven years of age.
10. *Children as victims of sexual abuse.* We hear the horrors daily where children are kidnapped and forced into sex rings. And in some cases, after being ravaged sexually, they are killed and buried.
11. *Children as victims of neglect.* Child neglect is still a growing concern despite efforts to curb it. Many parents do not seek to secure the health of their children and keep them safe.
12. *Children as victims of physical abuse.* Hitting and beating up on children can be devastating consequences.
13. *Children as victims of emotional abuse.* Destructive words, such as "You are no good," are often spoken to children. Negative words, labeling words have adverse effect on children and potentially follow them through life.

14. *Children whose parents are starstruck* (without balance). Forcing children into public life and public view, pressuring them into overachievement, disrespecting their will, can have a profound negative impact on children.

Too many adults today, trace their hurts, pain, dysfunctions, destruction, and cyclical evils to moments in their childhood when they were ill-treated, neglected, and exploited. One does not need a psychoanalyst like Sigmund Freud to tell us that what we see in our adult behavior is the result of the social conditions that have been experienced in childhood. Just watching the behaviors and listening to the stories of adults can tell us much about the histories of human lives. Because there are lifetime consequences for what happen to children, it is important that early analysis of some of the destructive elements be made in order to give the help and support necessary. In the long run, there can be a turn-around from some of these troubling traits listed below:

1. Their sense of values confusion—struggle between right and wrong.
2. Their loss of opportunity for peer interaction—their normal socialization with their friends denied.
3. Their sense of reality destroyed—they live in denial.
4. Their loss of the transitional states of their lives—they do not know whether they are children of adults.
5. Their sense of self-esteem compromised—they live in identity and crisis.
6. Their time for play passed.
7. Their vital energy is often used up before adulthood.
8. Their loss of the sense of profound joy.
9. Their loss of freedom grave—they are forced into seriousness.
10. Their acceptance of abnormal behaviors as normal.
11. Their loss of opportunity of child-adult relationship.
12. Their capacity for decision making is often skewed.

13. Their foundation for many maladaptive behaviors—obsessions, compulsions, and addictions are formed through their childhood experiences.
14. Their depressions are brought on from the difficult times they have faced, so difficult sometimes they become suicidal.
15. Their lack of capacity to determine boundaries.
16. Their codependency syndromes is often seen in their always trying to "be nice."
17. Their struggle with willpower.
18. Their general lack of courage.
19. Their life of self-resignation.
20. Their low level of performance.
21. Their general fear of the future.

The twenty-one conditions listed above are just a fraction of the multiple negative states that we call "stripping our children of innocence." The topic "stripped of innocence" evolved out of a class in Christian ethics that one of us taught. As the class opened up questions on sexual challenges, especially in the area of incest, it was painful to believe that even in the very class being taught, there were so many victims. The revelations of that moment are still mind-boggling years later. Interest in the subject heightened as the news media brought an awareness of thousands of children exposed to sexual and drug abuse. Our interest was even more intense; as we followed the scandal arising from the many months of revelations about sexual abuse and pedophilia by Roman Catholic priests in the United States and across the world. The thought that, in a few short years, one priest abused one hundred children and, in a few years, forty thousand priests abused more than ten thousand children in the dioceses, in the Eastern United States, was incomprehensible. When the television showed adult survivors crying for what had been done to them, it brought home in a forceful way what our homes, churches, and other corporate institutions need to do to deal with the plight of children. The question then at the point of class discussions, and the media revelations, is still relevant: "While we are fighting wars for our world's liberation, how do we liberate our children and keep them safe?"

As we ponder the fate of our children, we pose several questions that bring deep concerns. Among the many are these:

1. How can we fight to keep our children free and safe from the predatorial forces that are destroying them?
2. How can we make our children know that they are valued?
3. How can we make them know that we are working together to protect them?
4. How can we prevent child abuse through our ministries?
5. How can leaders rebuild the trust of parents in leadership so that they can leave their children with us?
6. How can we touch the lives of our children in order to save them?
7. How can our homes become better places of safety where our children who become deluded can grow?

In presenting these questions, the intent is to call for responsiveness from persons in positions of trust, and to challenge all of us in the way we value children. In each of our workshops and discussions, we seek to encourage youngsters, parents, churches, and public leaders of conscience to place the protection of children at the highest interest in their work.

It is our conviction that while we fight wars for our interests, multitudes of adults are struggling with the wounds they received in childhood. While we work for our own economic comfort, our children yearn for our love and attention. While we are enjoying our supposed adult entertainment, our children are exposed to the most tragic types of mental abuses. In effect, it is our hope that future workshops and discussions might be transforming for the life of even one person who has been stripped of innocence.

In order to give the kinds of help that our children need, parents and other responsible adults must understand that our children need someone to

- support them
- help them
- assist them
- encourage them
- defend them
- help them with visioning
- train them
- prepare them for the future
- motivate them
- challenge them
- rebuke them
- listen to them
- teach them respect
- help them understand the question of personal dignity
- affirm them
- recognize them
- wisely reward them
- encourage them
- empathize with them
- teach them integrity
- teach them accountability
- build their trust
- resolve conflicts.

Advocacy as a Major Task

Based on the above list, it should be understood that advocacy has been and continues to be a major task of parenting. If you are an effective parent, you are a powerful advocate. Many persons and institutions such as the court system (judges, attorneys, child welfare agents), the medics (doctors and nurses), educators (principals, teachers, social workers, and psychologists), and in the field of religion (pastors and their associates) are advocates. However, it must be reinforced that no one can be more important as advocates than parents.

Very often one does not pause to think of the multiple roles that parents must assume in behalf of their children. Certainly, if many did, they would not have taken on the task of parenting? Here are a few of the many things parents do or ought to do:

- Parents have visions for the future of their child/ren.
- Parents plan for the future of their child/ren.
- Parents know their child/ren better than anyone else. The school, the church, the community might be involved with the child/ren for a few years; but parents are involved all their lives.
- Parents play an active role in planning for their children's well-being.
- Parents are their child/ren's first teacher.
- Parents are their child/ren's most important role model.
- Parents are responsible for their child/ren's welfare.
- Parents have their child/ren's interest at heart.
- Parents are their child/ren's natural advocate.

Those who understand the above know that parents should make the best advocates.

Places Where Parental Advocacy Is Needed

There are several areas in which parental advocacy is needed for the protection of children. These are areas where parents need to be vigilant. They do not need training in these areas, but they must be willing to ask questions and seek directions from those who are capable of handling the systems. The most crucial areas of need are listed here:

- In the legal system
- In the educational system
- In the medical system
- In systems of potential abuse

Since many parents cannot mediate these systems by themselves, they too need advocates. These advocates who are familiar with these systems, can provide parents with support necessary to take the appropriate actions that are needed to resolve the problems they are facing.

To Be an Effective Advocate

Sometimes parents might be hesitant to seek help because they are not sure of the role of an advocate. However, to be an effective advocate, parents should:

- Be proactive, humble, transparent, thankful, and flexible.
- Seek counsel from people with a proven track record of wise decision and, if appropriate, expertise and experience.
- Be discerning.
- Learn what their rights are and what their child/ren's rights are.
- Use effective communication in advocating for their rights by engaging in active listening and being nonthreatening.
- Find the information to make appropriate decisions.
- Develop problem-solving techniques to overcome obstacles.
- Develop the confidence to do your own advocating.
- Take appropriate actions.
- Analyze problems and pinpoint areas of responsibility.
- Support your child's efforts toward independence.
- Learn about community resources and agencies.
- Network with other parents and groups for mutual support,
- Connect with your provincial/territorial learning.

If parents wait for others to advocate for their children and provide them with the necessary skills to be independent and become self-sufficient members of society, they are likely to be disappointed. Many parents are succumbing to the pressures of life, and often forget the real needs of their children. So, when we speak of advocacy, we will say more about what advocates need to do in particular circumstances.

Here, the point we make is that parents must be among the most powerful advocates of society who will make effective use of what is available to them.

QUESTIONS FOR REFLECTION

1. How would you describe the work of advocacy that you have had to do as a parent?
2. What kinds of skills do you feel would be most helpful to you as a parental advocate?
3. In what ways have you felt the need to coalesce with other parents in order to be effective advocates?

CHAPTER X

Understanding the Rules of the Game for Effective Advocacy

Clarifying Your Expectations

Every game has its rules. This was the point made in François Truffaut's film *The Rules of the Game*. The rules tell us how to play. They orient the minds of the spectators. Without rules, every game would be in confusion. They would lack structure, destiny, and  direction. They would be played in total disorder, or one might say that they could not be played at all.

God also has rules. In their most strict form, they are called The Ten Commandments (recorded in Exodus 20:1–17 and Deuteronomy 5:6–21). The Deuteronomic version of the ten rules as stated with a brief introduction in the New International Version of the Bible reads as follows:

Introduction. I am the LORD your God, who brought you out of Egypt, out of the land of slavery.

1. You shall have no other gods before me.
2. You shall not make for yourself an idol in the form of anything in heaven above or on the earth beneath or in the waters below. You shall not bow down to them or worship them; for I, the LORD your God, am a jealous God, punishing the children for the sin of the fathers to the third and fourth generation of those who hate me, but showing love to a thousand generations of those who love me and keep my commandments.
3. You shall not misuse the name of the LORD your God, for the LORD will not hold anyone guiltless who misuses his name.
4. Observe the Sabbath day by keeping it holy, as the LORD your God has commanded you. Six days you shall labor and do all your work, but the seventh day is a Sabbath to the LORD your God. On it you shall not do any work, neither you, nor your son or daughter, nor your manservant or maidservant, nor your ox, your donkey or any of your animals, nor the alien within your gates, so that your manservant and maidservant may rest, as you do. Remember that you were slaves in Egypt and that the LORD your God brought you out of there with a mighty hand and an outstretched arm. Therefore, the LORD your God has commanded you to observe the Sabbath day.

Ten Commandments

5. Honor your father and your mother, as the LORD your God has commanded you, so that you may live long and that it may go well with you in the land the LORD your God is giving you.
6. You shall not murder.
7. You shall not commit adultery.
8. You shall not steal.
9. You shall not give false testimony against your neighbor.
10. You shall not covet your neighbor's wife. You shall not set your desire on your neighbor's house or land, his manservant or maidservant, his ox or donkey, or anything that belongs to your neighbor.

What is it that makes these rules so different from the general rules of life's games? One suggestion is that while the general rules of life's games might change with time, context, and culture, the Ten Commandments never change within themselves, although how they are applied might be changed. In fact, from the Deuteronomic perspective, there are ordinances and statutes (for example, the health laws, food laws, laws of assembly, laws for the sacrificial system, and laws for property usage and so forth) that were given to show how the Commandments were to be applied to the life and history of Israel. Some of the ordinances and statutes lost their relevance over time, but the Ten Commandments in themselves have never lost their relevance. In effect, the Ten Commandments are non-negotiable rules, statutes, principles, or standards for how life can be lived in any age and in any social context. They are fundamental for the stability of the human community and the development of good characters. Therefore, one should do well to teach them to every generation of humanity. The instruction was given to Israel: "Teach them to your children, talk about them when you sit at home and when you walk along the road, when you lie down and when you get up." (Deut. 11:19 NIV).

As foundational rules, the Ten Commandments are given for relationship building with God and human beings. In fact, they sit at the heart of the Covenant with God and humanity. The Covenant is the supreme agreement between God and humanity. In the Covenant document, what is expected in the relationship is stated specifically. Thus, with the words of the Covenant are blessings for obedience and curses for disobedience (cf. Deuteronomy 28).

From what has been stated, we can extract why when parents relate to their children, they must make clear their expectations; that is, the rules of the game or the laws, statutes, or principles of life by which they and their children are to live. The child/ren must be clear on the principles for their individual behavior, how such principles impact the family as a whole, and society in general. They need to know that laws are given for relationship building, for protection and for safety. They need to understand rules in terms of commendation and prohibition. Yes, the points being made are that

- children need to know what is expected of them,
- they need to be given the expectations with clarity,
- they are to know that there are expectations that will be insisted upon,
- they need to understand the consequences of not fulfilling the expectations,
- they need to take full responsibility for their decision,
- they need to understand what it means to take responsibility,
- they need to learn early about what it means to be accountable.

Who Is in Charge?

It is important that a child knows what the rules are, and who is in charge. Sometime ago while delivering a series of lectures at a church, one of us observed a toddler in a stroller determinedly kicking his father. The extended period of kicking and crying brought much interest to us. We even mused that the toddler had some kind of disability. His curved position in the stroller enforced that assumption, for he seemed not to be able to turn in any other direction. But toward the end of the presentation, the toddler turned after getting his father's attention. Of course, nothing was wrong with wanting his father's attention. However, it was clear that the toddler had learned how to get attention negatively. It did not seem to matter to the father that the child was kicking him to get his attention. Obviously, there were no rules in place, as far as relationship building was concerned.

Ironically, the next morning, we visited a restaurant in the same city to have breakfast. There, we saw a boy of about seven years. He caught our interest as we noticed how he was placing his hands in his breakfast plate and purposefully scattering his egg and cereal all over the floor. As he continued, his father, in low tones, said, "Son, don't do that"; but the boy sensed a lack of authority in his father's voice and just continued what he was doing without acknowledgement. Both of us looked at each other and cringed because we both wanted to get up, look him in the eye, and say, "*Stop!*" We knew we could not do what we thought, but we kept glancing over to see if the parents understood how repulsive the actions of this child were to the other patrons who were also looking. The boy continued until he felt satisfied, and then he sat down to eat what was left of his meal, as if he did nothing wrong. From all appearances, the boy seemed quite normal, and the mother's response of "I don't know why he chooses to do this" confirmed our assumptions.

Often, people do not realize how much information an observer can gather about family interactions by just sitting in airports, restaurants, and other public spaces and being observant. One afternoon, we did not feel like cooking, so we went to a restaurant. As we waited to be served, we heard an elementary-age girl reprimanding her mother. She told her mother in no uncertain terms that it was "rude" to be talking about her in her absence. The little girl had stepped outside to find her father, and her mother was saying to a friend that her daughter does not like to eat. What interested us was that the girl did not seem to have any regard for her mother. She did not seem to care where she was or who heard her angry outburst on her mom. What children need to know is that they have a right to speak, but that there is a need for them to learn how to speak to any person, more-so their parents in public. They need to understand the rules of respect like they need to understand many other rules.

How does one behave in a restaurant, in a church, in a school, or in any other public space? How does one behave in the home or any other private space? We interviewed several parents as to what constitutes some simple rules of operation for the home, and here are some of the responses:

- Always say please when you ask for anything and thank you when you get it.
- Pick up toys after you use them and return them to their proper places.

- Be honest at all times. It is better to tell the truth than to lie.
- Speak respectfully to their siblings and peers.
- Learn to speak appropriately and listen when being spoken with/to.
- Keep rooms tidy—clean up when you mess up.
- Return things to where you have taken them from.
- Do not jump on furniture and sit on tables.
- Show respect for everyone.
- Complete any task that you have started.
- Be controlled when you use the Internet.
- Be selective in your choice of music.
- Be dignified in your dress.
- Be courteous in your speech.
- Ask for what you need. Don't just take it and feel it is okay with everyone.
- Don't go around barking at everyone.
- When upset, stop and think before responding to avoid getting into trouble.

Children need to know **who is in charge**. One needs not be an authoritarian parent to prove who is in charge. Neither does one need to be an indulgent parent in order to prove that the child has freedom. Many scholars, noting whether parents have been high or low on parental demandingness and responsiveness, have created a typology of four parenting styles, namely, authoritarian, authoritative, indulgent, and uninvolved. Some have noted that each of these parenting styles reflects different naturally occurring patterns of parental values, practices, and behaviors and a distinct balance of responsiveness and demandingness.

1. *Indulgent parents* (also referred to as "permissive" or "nondirective") are more responsive than they are demanding. They are nontraditional and lenient, do not require mature behavior, allow considerable self-regulation, and avoid confrontation. Indulgent parents may be further divided into

two types: democratic parents, who, though lenient, are more conscientious, engaged, and committed to the child, and nondirective parents.
2. *Authoritarian parents* are highly demanding and directive, but not responsive. "They are obedience and status oriented and expect their orders to be obeyed without explanation." These parents provide well-ordered and structured environments with clearly stated rules. Authoritarian parents can be divided into two types: nonauthoritarian-directive, who are directive but not intrusive or autocratic in their use of power, and authoritarian-directive, who are highly intrusive.
3. *Authoritative parents* are both demanding and responsive. "They monitor and impart clear standards for their children's conduct. They are assertive, but not intrusive and restrictive. Their disciplinary methods are supportive, rather than punitive. They want their children to be assertive as well as socially responsible, and self-regulated as well as cooperative."
4. *Uninvolved parents* are low in both responsiveness and demandingness. In extreme cases, this parenting style might encompass both rejecting-neglecting and neglectful parents, although most parents of this type fall within the normal range.

Discipline and behavior

The point we have reached is to note that each parenting style impacts discipline and behavior. To discipline means to teach, train, or instruct as well as to punish with the desire to change, restore, refine, or root out all that is malevolent. The book of Proverbs tells us that we are not to hold back discipline from our children so that they will not be led to destruction (Prov. 19:18). We are also told that to discipline them proves our love for them (Prov. 13:24). Often the tone of Proverbs and some of the texts on discipline in the Old Testament might seem to focus on punishment. However, the greatest focus on discipline is for prevention from destruction. As it said in Proverbs 22:15, the discipline is to preempt *foolishness.*

In whatever way the definition of discipline might be made, true discipline needs to be age sensitive, but it needs to be carried forward. For example, while a toddler needs to be told what to do, a teenager needs to be able to be given some freedom to make choices while understanding the burden of consequences. The more we ponder what's involved in discipline, the more we are convinced that it is a necessary component of advocacy.

While reading Larry Lichtenwalter's book, *David: Dancing Like a King,* the gripping reality came more and more to us that the failure of David's sons rested with David's laxity regarding discipline (2 Sam. 13:19). Of course, as great a king as David was, he failed in many ways in the area of self-discipline. The story of David's life is played out from unchecked sexual passion, to murder, to isolation, to anger; and then in his children, it mushroomed into rebellion, death, and agony. David's son Amnon, for example, was in love with his beautiful sister Tamar. Amnon was fixated on her beauty to the point of illness and inability to cope. His undisciplined attitude and uncontrolled passion led him to mope and scheme until he committed the abominable act. He faked being sick and then raped her. Having completed the act, his passion turned to intense hate. Instead of agonizing over his destructive behavior and listening to his sister's wise counsel, Amnon "despised" her. David became furious but did nothing else. Amnon was a grown man and responsible for his actions, yes, but a gross injustice had been done. The embarrassment that he caused his sister needed to be addressed. David's unwillingness to discipline led to a chain of events that almost cost him the kingdom. David's action or lack of action is one that every parent needs to face. Who will call a child to be accountable? How will justice be meted out in a family? David was found wanting as a father. He did not advocate for his daughter, who was wronged, and as the leader of Israel, he did not act. He gave others the license to do as he did.

In fact, Absalom, Tamar's brother, watched for two years as his father David did nothing to vindicate his sister. And he said nothing for the entire period of time as if he intended to do nothing about the rape of his sister. However, he was boiling with resentment and wished for vengeance. After two years, he took matters in his hands; and at the opportune time, he struck—he murdered his brother. King David became a despairing father. His daughter had been marred for life, one son was dead, and another son became a murderer and a fugitive. What a price to pay for not disciplining one's child/ren? That Absalom might have been appeased by David's intervention, one cannot say for sure, but it is to be believed that some intervention and discipline would have made a difference. When Absalom went into exile, he waited for some resolution; but once again, David did nothing. He did not rebuke, and he did not say I forgive. The more Absalom waited for a word from his father, the more he became angry and resentful. He then participated in a scheme that tricked David into bringing him home. By not acting, David allowed Absalom to continue from one wrong course to another until Absalom tried to kill David and take his throne. This led to the civil war that caused the death of Absalom and another 332,000 (cf. 2 Samuel 14).

The episodes of David's life, caused one commentator to say:

> The shameful crime of Amnon, the first-born, was permitted by David to pass unpunished and unrebuked. The law pronounced death upon the adulterer, and the unnatural crime of Amnon made him doubly guilty. But David, self-condemned for his own sin, failed to bring the offender to justice. For two full years Absalom, the natural protector of the sister so foully wronged, concealed his purpose of revenge, but only to strike more surely at the last. At a feast of the king's sons the drunken, incestuous Amnon was slain by his brother's command.
>
> Like other sons of David, Amnon had been left to selfish indulgence. He had sought to gratify every thought of his heart, regardless of the requirements of God. Notwithstanding his great sin, God had borne long with

him. For two years he had been granted opportunity for repentance; but he continued in sin, and with his guilt upon him, he was cut down by death, to await the awful tribunal of the judgment.

David had neglected the duty of punishing the crime of Amnon, and because of the unfaithfulness of the king and father and the impenitence of the son, the Lord permitted events to take their natural course, and did not restrain Absalom. When parents or rulers neglect the duty of punishing iniquity, God Himself will take the case in hand. His restraining power will be in a measure removed from the agencies of evil, so that a train of circumstances will arise which will punish sin with sin.

The evil results of David's unjust indulgence toward Amnon were not ended, for it was here that Absalom's alienation from his father began. After he fled to Geshur, David, feeling that the crime of his son demanded some punishment, refused him permission to return. And this had a tendency to increase rather than to lessen the inextricable evils in which the king had come to be involved. Absalom, energetic, ambitious, and unprincipled, shut out by his exile from participation in the affairs of the kingdom, soon gave himself up to dangerous scheming.[58]

David's irresolution, his compromising attitude, his do-nothing approach, his lack of resolve to confront and rebuke his son stand as reminder to many of the consequences of our failures to correct our

---

[58] Ellen White (1890, 1958), *Patriarchs and Prophets*, Washington, DC.: Review and Herald Publishing Association, 1958, 727-728.

children. It might be hard to take the initial step, but it is harder yet when we are left to stare at the path of destruction our cavalier attitudes have created. We should never maintain a wait-and-see attitude, for delay is danger. Again, Ellen White echoes this thought when she says of David's wait-and-see attitude:

> It was not wise for the king to leave a man of Absalom's character—ambitious, impulsive, and passionate—to brood for two years over supposed grievances. And David's action in permitting him to return to Jerusalem, and yet refusing to admit him to his presence, enlisted in his behalf the sympathies of the people.[59]

It brings pain when a parent finds himself/herself in the role of having to bring discipline to grown children, but a reality is that what is not done in the morning might have to be done in the evening. Of course, the proverb is still accepted that "the earlier a twig is bent, the easier it is to be trained." For, example when parents have to commit their child/ren to drug rehab, prison or other punitive situations for rehabilitation, it can be profoundly challenging.

While disciplining is crucial to child advocacy, there are several pointers that parents must bear in mind.

1. Establish a reason for discipline.
2. Think of discipline as an instrument of education.
3. Determine the kind of discipline that is suitable for the occasion/situation.
4. Vary the approach to discipline.
5. Remember that to render effective discipline demands calmness and kindness.
6. Discipline demands effective role modeling.

---

[59] Ibid. 729.

Parental Advocacy

7. Be careful of ignoring "occasional" bad behavior when disciplining.
8. Be consistent when you discipline.
9. Be credible when you discipline—how a parent lives corresponds with how effective that parent can discipline.
10. Allow room for failure when you discipline—do not always rescue.
11. Never let down your guard when you discipline.
12. When dealing with teenagers, give them some control over their decisions.
13. Focus on positives - wrong attitudes when not checked lead to a bad character.
14. Be sure that when one neglects to correct, one pays the consequences.
15. Do not accept flimsy excuses for inappropriate behaviors.
16. Learn how to affirm and give support.
17. Write letters and notes to your children, if you have to, but never fail to correct.
18. Do discipline the caring way—let all discipline be meaningful.

Punishing a child

An aspect of discipline that many parents and social scientists are failing to talk about in certain cultures of the world today is punishment. Punishment was understood in the traditional cultures as necessary for the development of character. However, in our contemporary metropolitan cultures, we have dropped the ball on punishment. And yet we find it quite contradictory that while we condemn parents when they punish their children to curb them at an early age, we have no problem when the police and other such entities have to do it in drastic forms in later years. While we do not extol extreme forms of punishment, we must admit that it has its place. One of the reasons that we think of punishment in a negative way is that we connect all punishment with "physical punishment" or even move it to the more negative level of "abuse." Some persons root punishment in the biblical injunction

"Don't spare the rod and spoil the child," stated in various ways in the biblical book of Proverbs (Prov. 13:24; 22:15; 20:30: 23:13, 14; 29:15). While the commendation might be to punish with a rod, there is no suggestion in the text that such is equated with "abuse" or "brutality." So, any act that seeks to be violent toward a child is to be considered outside the context of the commendation of Proverbs. Beyond that, the shepherd's rod that is often thought to be an instrument of punishment and correction was also an instrument of comfort (Ps. 23:4).

While contemporary views on punishment might differ; it seems that it is hardly possible to argue that at times, physical restraint or physical punishment might not be necessary in order to caution and correct a child. When every other form of restrain or discipline proves ineffective, one might find that some amount of physical restrain needs to be in place. What needs to be emphasized, however, is that

- punishment, as physical restraint, should never be used to seek vengeance;
- it should never be intended to bring physical harm;
- it should never be used to vent frustration, anger, or hurt;
- it needs to be carried forward with all the love that is available from the heart;
- let the one being punished know before you punish why such a punishment is being meted out;
- follow through on any promised punishment;
- do not exaggerate what you will do;
- affirm good behavior as you censor bad behavior;
- when there is resistance to your appeals, chart the bad and good behavior.

Time-Outs

We picked up a satire on "Modern Discipline" from an anonymous author some time ago that stated the following: "When I was a youngster," complained the frustrated father, shaking his head "I was disciplined by being sent to my room without supper. But our son has his own color TV, phone, CD player and computer in his room." The million-dollar question was asked, "So what do you do when he misbehaves?" And the response, "I send him to our room." Doesn't it make you laugh a lot?

When and How You Use Time-Outs?

- Make it short and do it in eye-view and earshot.
- Make it a time for reflection to be followed by a discussion to create change.
- State why such a behavior is punishable.
- Establish what can be done to change the behavior.
- Discuss what resources are needed to facilitate the change.
- Make sure the time-out is monitored.
- When the time-out is done, help the child to rejoin the community.

Too often children are sent to "time outs" and are not remembered when the "time outs" are over. The parents are too busy doing something else. The parents who say when you are ready you can come out," are saying that the decision is left up to the children. Often enough if the parents had total control the child might not have needed timeout in the first place.

- When you take away privileges, do not take them away ways that you feel guilty or self-punished.
- Be decisive in whatever form of punishment you offer to use.
- Be meaningful in the form of punishment you use.
- Punish sparingly; less the punishment loses significance.
- Before you punish, listen carefully to the one to be punished to establish the truth about that for which you wish to dole out punishment.

- Parents should not neglect their responsibility of training (correcting) then focus on punishment.

Making sure

What we have been concerned about in this discussion is that the discipline and punishment of our children are the basic facets of advocacy. Not to help our children develop wholesome character traits through disciplining, is reckless parenting, which leads to a cycle of dysfunctionality. To advocate for our children is ensuring that they develop the skills necessary for survival in an ever-changing world. This kind of advocacy demands that we make clear what are the rules of the game. That is, we help our children to play fairly the game of life, because every misplay is costly.

QUESTIONS FOR REFLECTION

1. How important is it to have clarity on the rules of the game for your child's development?
2. In reflecting on the methods of discipline you have used with your children; how effective do you think they have been?
3. What is the harshest punishment your parents ever gave to you? Do you think it was very helpful?

CHAPTER XI

How to do Educational Advocacy

One of the most significant areas of advocacy in which parents ought to be involved is education. Without parental involvement, many children are lost in the educational system. While parental involvement might vary with their children's level of development, parents need to be involved to help their children move forward. It needs to be understood that:

Educational advocacy

> The classroom teacher is the single most important person affecting your child's education. The teacher has tremendous influence on your child's happiness at school and is the person that spends one-on-one time with your child on a daily basis. It is extremely important for parents and teachers to work together to provide a good school experience for each child.
>
> Most teachers welcome the involvement of parents and want to hear your ideas. In fact, many teachers report that they are more motivated to teach a child whose parents are actively involved than one whose parents never seem

to care. If the teacher resists involvement, you need to put into practice, constructive communication. Praise the teacher for the good things going on and keep the lines of communication open by writing notes, making classroom visits, attending conferences, etc. Remember, you have the right to be involved, but exercise that right in a constructive way.[60]

Getting an education is the right of every child. It is not a privilege as many have thought. Individuals who have achieved academically are those who have been supported, directed, and even defended. As one listens to testimonies of those who have achieved, they have noted the involvement of their parents, guardians, or other surrogates who have advocated on their behalf.

Understanding the Goal of Educational Advocacy

Education is crucial for survival. It functions as one of the leading passports to a better life. It opens numerous opportunities for many individuals and ensure good job opportunities. Not long ago, individuals with a high school education had access to jobs that led them to enjoy the American dream. Today, that is not the reality since one's financial stability is directly tied to their academic achievements. If such is the case, then our children need to be prepared to meet the demands of an ever-changing job market, which is even becoming difficult for those with high educational attainments. In order for children to be adequately prepared to meet the demanding future, they need parental involvement and support. The tragedy, though, is that while some parents understand the interrelatedness of parental activism and children's achievement, many parents have abrogated their responsibilities, choosing rather

---

[60] Adopted from "Adopting for your Child with Learning Disabilities," Learning Disabilities of Canada (1998). Ottawa, Ontario, Canada. Exceptional Children's Assistance Center News Line.

to believe that the education of their children is the responsibility of the government and the educational system. However, such thoughts are mere misguided assumptions, for while laws do exist to help, the ultimate responsibility rests with parents. The mind-set of parents, the attitudes they communicate to their children, the importance they give to educational achievement, their commitment to be involved in the education of their children are crucial. No one knows their child/ren as parents do. Parents know their likes and dislikes; parents know more about their children's strengths and weaknesses as none other. In essence, parents have a piece of the puzzle that no other adult has.

The case we are seeking to establish is that parental responsibility, makes parental advocacy critical in children's education. While many parents might have some understanding of this, fear to take charge has a stranglehold on many so that their senses are numbed to the challenges their children are encountering and will encounter in order to obtain the best education possible. A major part of the fear factor for many parents is grounded in a lack of understanding of the educational system in which their children must be educated. While one might be quick to condemn such parents, it is worthy to note that such a fear might not be unfounded, especially among first-generation immigrant populations whose cultures are vastly different from the new culture in which they have brought their children. When one is intimated by an educational system it often leads to a wait-and-see attitude, a do-nothing attitude, and a feeling of inadequacy and apathy. Such postures are very unproductive ways of being helpful to our children. What then do we say to parents who harbor feelings of fear, and feelings of inadequacy? What do we say to those who say they lack the skills to be able to mediate the system? We strongly suggest that parents need to become proactive and therefore need to do whatever it takes to become effective participants.

The Effective Educational Advocate

A good place for parents to start their work of educational advocacy is to be knowledgeable about the system so that they will not be intimidated.

More importantly, one needs to know who their child/ren's teacher/s is/are. The following suggestions are ways in which parent might prepare for a meeting with a teacher:

1. Write out a list of what you want to discuss with the teacher.
2. When appropriate, praise the teacher for specific things you feel good about. For example, "Mrs. Brown, thank you for spending extra time with Johnny and working on his behavior. We really see results."
3. If you have a problem, discuss the specific things that bother you as they relate to your child. Do not generalize. Do not say to the teacher, "You are not teaching my child. This is going to be a wasted year." Instead, you say, "The math program does not seem to be working for Johnny. Is there a way we can change it to better meet his needs?"
4. Approach the teacher to discuss these concerns in a positive, non-threatening way.
5. Keep the focus on your child, not the teacher's shortcomings. For example, relate specifically how and why a particular behavior modification practice will not work with your child, instead of complaining about the teacher's poor application of a behavior modification program.
6. Offer assistance in the classroom when possible. Decide with the teacher if this involvement is appropriate for your child.
7. Offer your time and talents. For example, when possible, volunteer to be a grade mother/father assistant - help with a field trip, tape a textbook chapter for a student with learning disabilities, etc.
8. When you make requests or give suggestions, illustrate very specifically to the teacher how your requests or suggestions can be implemented. Follow up your requests or suggestions with a letter of thanks.
9. Attend all meetings and conferences.[61]

---

[61] Ibid.

Parental Advocacy

Here are some other suggestions that parents need to follow if they are going to be effective in their support for their child/ren:

- Encourage school attendance.
- Help your child/ren create an educational philosophy of life.
- Help your child/ren to stop the focus on permissive sexual passions.
- Help them to stop the focus on clothing.
- Help them to focus on meaningful work.
- Help them to learn to read good books and journals so that your child might see.
- Watch the amount of time your child spends with the modern gadgets.
- Help them to find appropriate places where they can find free and appropriate reading materials, in places such as, the local library, schools, churches, YMCA, YWCA. (If parents are motivated and willing to read, they can have all the information they need to be able to support their children's education).
- Make use of conferences and workshops. Very often school systems, advocacy groups, some churches, and other organizations convene informational sessions to provide parents with the tools that they will need to give support to their children. At such convocations, parents should listen carefully and ask questions. Many times, the sessions are informal so that parents will not be intimated but encouraged to seek clarifications on issues. In our travels, we have met many parents who told us that they were now better able to advocate for their children because of attending conferences and workshops that were made available to them.
- Connect with other parents as sources of information. Many individuals feel that what happens to their child/ren is their business. This is probably true to some extent; but we have found, and other parents have also told us, that when they thought their experiences were unique, they were wrong. When the stories were told, the experiences were similar. Others who are going through, or have gone through, can provide

tremendous support for others. They have firsthand experiences of how they overcame fear of the educational systems and found the information they needed to move ahead. Many others, who might not have had fears, can also give vital information on the proven strategies to mediate the system. Talk with other parents, and learn about the system. Well-informed parents are powerful resources for their children. When parents know their rights, when parents understand the working of their educational system, when parents understand that the future of their children rests heavily in their hands, they will not be afraid of overstepping their bounds in their efforts to work with, and in behalf of their children.

Having been teachers for several years, we give a word of caution that parents should not wait until their child/ren is/are in trouble at school before they meet the staff. Such meetings might not be friendly; for most often, parents hear all the negatives about their children, and then anger and frustration result. Such anger and frustration might not be targeted at the service providers, but at the child for having embarrassed and defamed the good name of their family by inappropriate behaviors. We have witnessed several times where parents became so angry at their child/ren that good sense and restraint were thrown out the window, and the parents vented in the wrong way. Again, we reiterate, meet the teachers, get a feel for their personalities, seek to understand their perspectives on principles, watch their body language, and try to determine if they are the individuals you want your child/ren to be around. Talk to them to ascertain the ways in which you as parents can facilitate the educational development of your children.

Where Are My Children When They Are Not Home?

While it is important to know the individuals with whom your children spend time in school, it is also necessary to know the environment in which your child/ren will be situated. Is it a child-friendly environment?

Is it a safe place for your child? Look at the physical plant; know the classrooms in which your child/ren will receive instruction. Are the rooms clean? Are there enough windows to provide light? Is there mold in the building? Are there rooms with broken walls and falling ceiling? Are there lavatories in close proximity? Are there enough escape doors in the event of a problem where they need to get out quickly? This is of special interest, especially in these days of school shootings and crisis situations. If no one sees them, no one will address them. We know that actions and changes will only come when alert parents begin to ask serious questions about factors that can impact their child/ren's education and safety. Many individuals might argue that certainly these conditions no longer exist, but one only needs to watch the news to learn the miserable conditions that still exist in many schools, particularly in low-income urban areas.

In deciding where to live, parents should check not only the physical environment but also the learning environment of their children. Check if your child/ren will have access to labs, digital space, libraries, and other features that will enhance their learning. Do children have access to books and other tools for learning? Is there a hostile environment or a welcoming one? What is the attitude of other children in classes?

Checking the learning environment might not be as easy as checking the physical plant, but it is certainly not out of the reach of interested parents. Parents, with the appropriate evaluative tools, can visit classrooms to observe and get a sense of the general classroom atmosphere and the level of interaction there. Parents can also visit as participants in certain activities. Many parents are not even aware that they are able to do this; and it is important that they do so, not frequently, of course, so that service providers, as well as the child/ren will know that Mom and Dad are serious about what goes on in school.

What Are My Children Learning When I Am Not the Teacher?

Another critical area of concern is what children are learning in school. What is the specific curriculum the child/ren will follow? That is, the specific subject matter to which they will be exposed and the kinds of activities in which they will be involved. This information is necessary in order to help parents understand whether what is being taught to their children is consistent with the beliefs and morals being taught at home. For example, many individuals might ridicule Jehovah's Witnesses, Muslims, Orthodox Jews and other such groups for their traditionalist and fundamentalist views. But one needs to admit that whether or not there is agreement with their particular stance, they are only ensuring that their children are not exposed to information that goes against their belief systems. They make sure that their children are excused from certain practices or subject matter taught in schools that go against their faith and practice. At least one of us has taught in school systems where children, for religious reasons, had to be excused from certain class contents. Of course, if parents do not ensure that their children are exempted, no one will voluntarily do so. Even though some parents might not fully understand everything, they can investigate school curricula to see whether what is being taught is consistent with the values they wish their children to develop.

Knowing about the course of study, particularly at higher levels, can give parents insights into the body of knowledge children will need for certain career preparation. That knowledge can help parents monitor whether their children are placed in the right classes. Parents need to ask early if, for example, the level of English, science, math their child is receiving will adequately prepare them for a career. If your son, your daughter wants to go to college, are they doing advanced placement (AP) math, science, etc., or are they doing just the general subjects? It is important that parents ask these questions so that they can rightly represent the needs of their children.

We recall two parents who moved into a new area and went to register their son in high school. The school taught three levels of English—I to III. The counselor registered the child for Level II English, noting that since the child was new to that environment, Level II would be easier. The parents accepted the suggestion but, before leaving, asked if their son would be able to move up to the other levels of English through the other grade levels, should he demonstrate in a few weeks that he can do so. The counselor's reply brought them concern as she noted that their son would have to be in Level II through the completion of high school. Immediately, both parents understood that that would diminish their son's chances for college and told the counselor, "Put him in Level III English and we will supply a tutor if needs be." The counselor, after much arguing, reluctantly registered their son in Level III with the caveat, "If your son doesn't perform, at the end of the semester, he will be demoted to Level II." The parents accepted the challenge, and at the end of the semester, their son's performance kept him in Level III. Those parents understood clearly that the path of ease is not always the better path to advocacy. We are not sure what the feeling of the counselor was, but we can only surmise that she might not have been too happy.

Vignettes of Advocacy

Having grown three sons from Jamaica to New York to Canada to Massachusetts, we learned very quickly that we had to advocate for them to ensure their preparation and success in life. Our advocacy spanned the grades from kindergarten through four years of college. We could relate several stories about our involvement at various levels, but we will only share three stories.

Knowing Is Power, but Not Knowing Is Folly

Our eldest son was in high school, and as we reviewed his grades, we noted that he was getting a failing grade for history—a subject that he loves. We asked for all his test papers, and after analyzing them carefully and questioning our son, we found that some five test papers had no questions, only responses. We noted too that each test had forty-five and sometimes fifty questions (not true or false). On further query, the reality of the situation hit us—the teacher stood and read each question while the students wrote the responses—some short responses, some one or two-word responses and others open-ended responses of about a paragraph. Some individuals might question what's wrong with that, and our response – a lot. But, being parents and teachers, it was our conviction that:

1. Students have varied learning styles; some are good listeners (auditory learners), but others have the need to see (visual learners). Some are touchy (tactile learners) and other a mix of all).
2. Some students need to check the questions against their responses to find whether they understood the questions correctly and responses accordingly.
3. Some students process information at a slower rate and therefore need to read questions several times.
4. Other students need to respond to easy questions first then proceed to the more difficult ones.
5. Some students write slowly and therefore need the questions so that they can work at their own pace.
6. Some students might even have hearing problems, and vision problems (perhaps minimal) but nonetheless a challenge for learning.

Note that we have isolated six kinds of learners, and that's not the full list; but realize that if your son or daughter were among any of the categories listed, he/she would have been deprived of the opportunity of doing their best.

After checking a few parents, we realized that they too were angry but not sure of how to approach their situation. Some called and complained to the principal, but apparently, the teacher assured the principal that the students were not adequately preparing for tests and that he had done his job as a teacher. Seemingly, the principal accepted the teacher's explanation, and things continued in the usual way. After hearing from several parents, we were not about to be satisfied with only making a complaint, we wanted an audience with both teacher and principal. We lost no time in securing an appointment with both the teacher and the principal. The day of the conference, we were with the samples of the exams responses that our son had given to us.

At the conference, we spoke with the teacher first, hoping that the issues could be resolved at that level; but apparently, he resented the fact that any parent would dare question his pedagogical skills. We were not asking for an apology but only an admission that perhaps other methods could have been employed. Instead, the teacher only sought to justify his approach of reading all his tests and quizzes, although the school had the possibility for duplicating materials for students. Needless to say, we were at our wits' end speaking with someone who disrespected our very presence. Finally, the principal came, and we handed over the tests we brought. We said nothing to him except to allow the evidence to speak. We noted the embarrassment and shock on the principal's face as the truth about his teacher's pedagogical skills unfolded. We voiced our concerns about the level of education our son was receiving and then left. The principal now was left with no recourse but to forward more inquiries and, at the end, release the teacher.

We are not gloating that our intervention in our son's education caused the loss of job for a teacher, but we had to do that which was necessary. And that's what we say to parents: "Support your child's education even if it means making some hard decisions." Seemingly, our intervention came at the right time—before the damage was irreparable. Our son went on to obtain undergraduate degrees in science and history. Our advocacy on behalf of our son was also helpful to other parents and their children.

We Know Our Children

Our second son loves art and spent much his time drawing. At the elementary level, his art production was evaluated as a tenth grader who had had art lessons. One day, while he was in the first grade, we were checking through what he had done in school that day and also what he had for homework. We noted that there was no work for science that he normally had, and there was instead lots of artwork. When we realized that he had no science homework, we asked why, and he told us he had none because the teacher had placed him in the art stream. Although we were new to that educational system, we immediately understood the implications for our child—our son was being tracked. We went to see the teacher with urgency and asked the basis for the placement. The teacher's response was, "He likes to draw." We requested that our son should be placed in the general classes where he would receive a broad-based education that includes the sciences. The teacher insisted that our son likes to draw and that was the best placement for him. She saw him as a future artist and therefore decided that he would remain in that grouping. But we knew our son and knew that she would not determine what or who he would be. That determination would be made appropriately by our son with our assistance. Not being able to move the teacher, the principal was the next level of appeal. The principal, in turn, had our son placed where we suggested he would receive the desired level of instruction. Our son is now a Psychiatric Nurse Practitioner and very passionate about his field. Does he still love to draw? Sure, he does. He is also an excellent saxophonist. He even spends more time playing the Sax than drawing. Yes, he is filled with artic gifts. But the evidence is that many times a child has more talents and gifts than even what parents and teachers know.

What's the implication if the above? Had we allowed the teacher to continue tracking our so at such an early stage of his life it would have followed him through elementary, middle, and high school. He would have likely missed out on his science foundation and would not have been able to take on a profession that involved science.

We Support Our Children

Our advice is to give support and guidance to all teachers in understanding our child/ren. The information parents hold is crucial for our child/ren's academic development.

Our last son was in his junior year in high school and was getting a failing grade in math. We thought it rather strange, because he was a child who enjoyed math. When we discussed the problem with his teacher, the response was, "He walks around and helps others and talks too much." Although we knew his math capabilities, we decided to go the extra mile to get what would make him successful. We asked about computer programs available for support since he liked to work on computers. The math teacher said there were none, but of course, we found that the school had programs; but he did not like the fact that we came to school, questioning the failing grade, and in addition, telling him about our son's learning style. We left and ordered a program for our son, although we knew the challenge was not in is lack of ability. The major challenge was our son's compulsive neatness, impacted the speed at which he worked. His work had to be neat, each number lined up correctly, and the appearance of the work on the paper was crucial. Being a special education teacher, his mom found the problem and requested an accommodation for testing while she would work with him to provide skills for task completion. You should know the answer by now. The teacher denied request for the simple accommodation. So, at the end of the semester, our son had a failing grade, although he did much better on the final.

Our son had just lost all confidence in his ability in spite of our support. He saw himself as dumb. We now had a tough choice to make:

1. Uproot him from his friends and give him a new start.
2. Leave him to face the same teacher for his senior year and watch him fail again.

We made our choice. Tough choices for a child's future and consequences can be enormous. We dialogued with our son and decided on summer school at another location. His confidence in himself came back, because at the end of the summer course, he had an A. In that class, the teacher used him as a resource for his mates. We could see the difference in his attitude—he was cheerful and felt good about his skills. Of course, after the summer, our resolve was tested. Sensing that our son would not be returning, friends from his former school pleaded, some teachers cajoled, and our son was yielding to the pressure to return. We dialogued with him and helped him to see the consequences with the same math teacher with whom he faced challenges. After intense moments of dialogue, our son agreed that to return was to jeopardize his completion of high school, so off he went to another school to complete his senior year. One day in reflection, he asked, "Mom, so what was happening to me at the other school why I was failing math?" Mom assured him that the challenge was not with him. She did not berate the teacher, although we felt that there were underlays of systemic racism. Our interventions paid great dividends for today our son's lifework is in a math-related fields.

We could relate stories of friends who have had to do the same, but time and space are limited. But what we want you to take from these vignettes is the importance of being a proactive advocate for your child. The importance of knowing what is happening to your child in school, of knowing what your child is learning and giving support, are crucial. Know also that at times, when you cannot resolve with a teacher, your child needs your wise support. If it means removing the child from the negative environment, do it. It might be painful to the child who has formed many linkages, but you will have to help your child see the greater good—the long-term impact. Assure the child that occasions for meeting with his/her friends will be encouraged so that the child does not feel abandoned.

Teachers Want Your Help

An aspect of parental advocacy that many teachers welcome is some direct help from parents in school-based activities. There are many opportunities for such involvement. However, parents need not worry about the extensiveness of involvement and their availability. Here are some simple ways in which parents can give help to teachers:

1. Volunteer to be a chaperone on field trips. Teachers appreciate when parents can take the time to travel with them since it provides additional adult security for children. But the benefits are not limited to teachers but also a tremendous learning experience for parents who might not have had the opportunity

to visit such places. It also gives parents firsthand knowledge to the kinds of exposure that their children are receiving.
2. Participate in special class projects maybe by preparing a special dish or other items. This kind of involvement might not necessitate parents leaving home, but we have seen firsthand the excitement in some parents when they prepared dishes as part of a school project. Many even took time to come in and enjoy the demonstrations.
3. Volunteer to share a skill with the class, such as craft, scrapbooking, knitting, painting, etc.
4. Volunteer as a reader or a story teller or dramatist.

Some parents might not be able to be involved in the ways suggested, but we do make the argument that every parent should make the effort to attend special in-school performances in which their child/ren participate. Go:

- when they are doing musicals,
- when they are presenting plays,
- when they are doing their project presentations,
- when their team is playing.

Children feel a sense of pride when they see their parents sitting in the audience, cheering them on. In our travels and many workshops, we have often heard complaints of "My parents never came to my school play" or "My parents never came to my graduation." Attending when your child sings on the choir might seem a small matter to us as adults, but parental presence is etched on that child's memory walls. Support is a part of educational advocacy because it says to children that parents care about what is going on in their child's school life; that parents have an interest in what their children do in school. Parents might give clothing, money, and all sorts of temporal rewards; but those do not replace parental support, that is, being physically there. It is noteworthy that the kind of support discussed is not just at the lower grade levels but also at the higher levels.

If this is the position taken, then note that parents will be haunted years later, when the catalog of missed opportunities is replayed.

Being a part of a Parent-Teacher Association (PTA) is a powerful tool for parental advocacy, yet one that is not utilized by many parents. PTA membership can be quite influential, impacting policies that govern schools. At this level, they are able to participate in some of the decisions that impact the school. They also become involved in several projects—such as fund-raising, beautification projects, scholarship funds, book drives, etc. The association also avails parents to the various services that can provide them with knowledge they can utilize to enhance their children's education.

A cornerstone of what is expected of parents is for them to have high expectations for their children. Parents will not give support, they will not seek to mediate difficult situations, and they will not be involved in their children's education to the fullest unless they set high expectations for their children. Children will rarely rise higher than what parents have in mind for them. Parents who have no expectations for their children or set low goals for their children are indirectly saying that that is what they want them to achieve. The caution, however, is that while expectations must be high, they must be realistic. Many parents push their children over the edge by setting unfair expectations. Each parent should know his or her child/ren's capabilities, and if they lack discerning skills, they must know that there are professionals who can help. Parents are to understand their child/children's level of cognitive and intellectual capabilities, give them the support to achieve to their level of development. The caution too is not to accept mediocrity or laziness but encourage children to be the best of whatever they can accomplish.

> **Children will rarely rise higher than what parents have in mind for them.**

It's Only Just Begun

A troubling fact in society, even today, is that too often completion of high school signals the end of parental advocacy and participation.

Many parents do not participate in the decision for which schools their child/ren will attend, how such schooling will be paid for, and what course of study their child/ren will follow. Yes, many parents might not be qualified to make those determinations, but they can certainly find counselors who will help their children to find sources of funding, appropriate schools that will be suited for the course of study they seek to pursue. At that level, parents should still be knowledgeable about what is happening to their children. Again, at the college level, know the school where your child will attend. Visit the campus to see if it is right for your child. Ask if the environment will be conducive to learning.

As parents, we made that mistake when our eldest son completed college and entered graduate school. The school was near home, so we did not bother to check it out. Of course, we knew the course of study he would follow, how schooling would be paid for; but we did not bother to check the learning environment—who would be his classmate, would he be able to form friendships there, who would be his teachers. After a year, our son dropped out, and we wondered why. A few years later, we attended a graduation ceremony, and as we watched, the reality of his plight hit us. He would not have made it at that young age. The composition of the faculty and student population of his particular field of study told us why he dropped out. We had failed him by not first going on campus to check to see what he was getting into. We were saddened that a child, for whom we advocated from kindergarten through college, was literally tossed to the wolves that almost overcame him. We are thankful that he completed his work at a different location, but he certainly could have been spared that episode had we continued what we knew especially because of his tender age at that time and his personality.

Do You Have a Child with Special Needs?

It is an overwhelming task for parents to be advocates for their children's education, but it is even more challenging when parents have children with special challenges that call for specific kinds of services in order for them to access education. Parents who have children with disabilities might feel that they are journeying on a lonely and unfamiliar path without any sense of direction. They might feel that the road ahead is uncertain and the future for their child grim. But if such are the feelings, parents need not despair because they are never alone on the journey, and better yet, there are numerous resources and support systems in place to buttress the education of children with disability. The major challenge, however, is not knowing how to access information and, even if they are able to access it, how best to use it. As such, the effort will be made here to give a few pointers that will help some parents face and address the challenges they might encounter in getting services for their children.

Parents can become knowledgeable and effective advocates for their children if they will take the time to do the search. It can be time-consuming and, at times, frustrating; but if they have the determination and the desire, they will obtain the road map that will get them moving toward their destination. The Individuals with Disabilities Education Act, commonly known as IDEA, is a landmark legislation that gives credence to the fight for children with disability. IDEA and the No Child Left Behind (NCLD) legislations have opened doors that were previously closed to children with disabilities. These legislations clearly state that all children, disabled or non-disabled, are entitled to Free and Appropriate Public Education (FAPE) in the least restrictive environment (LRE), meaning education must be provided in locations with their non-disabled peers as much as is possible and must meet the needs of the particular disability. Parents need not worry as to whether their child will be accepted by a public institution since that is a given. The major challenge for parents as advocates is to become knowledgeable about their rights in order to ensure that their children receive the services to which they are entitled.

To Know Is to Act—Identify the Problem

In order for parents to be true advocates for their child, there is need to identify the particular challenge/challenges that can potentially impact education negatively. If parents understand how a child develops normally, they will be able to detect when something is wrong. In order to ascertain whether or not a child is developing normally, parents need to be on the alert. If parents have a hunch that something might be wrong, they are encouraged not to sit and say, "Well, he/she will grow it out," as is the tendency many times. Act on your hunch by being more observant, noting all the signs that what you sense could be abnormal. Not only should careful note be taken, but inform the pediatrician who in turn will ask intense questions and do careful evaluation to determine if a disability is presenting itself. If the medical findings warrant further steps, the medical practitioner should provide information for other services that will be needed to ensure the success of your child.

As part of early-identification systems, the government has what it terms "Child Find."[62] Parents who have a hunch can also call the system to have their child evaluated. Teachers also can make a referral for an evaluation, but here, parents need to know that their child cannot be identified without their written consent. Know then that parental alertness will initiate early intervention, which is the key to the progress of the child in the long run.

What Do Parents Need to Know about Individualized Family Services Plans and Individualized Educational Plans?

The Individualized Family Service Plan (IFSP) is mandated by the federal law—IDEA. It provides early-intervention services for children from zero to three who are identified as having a disability that warrants special kinds of services. While it details information on the services that are available and necessary for the successful development of the child with a disability, it also allows for parental participation and gives them support so that families can be helpful in the development of

---

[62] www.ed.gov/parents/needs/speced/iepguide/index.html notes that the state must identify, locate and evaluate all children in the state in need of special education and related services.

the child. At this level, family support is not a maybe; it is a must, for outside services alone cannot provide the only source of intervention. It is noted that an IFSP must contain information about the following:

1. The infant's or toddler's present levels of physical, cognitive, communication, social or emotional, and adaptive development.
2. The family's resources, priorities, and concerns relating to enhancing the development of the infant or toddler.
3. The major outcomes expected to be achieved for the infant or toddler and his or her family, as well as criteria for determining progress made toward such outcomes. Any revisions of either outcomes or services to achieve them must also be included.
4. The specific early-intervention services necessary to meet the unique needs of the infant or toddler and the family, including the frequency, intensity, and method of delivery.
5. The natural environments in which the early-intervention services will be provided, including a justification of the extent, if any, to which the services will not be provided.
6. The date the services will begin and their anticipated duration.
7. The identification of the service coordinator from the profession most immediately relevant to the infant's or toddler's family's needs, who will be responsible for the coordination and implementation of the plan with the other agencies and persons.
8. The steps to be taken to support the transition of the toddler with a disability to preschool or other appropriate services.[63]

An IFSP service coordinator is provided to help the family get the services and supports that the child needs as described on the IFSP until the child turns three or until he or she no longer needs early intervention. The service coordinator also provides knowledge of the law of community resources and will help connect the family with other parents.

---

[63] See, "Guidelines for the Individualized Family Service Plan," http://www.ldanatl.org/aboutld/professionals/guidelines.asp.

Should parents desire more details on IFSP, they should visit available Web sites[64] or a professional.

What's an Individual Education Plan?

Children older than three years who have been identified with disabilities are placed on an Individualized Educational Program (IEP) also mandated by IDEA. The IEP ensures that a child with a disability will receive services and support throughout high school. The IEP entails several steps to ensure that (a) that appropriate services are provided, (b) safeguard against misclassification for in times past children were placed in special classes even though there was the absence of a disability, (c) ensure parental participation in the process. The modified chart below[65] gives a brief breakdown of the steps involved:

PROCESS	SIGNIFICANCE
1. Referral/ Identification	Steps taken by state agencies, parents, teachers, other school professionals, pediatrician, and other sources that have contact with the student. The purpose is to identify whether a student might be in need of special education and related services.
2. Evaluation	Parents must give their consent before the evaluation process can begin. If consent is given, then assessment will be carried out by qualified professionals who will look at the student in the areas that relate to the suspected area of disability.
3. Eligibility decisions	Parents and qualified professionals look at the results of the evaluation and together decide if the child has a disability that needs special education services. If parents disagree with the evaluation, they can challenge it and ask for an Independent Educational Evaluation.

---

[64] www.ed.gov/parents/needs/speced/iepguide/index.html.
[65] Ibid.

4. Eligible? IEP Meeting scheduled	If the team determines that the student has a disability that needs special education and related services, an IEP meeting is scheduled. Meeting includes as follows: • Parents can take advocates who understand the process and have intimate knowledge about the child • Other team members such as psychologist, teachers, school nurse
IEP development meeting	Team members talk about the needs of the student. The goals and objectives are written, and the kinds of services are laid out. All information should be explained clearly to parents so that they can make informed decisions. They need to know the kinds of services that will be provided so that the child can be educated appropriately. If parents a agree with the IEP as written and explained, they sign. If there is disagreement about the IEP and placement, parents can discuss their concerns with the team. If no agreement is reached, the parents or the school system asks for a due process hearing where the case will be mediated. In many instances, parents and team can settle a disagreement before it gets to a due process hearing since that helps to delay the implementation of services.
6. Implementation	The student's program and services begin. The service providers have access to the IEP and make sure that the child receives the services outlined in the IEP. Parents also receive a copy of the IEP. Many parents become watchdogs to ensure that their child gets the services and supports specified in the IEP.
7. Tracking progress	Frequent progress reports (quarterly, bimonthly, monthly) depending on the need, are used to determine the progress the student is making toward his/her annual goal. Parents should receive these progress reports.

Parental Advocacy

8. Annual review	The IEP is reviewed at least once per year by the team and parents to make sure that the student is meeting the goals and objectives as specified? in the IEP.

Working with children with disability can be challenging, but parents must be willing to participate to the best of their abilities. Too often, many parents feel that their collaboration with the education system is not necessary. Such a belief is a misconception of parental advocacy and responsibility. At the very least, parents need to be alert and understand what is it that their child/ren is/are receiving or should receive and must be a part of the process if the child/ren is/are going to be successful. Parents need to have some level of understanding as to what constitutes an IEP, and they should never be afraid to ask questions about the kinds of services their child/ren is/are receiving; for after all, it's their child/ren's life and education at stake. Parental participation in the development of their children is crucial, and the success of children with disabilities is directly related to the level of parental support. Those parents who separate themselves from being involved in the process rob their children of the possibilities for being successful. The following story demonstrates the importance of parental involvement in providing adequate service for children with disability.

Mrs. Brown's (alias) daughter Monique (alias) was diagnosed with dyslexia and therefore needed special education services. The team met and constructed IEP providing services for Monique in a self-contained setting that was considered to be the most appropriate setting for her to receive the services she needed. Mrs. Brown refused to sign the document stating that her daughter should be placed in a setting with non-disabled students where she could have the support and models of other students. Of course, Monique's scores showed that her reading level was at the third grade, and therefore, she would not be able to handle reading at seventh - or eight-grade levels; but Mrs. Brown was determined that her daughter would not be placed in the setting described in the IEP. Mrs. Brown's concern for the well-being of her daughter pushed her to seek help from advocates who were better equipped to take on the school system. Her determination paid off as the decision was made to place Monique in an inclusive classroom on a temporary basis where she would receive services with non-disabled peers. The compromise was that Monique would receive all subjects except math in regular classroom settings and math in a self-contained classroom. Mom knew Monique was weak in math as was the case with her. Her initial opposition to self-contained math class was dropped. All support services were put in place, and Mrs. Brown made sure that Monique was getting all that was specified in the new IEP. At the end of the first term, Monique was successful in her classes, making better grades than many of her otherly-abled peers; and needless to say, after two years, Monique graduated from middle school, receiving honors in some of her subjects.

Whereas one might have been tempted to classify Mrs. Brown as annoying and probably a nuisance to some, one must agree that what mattered most was the success of her daughter. Mrs. Brown, despite how some might have seen her, demonstrated the fortitude and the tenacity that parents need to be advocates for their children. And what is noteworthy is the fact that she had only a ninth-grade education; she had no money, but she had one thing in mind—the success of her daughter—and she was determined that no one would prevent her from seeing to that. Mrs. Brown knew something about her daughter that no test score could reveal. She knew something that would have taken time for teachers to find. That piece of the puzzle was that Monique had very good listening skills and could remember much of what she heard. We commend Mrs. Brown as a good example of a parent advocate who kept in communication with her daughter's service providers. If Monique was unable to complete a homework assignment and Mom could not help, teachers were notified in writing about the particular problem so that Monique could get support with information that Mom could not help her with. At times, service providers felt overwhelmed by Mrs. Brown's constant insistence; but in the end, many had to admit that in spite of the frustrations with her, she did what she needed to do.

Not every parent will have the drive that Mrs. Brown had, but parents can learn to use the legislations enacted for the support of children with disabilities. If laws are on the books and parents do not understand how to access them, of what good will they be? Having a child with a disability brings concern and necessitates hard work, but we note that having a child with a disability is no cause for apathy and hopelessness.

Beyond Individual Educational Plan, What?

Support for children with disability does not end. Although IEP services for individuals with disabilities end at the completion of high school—and incidentally, children with disabilities have until age twenty-one to complete high school—there are other services provided for those who are capable and wish to pursue a college and graduate education or vocational skills. The Americans with Disabilities Act (ADA) makes provisions for those individuals who will need support to access additional education. In ensuring that students with disabilities receive services, parents need to be involved as well. Parents also need to note that their input in the selection of colleges is vital to their child with a disability. A proactive approach is important since finding the right school is crucial, for not all schools will provide the same level of support. Although ADA has provisions for some accommodations, some schools provide only the bare minimum. Understanding the needs of your child will help you to determine which schools will provide what your child needs. We note, therefore, that parents need to study carefully with their child the choice of school for higher education. Even though some parents might not have the skills, for whatever reason, to be involved in the correct choice of school, they can still be involved by seeking help from counselors, teachers, other parents, and anyone who has a clear understanding of the system. And one might be pleasantly surprised to find the level of willingness of many individuals to help parents who need added support to see their children with disabilities through the educational system.

As educators, we have worked at various levels from elementary school through college and watched with interest how some parents advocate for the needs of their children with disabilities by making sure that those children will have what is necessary. We have seen parents withdrawing children because of the lack of proper support and locating them in other settings where they felt the needs would be adequately met. On the other hand, we have seen and heard parents despairing but doing nothing to change the situation. Tough as it might seem, mere complaining, self-pity, and despairing will not help. Give positive support in whatever way you can because children can achieve success to varying degrees, depending on the level of disability. One only needs to read magazines, listen to talk show interviews, observe the environment in which they live; and they will find a long list of successful individuals who have disabilities. There are many in various professions who have various kinds of disabilities, and if one had the chance to interview them, all one would hear are success stories despite the struggles with their disabilities.

There are no easy answers to having children with disabilities, but we surely say that when parents avail themselves of the knowledge and information that is provided, they can help their children to accept who they are and work to their fullest potential to achieve the levels of success to which they aspire.

QUESTIONS FOR REFLECTION

1. What rights do you have as a parental advocate in the educational context?
2. What kinds of questions should a parental advocate ask in relation to the education of their child?
3. How necessary is it for a parent with a gifted child to do advocacy?

Chapter XII

Dealing with the Church as an Agency of Advocacy

If you belong to a church and is already convinced of its power as an agency of parental and child advocacy, maybe you do not need to read any further concerning the present discussion. In any case, let us encourage you a little to read on. If you are reading this sentence, you might find in the discussion something that might inspire you. It will also help you to challenge someone else who might be taking their church experience for granted. The discussion might also help you to bring encouragement to the leadership of your church (particularly your local congregation) so that it might offer better services in the areas of advocacy.

The general question that requires an honest answer is, "Does having membership in a church give a person an advantage over persons outside the church?" If you are a member of a church, the answer will be easy. However, if you are not a member of a church, you might say like one couple who responded to our question: "The church might be important and have its place, but we get our faith nurtured at home as we read the Bible together." We asked a further question, "What will you do when you have children?" The couples response was, "If we have children, then that is a different question. Churches are always good for kids." On hearing the answer, one of us chimed in, "Do you really mean church is for kids?" "Well," said one of the couple, "We don't mean it that way, but you know adults have so much to do, so we need to get the children all they can get out of church before they become adults."

Is the Church for Kids?

The comment is quite interesting, you might say. In fact, you might feel that the couple's answer is inconsequential, but such is what many adults, especially in our metropolitan western world, have been arguing for many decades. In some traditional cultures, the argument goes that church is for women and children, so send the children to church or drop them off with some trusted friend while the men stay home and do adult things, like watching football, soccer, baseball, drag race, or some other game. It is interesting to note that two of America's usual substitutes for worship experiences are football and baseball; in other places, different games are chosen. The point is that there is an ironic way in which religion and the world of sports come together, and another subtle way in which they compartmentalize the world into the sacred and the secular.

Understanding the Challenge of the Compartmentalized Life

Before we focus on the question whether or not having membership in the church gives a person an advantage over those outside the church, let us remind readers of one of the great challenges in American life, namely, that there is a vast divide between church and public education. While we do not promote teaching religion in public schools in the way that such teaching might happen in our culture of contradictions, pluralism, and denominationalism, yet the tragedy we find is that in our contemporary culture, the field of education has been dictated by secularists. As such, children who attend secular institutions and who have no serious church life are left without the blessings that the church should bring to their lives. This, for us, is good reason to promote church school education and church affiliation. The reality is that faith/religion matters.

Church Affiliation

The central question for discussion is, whether there is an advantage in church membership for parents and children—that is especially focused on the issue of advocacy. In posing the question in this way, one might assume that all one is saying about the church is that it is merely for personal advantage and not so much to lead people to the kingdom of God. However, anyone making the latter assumption should bear in mind that there is no question in our minds as to what the church is, and what it is for. Our understanding is clear that the church is "God's appointed agency for salvation for humanity;" it is further described as "the repository of the riches of the grace of Christ" and "God's fortress, His city of refuge, which He holds in a revolted world." Although we do not argue the Catholic tradition that, "there is no salvation outside the church," we accept that through the church, God brings people to salvation. In the terms spoken of by Dr. Bushnell more than a hundred years ago, the kingdom of God is to grow by two means, namely, conversion and propagation. The latter is to be emphasized as much as the former. In the latter context, Bushnell insists, "Natural affections are not enough to be effective as parents." What is needed is a sense of the love of God. On this basis, Bushnell rationalized his understanding of religious education.

What the Church Does

The four great reasons for the existence of the church are spoken of as follows:

Worship. The church recognizes as central to its life the act of worship. In correspondence with the understanding that worship is at the central core of what it means to be human, every act of the church's corporate life focuses on worship. We should encourage people to attend church for worship.

Proclamation. This is the sharing of the gospel through preaching and teaching, which seeks the salvation of humanity. This is the most significant corporate task of the church—to share the love of God with humanity. The apostle Paul says, "So then faith *comes* by hearing, and hearing by the word of God." (Romans 10:17 NKJV). We should encourage church attendance so that people can be nurtured in the word of God.

Fellowship. A profound reality of church life is the building of community fellowship. People who are affiliated with the church recognize themselves as brothers and sisters. While such language is not as explicitly used in the secularized cultures of our day, there is still a clear understanding that church is a brotherhood and sisterhood. Church offers a place to have a sense of belonging.

Edification. One of the most notable functions of the church is that of edification. Edification has to do with giving guidance or instruction in multiple areas of life's education. When we say life's education, we include matters of the family, health, economics and anything that involves the daily life of people as they have to live in the world.

The Advantages of Being in the Church

Let us not forget the question we are pursuing is, namely, "Does having membership in the church give a person an advantage over persons outside the church?" Because we do not intend to write a theological treatise, we simply list the answers that we have gathered from a number of persons we interviewed over the years. What does church mean for them, we ask? The answers are of interest:

1. **A healthy social context**. The church is the healthiest social context for faith development.
2. **A place of belonging**. The church gives us a sense of belonging; it is like being in a family. It is a place where children and parents can be most often together in intergenerational experiences.
3. **A context of intimate friendships**. The church gives us intimate friendships; it helps us find those with who we have a mutual sense of trust.
4. **A place for community building**. The church gives us community. In sociological terms, *community* is defined as a place where multiple services are provided: religious, educational, social and so on. All these services and more are provided by most churches.
5. **A place for fellowship**. The church offers us fellowship—that is, a place to share in warm, open feelings. Perhaps one of the most important reasons for people to participate in a local congregation is that people need each other.
6. **A place of bonding**. One of the ironies of church life is the fact that somehow it provides possibilities for the maintenance of cultural and ethnic identities. Although there is much emphasis in the church on kingdom identity, yet cultural and ethnic identities are maintained as part of congregational life.
7. **A place for identity development**. The church provides a context of identity. It is a place where a person can get a sense of their uniqueness, develop their character, personality, and gifts.
8. **A place for involvement**. In the church, a person can get involved in congregational activities—such as finding a place in a variety of ministries, clubs, support and service groups, mission activities, and other kinds of opportunity activities.
9. **A place for learning leadership**. The church is one place where parents and children can learn leadership together. The children

can watch their parents in leadership positions as parents watch their children develop in leadership positions.

10. **A place for finding good counseling.** The church is one place where parents and children can receive free counseling. Often enough, the church has a high concentration of health and human services persons, educators, and other professionals who are capable of giving counsel. Alongside the pastor, these individuals are powerful advice-givers.
11. **A place to find positive mentorship.** The church is a place where each one can find many parents. What Hillary Clinton stated in her book *It Takes a Village* is also true in the church. The context can be intimate enough that parents will find mentors for themselves and their children. Where such mentorships are not naturally provided, they can be easily constructed.
12. **A place to build positive peer relationships.** If one should think of any context where one is to find the most positive relationships, one has to look to the church. Those who go to church have a system of values that is not naturally found in the competitive world.
13. **A context where many free seminars and workshops are provided.** Churches often provide many free seminars and workshops on parenting and child development. Many churches encourage parental love seminars, financial seminars, seminars on dating, workshops on worship in the home, and other aspects of family education. Families need to take advantage of these opportunities, for this might be the only family education classes that they will ever attend.
14. **A place with children departments**. We cannot overstate the value of the children's divisions of Sabbath/Sunday schools. Children who participate in these situations get an extensive opportunity for education. The experiences might not only offer spiritual advantages, but serve many aspects of the educational development.

15. **A place with generally safer environment.** In these days when abusiveness is so rampant in public spaces, one has to still speak of the comparative safety of the church environment. The cases of molestation and abuse that occurred in the Roman Catholic Church over the years are not be taken as the norm among Christian churches. In recognition of the increase in predatorial attitudes and the need for protecting the children, churches are making sure that those who work with children receive background clearance.
16. **A context where one is taught to serve others.** The church gives us opportunities to serve, which help us grow in ways we did not expect. In general, the value that we get out of a local congregation is in proportion to the amount of involvement we give to it. The church prepares and motivates us to serve in public community.
17. **A context for religious education.** One of the greatest advantages of being affiliated with the church is the possibility for participating in its system of education. Most youngsters who attend a religious system of education receive tuition subsidy. It is true that the cost might seem more than what is paid in other systems, but someone says, "If you think the cost is high, try the alternative." Sometimes parents can be so focused on the cost that they do not think of all the other benefits that their child/ren is/are receiving. Character building is as important as the academic subjects. In this context there are numerous opportunities to participate in morning worship, singing spiritual tunes, or going on a school mission trip that is church-affiliated.
18. **A context for linking parents and children in a common community through which multiple services can be obtained.** The church is a network community. It often has connections with multiple external agencies and can make referrals to those who attend or seek its assistance.

Using the Resources as Described

The suggestions above are only a few aspects of the advantages that are possible to parents and children in their churches. The question now is not whether there are advantages but whether individuals are using the advantages as they ought to. Too many of us neglect the benefits that churches provide. If as a parent you are affiliated with a church, make sure that you use the resources and network available to you. Also, support the church in ways that no one will think you are abusing the resources of the church. Do not only call upon its services when you find yourself or your children in trouble. Church folks are often very generous, even when they are not respected; just think what it might mean when they are respected. Even Jesus commented concerning the ten lepers that he had healed, "Were there not ten cleansed, but where are the nine?" (Luke 17:17).

The Church's Opportunity

In a directed study on the impact of parents on the spiritual development of their children, George Barna reports that millions of parents are unaware of the breadth of spiritual needs their children have.[66] Further reflection on the report states that of the 51 million children under the age of 18 who live in the United States, more than 40 million of them do not know Jesus Christ as their savior, which suggests that there are some basic unmet spiritual needs that parents are overlooking. This is one of the most significant and fertile mission fields in the nation, yet the very people who claim responsibility for the spiritual growth of those children are doing little about it beyond dropping their kids off

---

[66] See, "Parents Accept Responsibility for their Child's Spiritual Development, but Struggle with Effectiveness," http://www.barna.org/FlexPage.aspx?Page=BarnaUpdate&BarnaUpdateID=138.

at church. Churches could help more by being increasingly proactive in preparing parents to handle that responsibility wisely.[67]

Barna's research also indicates that sometimes parents are not able to guide their children spiritually because the parents are struggling with their own faith development. "When it comes to raising children to be spiritually mature, the old adage, 'you can't give what you don't have,' is pertinent for millions of families. Most parents proclaim that the spiritual nurturing of their children is their job, but are very happy to let their church shape the child's faith," according to the researcher. "Unfortunately, no matter how hard a church tries, it is incapable of bringing a child to complete spiritual maturity: that is the job of the family. The more willing churches are to play the co-dependent role in this drama, the less likely we are to see spiritually healthy families and a generation of young people who grow into mature believers."[68]

Taking Care to Access the Advantages of the Church

The church must make every effort to meet the needs of anxious parents who wish to advocate for their children. However, the point here is not so much to speak to churches concerning their role as it is to speak to parents about taking care to access the advantages provided by their church. In fact, in a concluding note, it might be of interest to observe the longitudinal studies that have been done on how parents' religious history and church affiliation have impacted their children over against parents who are not so connected with the church. Such studies suggest that parents who are church affiliated have children who are much more positive in their attitudes and stable in their lives. Even if such children rebel for a while, their consciences will challenge them to return to their roots. In the words of the wise man Solomon, "Train up a child

---

[67] Ibid.
[68] Ibid.

in the way he should go, and when he is old, he will not depart from it" (Pro. 22:6 NKJV).

QUESTIONS FOR REFLECTION

1. As an agency of advocacy, what important values do you think the church can provide you?
2. How effective is your church in promoting an ethic of strong, committed relationships and responsible parenthood?
3. What resources has your church provided to assist you with advocacy?

Chapter XIII

Using Scripture as a Tool for Advocacy

In generations before the latter half of the twentieth century, Scripture was seen as the most ideal tool for advocacy. It was used in nearly every home, church, and school as the preferred tool from which the principles and values of life were extracted. However, with Dr. Benjamin Spock's 1945 publication that influenced a new generation, parents were encouraged not to inhibit their children's freedom or to punish them. Since Spock's publication many other resources have been presented by psychologists and other social scientists as more valuable than Scripture. In fact, many parents today are just confused by the variety of child development material being proliferated, some of which are based on fictional ideals.[69] While we have no interest in entering into a debate that seeks to call for Scripture to be returned to public schools,

---

[69] Children are imaginative, and magical and fictional resources have a great appeal to them. However, if we do not help them to engage in the search for truth they will stay in the world of non-reality. This is of special significance in a world where the minds of many are now being infected by fake news.

yet we seek to assert that Scripture is the one uncontestable positive resource that has been most effective for the training, development, and advocacy of children. The testimony of such characters like Augustine, Martin Luther, and John Wesley tells what Scripture did for them personally and to their generation. So while we do not care to argue with those who have sought to attack Scripture and call for its ban because of their claim that it gives to children a negative portrayal of war, sex, and violence, we simply propose that the latter evaluation arises from persons who misinterpret and misunderstand Scripture and who predispose themselves to be indifferent to anything that is not of a humanistic origin. We argue that we are most favorable to the view that Scripture is the greatest book for advocacy because we have seen its positive bearing in our lives and that of our children.

The Bible Is a Book about Advocacy

It is very concerned about questions of justice:

- The rights of slaves (Ex 3:1–12; Exod. 12:44; Lev. 19:20; Prov. 30:10; Prov. 1:16)
- The rights of resident aliens (Exod. 22:21–23; Mark 12:28–34; Luke 10:25–37)
- The rights of those who suffer the miscarriage of justice or better stated the right practice of justice (Exod. 23:1–9; Deut. 16:18–20; Matt. 23:23; Luke 16:19–31; Luke 19:1–10; John 8:1–11)
- The rights of the poor (Lev. 19:9–10; Prov. 21:13; Isa. 3:13–15; Ezek. 22:23–31; Amos 8:4–8; Matt. 25:31–46; Luke 4:16–21)
- The rights of those caught up in debt (Deut. 15:1–11)
- The rights of women (Genesis 1:18; 2:27-28; Exodus 20:12; Luke 8:1-2; Matthew 27:55-56).
- The rights of the fatherless (Isa. 58:1–14)
- The rights of children (Ps. 127:3; Lev. 25:46; Prov. 22:6; Mark 10:16; Matt. 19:14; Luke 18;16)

The Call for the Advocacy of Children

In speaking to the topic of our concern, which is the advocacy of children, the Bible is full of advocacy instructions. Here is a sampling of textual instructions.

- Teach them [that is, the children] the decrees and laws, and show them the way to live and the duties they are to perform. (Exod. 18:20)
- Do not take advantage of a widow or an orphan. If you do and they cry out to me, I will certainly hear their cry. (Exod. 22:22–23)
- The secret things belong to the LORD our God, but the things revealed belong to us and to our children forever, that we may follow all the words of this law. (Deut. 29:29)
- Assemble the people—men, women and children, and the aliens living in your towns—so they can listen and learn to fear the LORD your God and follow carefully all the words of this law. Their children, who do not know this law, must hear it and learn to fear the LORD your God as long as you live in the land you are crossing the Jordan to possess. (Deut. 31:12–13)
- But you, O God, do see trouble and grief; you consider it to take it in hand. The victim commits himself to you; you are the helper of the fatherless. (Ps. 10:14)
- He will defend the afflicted among the people and save the children of the needy; he will crush the oppressor. (Ps 72:4).
- The LORD watches over the alien and sustains the fatherless and the widow, but he frustrates the ways of the wicked. (Ps. 146:9).
- A good man leaves an inheritance for his children's children. (Prov. 13:22)
- Train up a child in the way he should go, even when he is old, he will not depart from it. (Prov. 22:6).
- Foolishness is bound up in the heart of a child; the rod of discipline will remove it far from him. (Prov. 22:15)

- My eyes fail from weeping, I am in torment within, my heart is poured out on the ground because my people are destroyed, because children and infants faint in the streets of the city. (Lam. 2:11).
- And if anyone gives even a cup of cold water to one of these little ones because he is my disciple, I tell you the truth, he will certainly not lose his reward. (Matt. 10:42)
- He called a little child and had him stand among them. And he said: "I tell you the truth, unless you change and become like little children, you will never enter the kingdom of heaven. Therefore, whoever humbles himself like this child is the greatest in the kingdom of heaven. And whoever welcomes a little child like this in my name welcomes me. But if anyone causes one of these little ones who believe in me to sin, it would be better for him to have a large millstone hung around his neck and to be drowned in the depths of the sea. (Matt. 18:2–6).
- Children, obey your parents in the Lord, for this is right. (Eph. 6:1)
- Children, obey your parents in everything, for this pleases the Lord. (Col. 3:20)
- Fathers, do not exasperate your children; instead bring them up in the training and instruction of the Lord. (Eph. 6:4)
- Religion that God our Father accepts as pure and faultless is this: to look after orphans and widows in their distress and to keep oneself from being polluted by the world. (James 1:27).

The texts cited speak well to the responsibility of parents to teach and advocate for their children. While we live in an age when more and more parents are reneging on their responsibilities and passing them on to the church and other social agencies, parents who are serious about the success of their children will not fail to use the Bible as a most valuable tool. While at times we might need to speak to the church and the other social agencies concerning their responsibilities, the point of emphasis here focuses on what parents need to do from the perspective of the Bible. If as parents we are not careful about our God-given task to make Scripture as central a source of education, we will leave a heritage of destruction on our children. Let us not forget the power of Scripture to do the following:

1. Teach the development of the love and the fear of God. These alternatives are not to be seen as a contradiction. There is no contradiction between the softening of our souls by love for God and our respect for divine authority. If at no time in history there is need for affection and awe, it is now.
2. Instruct in the understanding of true wisdom. There is a wisdom that comes from the world of human experience, but it can never be compared with that which comes through the revelation of God.
3. Build a clear perspective on the stewardship of life. The understanding that theology should precede anthropology, sociology, and ethics is a necessary reality here. For when our children do not know where they are from, they can never truly know what they are doing here and where they need to go.
4. Create understanding of the principles of piety and purity. There is a lot that we learn from the commentary in 1 Samuel 3:1: "When the word of the Lord was rear in those day," the people and the priesthood became so corrupted that all kinds of violent acts were taking place even inside the tabernacle at Shiloh.
5. Help with the softening of the heart. So many books have been written on the civilizing power of Scripture to reshape personal lives, that we need not give a lengthy commentary here, but if one is in doubt, one should just test it on one's own life or that of a child and see the difference.
6. Develop the conscience. Conscience is something that is added to our being. It develops within the social contexts in which we live. Most often (or maybe we are to say always) such social contexts are deficient and need something more to purify whatever is extracted from them. What is better than a word revealed by God? Nothing. Thus, we can say, here is the value of Scripture.

7. Create an understanding of things of infinite value. In our culture where so many icons (idols), such as sports, television, internet, YouTube, smartphone and social media compete for our interest, and that of our children, we need to have one force that can help them to critique the icons, and nothing is better than Scripture.
8. Give rebuke and counsel. The balance between rebuke and counsel is found everywhere in the Scripture, even where it describes the cross where justice and mercy met together. It is thus a pathetic thing that Scripture is used so little to gain the balance in our rebuke and counsel with our children. No wonder that so often, we tear the two principles of rebuke and counsel apart.
9. Help with guidance in decision making. Multiple books are on the market that tell us how to do this and how to do that, and there are mass media advisers (TV, Internet and Radio) everywhere; however, there is no better tool that can be found than the word that is inspired and revealed by God. Thus, Scripture is the best source of guidance and advice anywhere.
10. Develop character. All communities of religious persons understand that the ultimate goal of their religious texts is nothing more than the development of the character of the generation to come. It is more than unfortunate that within our Western world where Bibles proliferate, and we proclaim the dominance of a Christian culture, that we find so little time to use the scripture. However, Scripture is still the number one tool for positive, moral, spiritual character development.

One of the most profound reflections on the purpose of the Scripture in education that we have reads:

> It is a law of the mind that it gradually adapts itself to the subjects upon which it is trained to dwell. If occupied with commonplace matters only, it will become dwarfed

and enfeebled. If never required to grapple with difficult problems, it will after a time almost lose the power of growth. As an educating power the Bible is without a rival. In the word of God, the mind finds subject for the deepest thought, the loftiest aspiration. The Bible is the most instructive history that men possess. It came fresh from the fountain of eternal truth, and a divine hand has preserved its purity through all the ages. It lights up the far-distant past, where human research seeks vainly to penetrate. In God's word we behold the power that laid the foundation of the earth and that stretched out the heavens. Here only can we find a history of our race unsullied by human prejudice or human pride. Here are recorded the struggles, the defeats, and the victories of the greatest men this world has ever known. Here the great problems of duty and destiny are unfolded. The curtain that separates the visible from the invisible world is lifted, and we behold the conflict of the opposing forces of good and evil, from the first entrance of sin to the final triumph of righteousness and truth; and all is but a revelation of the character of God. In the reverent contemplation of the truths presented in His word the mind of the student is brought into communion with the infinite mind. Such a study will not only refine and ennoble the character, but it cannot fail to expand and invigorate the mental powers.[70]

The teaching of the Bible has a vital bearing upon man's prosperity in all the relations of this life. It unfolds the principles that are the cornerstone of a nation's

---

[70] Ellen White, (1890, 1958), *Patriarchs and Prophets*, Washington, D. C.: Review and Herald Publishing Association, 599.

prosperity—principles with which is bound up the well-being of society, and which are the safeguard of the family—principles without which no man can attain usefulness, happiness, and honor in this life, or can hope to secure the future, immortal life. There is no position in life, no phase of human experience, for which the teaching of the Bible is not an essential preparation. Studied and obeyed, the word of God would give to the world men of stronger and more active intellect than will the closest application to all the subjects that human philosophy embraces. It would give men of strength and solidity of character, of keen perception and sound judgment—men who would be an honor to God and a blessing to the world.[71]

Grounding Whatever We Do in Scripture

What we have been arguing is to ground our work of advocacy in Scripture. In this way, we will be using the best resource that is available to bring into balance any action we take to make a difference in the lives of our children. A foundation built on a document of faith surpasses any other foundation. Thus, while there are those who view and use Scripture in a negative way to do their work, there is need to remember that the Bible is a book with a very positive message. What parents need to do is to study it day by day, and use its knowledge, wisdom, instruction, counsel, guidance, and direction, so that in all we do, we might be as effective as God wishes us to be.

---

[71] Ibid.

Our Call to Advocacy

How well we care for, protect, and advocate for our children reflect our understanding of the responsibility that God has given to us. We are told in Scripture:

> And whoever welcomes a little child like this in my name welcomes me. But if anyone causes one of these little ones who believe in me to sin, it would be better for him to have a large millstone hung around his neck and to be drowned in the depths of the sea. (Matthew. 18:5–6 KJV)

Whoever neglects their responsibility is under the judgment of God. The reality is that the depravity of human hearts has reached such a point today that our children have to be protected at every moment of their lives. So, while we take time to recognize them, affirm them, model for them, and instruct them, we also must take the time to assure their safety and security. We are sure that for any neglect of our responsibility we will receive the just judgment of God.

QUESTIONS FOR REFLECTION

1. Can you point to any way that you have found the scripture helpful as a tool of advocacy?
2. What are some of the most effective teachings that you have found in scripture on the value of children?
3. What are some of the rights that scripture proclaims for children?

Chapter XIV

Using Prayer as a Tool of Advocacy

Praying for Our Children

The birth of a child often brings joy to a family. Within days of each birth, many rituals are celebrated including that of taking the child to a house of prayer for a pastor or priest to pray for the blessing and protection of the child. The ceremonies of blessing are usually attended by many family members and friends who state their commitment to join the parents with continuing prayer and support. It is rather pathetic that many forget to continue in prayer with persistence; for the profound challenges of growing our children certainly need  those prayers for prudence, provision, power, and protection. Ask any godly parent what made the difference in their child's life, and they will often answer with one word—*prayer*. The Bible gives clear records of parents and other individuals who interceded in behalf of their children.

Job prayed for his children. "His sons used to go and hold feasts in one another's houses in turn; and they would send and invite their three sisters to eat with them. And when the feasts had run their course, Job would send and sanctify them, and he would rise early in the morning and offer burnt offerings according to the number of them all; for Job said, 'It may be that my children have sinned, and cursed God in their hearts.' This is what Job did." (Job 1:4–5).

Hannah interceded that God would give her a child. Eli accused her of being drunk when she attended the tabernacle service and was interceding with God for a child. God saw her pain, and gave her Samuel. When Samuel grew to the age of twelve, she took him to the tabernacle and handed him over to Eli, who found him to be a most diligent hand in preparation for the priesthood. It is said that Hannah continued to keep her heart upon Samuel, and once each year, she visited the tabernacle at Shiloh to take him a new garment. Samuel became one of the greatest judges and prophets of Israel (1 Sam. 1:2).

Elijah prayed for a woman to have a child, and when the child grew into a lad, he became sick and died. Then Elijah prayed again, and the child was brought to life. The joy of the mother was profound, for she knew that God had responded to the prayers of the prophet (1 Kings 17:24).

Jesus told the disciples to allow the mothers to bring their children to him and not to stop them. He said, "Let the children come to me and don't stop them, for to such the kingdom of heaven belongs" (Matt. 18:16). He knew too well that prayer lifted burdens from the hearts of mothers and gave them assurance of the protection of God.

Prayer as Advocacy

In effect, it is a historical fact that prayer has been one of the most powerful tools of guidance and direction that parents have used in the life of their children. Prayer is seeking the presence of God. It is depending on God's power, providence, and protection. It is seeking God's peace, holding God to his promises, giving praise to God, and asking God's guidance for the way forward in one's personal life and in the lives of others. To state this in the frame of our present discussion, prayer has been and is used as the most effective tool of advocacy by parents for their children.

The Prayer Advocate

Of interest, is the fact that one of the most fascinating pictures of God, as revealed in Jesus Christ, is that of an advocate. The apostle John states, "My little children, these things I write to you, so that you may not sin. And if anyone sins, we have an Advocate with the Father, Jesus Christ the righteous. And He Himself is the propitiation for our sins, and not for ours only but also for the whole world" (1 John 2:1–2). This means that the very idea of advocacy is bound up with God. An advocate, as has been noted, offers intercession for another or speaks up for another. An advocate also seeks to defend another or pleads for another. An unfortunate conception of Christ as advocate, as seen by some theologians, is the notion that Christ's intercessory work before the Father amounts to Christ begging the Father to accept us. But such a picture of the divine advocacy misappropriates the fact that God seeks to defend his children from the dragon that roams the world. The reality is that as Christ is our advocate (cf. Rom. 8:33), so is the Father (cf. Rom. 8:31). Thus, when we pray to God, we can enter into the heavenly courtroom where Christ, through the Holy Spirit, stands up for us. Whatever else might be projected through the mystery of the relationship between God the Father, God the Son, and God the Holy Spirit, it is quite clear that the conception of the heavenly advocate has profound significance for anyone who seeks to pray (Rom. 8:26).

The prayers we pray are reflective of how we conceptualize God. If we see God as a loving, caring, protective, intimate father, we, and those who imitate us, will pray to him in a personal way. If, on the other hand, we see God as a distant, autocratic, oppressive figure, our prayers will be offered to him in an apprehensive way. A question that is pertinent here is, "How do we image God to our children?" According to Erik Erikson, human development begins with (1) basic trust (ages zero to one and one-half), then moves to (2) autonomy (two to six), then (3) industry (seven to twelve), then (4) identity (thirteen to twenty-one), then (5) intimacy, then (6) generativity (thirty-five to sixty), and finally, (7) integrity. An analysis of these emotional stages might illustrate that at every stage, God is conceptualized in different ways. James Fowler makes the point that faith begins from a preoperational stage where one forms attachments, to the concrete operational stage, then to the time of early formal operations, to that of formal operations, and then within the latter, there are a variety of formal stages that lead to the most mature—that of universal faith.

PREOPERATIONAL	CONCRETE	EARLY FORMAL	FORMAL	UNIVERSAL
Between ages of two to six years, children like to imitate, role-play and are very symbolic focused.

They conceptualize faith in the ways that their parents speak of it. What they hear is what they say. Most of their prayers say, "Bless Mommy and Daddy and my brother and sister." | Between ages seven to eleven, a child begins to think logically about events but often has difficulty with deductive or abstract reasoning.

Faith is conceptualized in very physical ways. They have to see it to believe it. They thank God for their toys and other gifts. | This stage covers adolescence. Children begin to let go of concrete experiences and reach out for the abstract. In this stage, their faith looks more like that of their peers rather than that of their parents. They thank God for the grades they make in school and anything that makes them look successful. | The stage covers young adulthood when serious attention is given to outcomes and consequences of behavior.

Children are able to systematically solve a problem.

Moral issues and ethical issues are given high consideration. | In this stage, a person is much more focused on love and justice than at any other stage.

Service to others becomes most significant.

Where injustice is seen, an obligation is felt to disobey unjust laws. |

The preoperational stage is where children make their foundational connection with God. As parents and caregivers, we should make sure that when we teach children to pray, we teach concepts of God that can be developed in the most positive way.

We have been quite apprehensive to share the following story, assuming that it is true, but we do so if it might support the point we seek to make about God. One of our brothers, who toasted us at one of our sons' wedding told it. He had lived with us when he was a youngster and felt he now had the audacity to share a family secret. He told it in such a manner that brought a lot of laughter but, at the same time, reminded us of how immature we were at the start of our parenting. We were quite excited at how our first son's development was progressing. He was our gift, "a little prodigy," who we wanted to mold as God would have us do. He had barely passed a year and a half but was beginning to talk so much that we thought it was time to help him learn to pray the children's prayer. As our brother told, for one week, we tried to help him say "Dear Jesus" prayer. Although, as we said, our son would say multiple other things through the day, but when we came to the time of prayer, he had no interest in our promptings. One evening, after his mother (June) tried to help him pray and he refused to respond, in utter frustration, she blurted out, "Child, are you an idiot?" The saga of resistance continued night after night, and finally as the story goes, Dad (DK) decided, well, Mom might not be a good-enough teacher, so he took over. Needless to say, the same response was offered. Dad then blurted out, "Son, stop acting like an idiot." With the constant frustration, we left off trying for a couple of days. Then another week, we tried again. Apparently, our son seemed quite satisfied that he had frustrated us long enough so, as we knelt down, without any prompt, he blurted out, "Dear Jesus, are you an idiot?" Our brother said we became so embarrassed that we did not know what to do next. We opened our eyes and stared at each other for a while and then started to pray.

We really have no recollection of the incident, but do not put it beyond any possibility of our wanting to be the perfect parents. However, it was there that we learned a fast lesson in how not to teach a child to pray. Our son had no way of knowing that "Are you an idiot" was not a part of the "Dear Jesus" prayer. We dare say, with every apology, such words should never be uttered from any parent to their children. It is sad, even outside of the context of prayer, to put any such negative label on a child. If the story did occur, then we admit that in our anxiety, we made a mess; but we were able to correct our ways and make sure that our son came to learn that Jesus is not an idiot. He soon learned the "Gentle Jesus, meek and mild" prayer and quickly prayed using his own words.

Gentle Jesus, Meek and Mild

Yes, one of the simplest prayers taught to many children in traditional Christian homes is this:

> Gentle Jesus, meek and mild
> Look upon a little child
> Pity my simplicity
> Bless me when I come to thee.

This can be a great prayer to place on the lips of children at the start of their lives, but we must take care that they do not grow to believe that the Gentle Jesus is for children, while the Our Father we teach to adults depicts a different God. We must take care that our children learn intimacy with God, but do not get the idea that Jesus is gentle while God the Father is the angry punisher. Any such misconception ought to be corrected from very early in their lives. Scripture declares that Jesus is the incarnate God (Isa. 7:14, 9:6; Matt. 1:22, 23; John 1:1–3, 14; 14:9; Col. 1:16–20), the one who came to bring the Father close to us. He is God in the flesh, to give us a face of God that was lost to many persons in ancient times and may be in ours.

The Model Prayer

In fact, in the Model Prayer, as taught to the disciples, Jesus introduces us to the most striking picture of the intimacy of God, by letting us know that God is Our Father – Abba Father – Papa. Such a picture transcends any representation of fatherhood that is to be found in any father on earth.

> Our Father
> Which art in heaven,
> Hallowed be thy name.
>
> Thy kingdom come
> Thy will be done
> On earth, as it is in heaven.
>
> Give us this day our daily bread.
> And forgive us our debts,
> As we forgive
> Our debtors.
>
> And lead us not into temptation,
> But deliver us from evil:
> For thine is the kingdom,
> The power, and the glory,
> Forever,
> Amen. (Matt. 6:9–13 cf. Luke 11:2–4)

There are many aspects to this prayer, and each says something about the fatherhood of God. It is very interesting to note the movements in the prayer.

Our Father. The fatherhood of God introduces us to the intimacy of relationship that is possible with God, the access that we have to God, and the confidence with which we can go to God. We each can claim God as our own. He is a personal God.

Which is in heaven. The transcendence of God moves God beyond the commonality of earthly fathers who sometimes fail to reflect God and therefore create resentment and rejection from their children. Of course, this distancing of God can be difficult for children because it puts God where he sometimes seems hard to be reached. So, the reminder often needs to be made that God is not just **out there**, but is also **present here**, with us.

Hallowed be your name. The distinctiveness of God shows the respect and reverence that one must have for God. The foremost need of our contemporary culture is respect for God. That means, not using God's name tritely. Like the third commandment says, "You shall not take the name of the Lord your God in vain; for the Lord will not hold anyone guiltless that takes his name in vain" (Exod. 20:7).

Your kingdom come. The rule of God is the reminder that God has a universal plan for this earth, and that such a plan will only be fulfilled when the kingdom of God is established in the earth. Often when we think of a kingdom, we think of something that involves great land mass, army and armory, palaces and castles, flags and banners, automobiles, warships and planes, drones and spy satellites, presidents and prime ministers, kings and queens and fair maidens, and so on. But such reflection is about human kingdoms that are established for temporary times. This part of the prayer calls us to direct our children to the establishment of the kingdom of God.

Your will be done on earth as it in heaven. The will of God allows us to understand that there needs to be alignment between that which is done on earth and what is done in heaven. This is most significant in any life of prayer. To be favored of God means that we stand in a heavenly position, thinking our thoughts like God. We can then seek to be in agreement with God's heavenly will. Children need to be taught more than ever that there is a will that is higher than theirs.

Give us this day our daily bread. The providential care of God makes the point that God is an effective provider. He is interested in the salvation of our souls, but he is also interested in our material well-being.

He sees our struggles to find daily sustenance and provides for us. Who gives us bread? It is not Castro or some other personage, but God.

And forgive us our debts as we forgive our debtors. The forgiveness of God portrays God as a Forgiving Father who expects us to live with forgiveness toward each other. In effect, we need to take cognizance of our indebtedness toward God so that we might forgive those who have offended us. And we need to teach our children that there is not only forgiveness with God, but that we must be live as forgivers.

And lead us not into temptation. The protective power of God shows that we can depend upon God for protection from the traps that have been set for us. To receive the divine protection, we must be in subjection to the authority of God. Traps are all around us. Sometimes we cannot see them. And we cannot resist them in our own power. We need divine power in order to overcome them. Here children need to know God watches over them.

Yours is the kingdom. The sovereign rule of God. For the millennia that this earth has been in existence, the powers of evil have sought to usurp the authority of God. The power of rebellion started in heaven and has been manifested on earth, through Satan. To pray with authority is to bring heavenly energy into the prayer. The Holy Spirit brings the divine authority, so we need to ask for the Holy Spirit. Only this authority can help us confront the demonic powers of earth.

The power and the glory. The fear and respect of God means having a sense of awe and wonder concerning the divine is most important for anyone who prays. Awe and wonder lead to reverence and worship. However, in our secularized world, much awe and wonder are gone out of life. Because of that, irreverence and contempt for God are creeping into our life experiences. We must, therefore, be committed to recapture the spiritual moments of life for ourselves and teach them to our children. Let us learn how we can truly glorify God and be obedient to him. We repeat, disrespect, disloyalty, and disobedience go together; so, in all things, let us focus on God as the one who is utterly distinct from us.

Forever and ever. The perpetuity of God is often compared to romantic relationships that only last for a short time. However, the concept is truly what it is when it is used to describe the perpetuity of God and the eternity of the promises, he offers to us. To live in the "forever" of God is to hold on to his promises, no matter what. "For as many as are the *promises* of God, in Him they are *yes*; therefore, also through Him is our *Amen* to the glory of God through us" (2 Cor. 1:20 NASB; italics added).

Amen. The amen of God is the way the Model Prayer closes and the way that most persons close their prayers. What is meant is that the prayers are verified in God, who is truthful and faithful. Every spiritual promise is fulfilled in God. If God cannot be trusted, there is no need to pray, "Amen. So, let it be." We are to trust God and encourage those with whom we pray to be grateful for every blessing that God offers to us. We need to teach our children that they are to put aside complaining and murmuring and praise the Lord for what he has done for us/them.

The Way to Begin Teaching Prayer

Modeling prayer. The prayer we have been discussing above is called "The Model Prayer." It is the prayer that Jesus taught his disciples. While he did not mean that they should always pray this prayer, he used it as a starting point to help his disciples develop the basics of prayer. When children pray, they mimic what they see and hear. Allow your children to see or hear you praying and they will pray. Such modeling is the best introduction to the prayer life of a child. Susannah Wesley, mother of the famous Wesley brothers—John, the evangelist and Charles, the hymn writer—made prayer her chief support. She prayed for two hours each day. She made time to pray. What is significant is that her children saw her in prayer, and when she could not find room to pray, she flipped her apron over her head and interceded with God. No doubt, Susannah who was a preacher's child saw her parents in prayer, and when she had her family, she carried forward the tradition. It is evident that her prayers impacted the lives of her sons, for they laid the foundation of the Methodist Church. Following are some suggestions as to how we might advocate with our children in prayer.

Praying with our children. At the earliest, pray with them. Begin to pray with your children even before you think that they can understand. Teach them the attitudes that are most consistent with prayer. Let them kneel when appropriate so that they will understand the significance of reverence, namely, that God is to be respected as absolute authority. Teach them to fold the hands so that they will not be fiddling around during the time of prayer. Teach them to close their eyes so that they might keep out distractions. As they grow older, they might learn how to negotiate these gestures, but when they are younger, they need to move from *ritualization* to *ritual*, just as they learn when to speak and when to be silent at a dinner table.

Praying for our children. Children like to hear their names in prayer. As old as we are, we still like to hear our names in our parents' prayers. When we would go to visit our mother in Florida, we felt blessed when in the wee hours of the morning we heard her calling each child's name in prayer. The following bluegrass lyrics attest to the power of parental prayer, and the impact it has on a child when he/she hears their name in the prayer of a parent.

> While kneeling by her beside in a cottage on the hill
> My mother prayed her blessing for me there
> She was talking then with Jesus while everything was still
> And I heard my mother call my name in prayer
>
> Yes, I heard my mother call my name in prayer
> She was pouring out her heart to Jesus there
> Then I gave my heart to Him and He saved my soul from sin
> For I heard my mother call my name in prayer
>
> She was anxious for her boy to be just what he ought to be
> And she asked the lord to take Him in His care
> Just the words I can't remember but I know she prayed for me
> For I heard my mother call my name in prayer

Refrain
Then I gave my heart to Jesus and I'm living now for him
And someday I'll go and meet him in the air
For he heard my mother praying and he saved my soul from sin
Yes, he heard my mother call my name in prayer
(Bluegrass lyrics)

Teaching your children to pray at special times:

- In family worship - Give them opportunity to pray.
- Going to bed at nights – Let them know that their last activity before sleep is prayer.
- Waking up in the mornings – Let them know that their first activity in the mornings is prayer.

Teach your children to pray anywhere:

- Let them pray — in the car, while walking, in the kitchen, at the playground, and in school.

Teach them basic prayer vocabulary:

- Give them the appropriate way to address God, thus allowing them to know that God is special. If children learn how to speak to their earthly parents with respect, they will learn quickly how to talk. As children growing up in Sabbath School, one of the early songs we learned was:

    I talk to Grandma on the phone
    On the phone, on the phone,
    I talk to Grandma on the phone
    And she hears me I know.

> I talk to Jesus when I pray,
> When I pray, when I pray
> I talk to Jesus when I pray
> And he hears me I know.

The above suggests that it is as easy to pray as it is to talk to grandparents on the phone. Here are some additional points in teaching children how to pray:

- Teach them how to be natural in prayer. Be real. Be simple.
- Teach them the components of prayer. Let them know that there is a place for praise, thanksgiving, confession, forgiveness, and communion in prayer.
- Teach them how to seek God's guidance in prayer.
- Teach the role of the Holy Spirit in answering prayers.
- Teach that praying to God is different from praying to Santa Claus.
- Teach children that they might write out their prayers.
- Teach them how to include others into their prayers.
- Teach them to pray for their friends, for the sick, for their neighbors, for their teachers, and just helping them to be mindful of others.
- Teach them the relationship between prayers and forgiveness.
- Teach them that prayer is dialogue—talk and listen to Jesus.
- Teach them about the time and length of prayer.
- Teach them that prayer is a power that helps dreams come true. Nothing is too simple or too great to talk to tell Jesus.
- Teach them to pray when things are going well.
- Teach them to pray when things are tough.
- Teach them that they can pray to identify their gifts.
- Teach them the value of submitting to the will of God in prayer.
- Teach them that prayer is waiting upon God.
- Teach them the relationship between prayer and action.
- Teach them how to approach the High and Lofty One.
- Teach them that prayer is not a time for joke or laughter. It is a time to be respectful and reverent.

Listening to Your Children's Prayers

We should not only teach children to pray, but also listen to them pray. Listening to children's prayers can teach us much about the maturing faith of the children. Listen if they are saying, "Our Father, which in heaven, Harold be your name." Listen if they are just praying if they are just praying for getting a good grade in school. Listen if all they consider reason for praise are material blessings. Listen, if they are growing in prayer. By listening you can learn a lot.

Several years ago, when we lived in Canada, we learned the importance of listening to our children's prayers. We had moved from New York City, where we lived for ten years, and settled in a neighborhood where we thought our children were adjusting. About nine months later, our second son prayed, "Lord, help us to find friends." When this prayer continued for several nights, the reality of the situation struck us. They were not adjusting as we thought they should have, because they needed friends. After discussing together as parents, we knew what adjustments we needed to make.

Many parents are not careful to listen to their children, but listening to them is one habit that every parent should practice. Parents, the watchword is to *listen! listen! listen!* for children are not hypocritical; they will tell how they feel. If it does not come out in normal conversations, it will certainly come out in prayers. We have heard of a little boy, when asked to pray at the end of a children story hour, saying "God will you take the demons out of my father." We do not know the truth or falsehood, of the story. But, however, it is, it is clear that the child was calling for some intervention. As we listen let us learn to take appropriate action, if we wish to be effective advocates.

Drawing Up the Battle Lines

We are living in times when the need for prayer for our children is never more urgent. Parents need discerning skills in order to attack the forces that seek to engulf our children. We must become truly aware of and act on the following:

1. Promiscuous and aberrant sexual behaviors
2. Harmful relationships
3. Addictions of any kind
4. Deviant behaviors of all kinds

Here are some approaches that we should take in order to be victorious in the battle for our children.

- Always maintain a prayerful attitude.
- Pray from the heart, not just from your head.
- Meditate upon the needs of your own soul.
- Be persistent and persevering.
- Be earnest—supplicate.
- Confess your mistakes and sins.
- Let God know that you are seeking his counsel.
- Remember the promises of God—hold on to them.
- Be plain and simple.
- Make sure you concentrate yourself.
- Try to understand Satan's effort to build distractions, deceptions, and destructions in your prayer life.

Kinds of Prayers We Need to Pray for Children

1. Prayers of Thanksgiving

Out of them shall come thanksgiving, and the sound of merrymakers? I will make them many and they will not be few; I will make them honored and they shall not be disdained (Jer. 30:19).

Many times, when God rescues our children, we neglect to be thankful. We must have an attitude of gratitude and allow our children to sense such gratitude. 1 Samuel, chapter 2, records Hannah's prayer of gratitude in a beautiful way. In chapter 1, she prayed for a child, and when she received the blessing, she lifted her voice in praise and thanksgiving. In gratitude for giving her a son, Hannah gave back the child she asked for to the service of God. Samuel grew knowing that he was special—that he was an answer to prayer and that he was an offering to God. These days, we teach our children to be thankful for material things, and there is nothing wrong with that, but we need to teach them to be thankful for the deeper blessings of God—their existence, the protection of God, the freedoms they enjoy, the ability to think, the ability to hear, strength for each day and the will to confront the world of evil. And as parents, we need to thank God for our children when we sense that they are mindful of doing God's will.

2. Prayers of Confession

One of the most powerful prayers of the Bible is Daniel's prayer of confession. We will not repeat the whole prayer here, but note the part in Daniel 4:9. "I prayed to the Lord my God and made confession, saying, 'Ah, Lord, great and awesome God, keeping covenant and steadfast love with those who love you and keep your commandments.'" It is always important to admit that we have sinned and come short of God's glory as parents. Admitting wrong is never easy, but necessary in order to feel forgiven. In fact, the spirit of forgiveness needs to be taught for the emotional and physical benefits that comes to a person who confesses and forgives. When guilt and resentment are removed by forgiveness a person can live a healthy life. Children should be taught confessional prayers instead of making excuses, as many adults do.

3. **Prayers for Protection**

   The Psalmist says, "But let all who take refuge in you rejoice; let them ever sing for joy. Spread your protection over them, so that those who love your name may exult in you" (Ps. 5:11). Metaphors for the protection of God proliferate throughout the Bible. I like to read Psalm 91, for example, where I find metaphors such as God as a "shelter," "shadow," "refuge," "fortress," 'shield," and "buckler," etc., all clumped together. In this Psalm, the Psalmist asks God to keep his children from the diseases, affliction, the arrows of warfare, the traps of the night stalker, and the mouth of the dragon. In these times of terror, when crime and violence are rampant in the earth, it is important to pray prayers of protection.

4. **Prayers for Discernment**

   The Apostle James says, "If any one lacks wisdom, let him ask of God who gives to all liberally and without reproach, and it will be given to him" (James 1:5). There are several songs that give us the sense that we lack discernment and need the power of God for restoration. The contemporary song by Steve Green "Touch Your People Once Again," is very meaningful to us.

   > We need wisdom we need power
   > And true love for each other
   > We have had so many big but empty word
   > So, we come before Your face Asking for Your grace
   > Bring Your people to a state of kingdom life
   > Restore Your church again

Chorus

Touch Your people once again
With Your precious holy hand, we pray
Let Your kingdom shine upon this earth
Through a living glorious church
Not for temporary deeds
But to restore authority and power
Let a mighty rushing wind blow in
Touch your people once again

Lord You see Your tired servants
And the broken wounded soldiers
Oh, how much we need Your precious healing hand
We need the power of the cross
As the only source for us
When we stand up facing final battle cry
Restore your church again

Chorus

Touch Your people once again
With Your precious holy hand, we pray
Let Your kingdom shine upon this earth
Through a living glorious church
Not for temporary deeds
But to restore authority and power
Let a mighty rushing wind blow in
Touch your people once again

5. Prayers of Intercession

The apostle Peter says, "The end of all things is upon us, therefore be serious and discipline yourselves for the sake of your prayers" (1 Pet. 4:7). In this context we say that parents need to stand before God for their children and before their children for God. This is what advocacy means. Parents, in this sense are "go-betweens". The intercession of parents must have a sense of urgency. They are pleading with God for the life of their children. The Bible is replete with examples of intercessions. When Stephen was being stoned, he did not pray for his protection, but rather he interceded with God on behalf of those who were hurting him (Acts 7:60). Sometimes this is what parents have to do for their children who are hurting them. Moses's interceded for his people when, because of their impatience, they made a golden calf and worshipped it instead of the true and living God. God was intent on destroying the rebellious people, but Moses stepped between an angry God and a sinful people and "the Lord relented" (Exodus 32:11–14). Parents need to step in the gap and intercede in behalf of children in whatever the challenges they encounter. Parents don't need to know the specific challenges, but must know that they are that constant go between. Many times, there comes an urge to pray for a child, and without stopping to ask why, parents need to stop in their track and intercede. Sometimes they might not know why, and in some instances, they find out later. Be persistent parents and have a passion for the needs of your children and of others.

A powerful story on intercession is that of a mother whose child sustained an accident and was badly hurt. She did everything, but all failed. Her child, her only child, was dying. As the story goes, the mother fell on her knees and passionately pleaded with God for the life of her child. She said, "God, are you going to allow my only child to go from me?" God heard her plea, and the child lived. Be mindful, however, that not every prayer of intercession is answered the way we want it. David interceded for his child, but the child died (see 2 Samuel 2). Know that God, in his wisdom, does what is best for us.

6. Prayer of Faith

John Westerhoff III argues that if parents want their children to grow up with mature faith, they need to show that their relationship with God is strong. We recommend this for the life of prayer. Prayer of faith is stepping out and believing that whatever we ask we will receive. We need to demonstrate in our lives that our faith is strong. Demonstrate to children that when we trust God, he will take care. When we talk of faith, the story of George Mueller should ring loud and clear. He ran several orphanages based only on faith even when many called him foolish. There were times when the cupboards were bare and hungry faces looking at him, but instead of giving in, he would have the children set the table and pray; and sure enough, God came through every time. We need to make prayers of faith a pillar in our homes, for "the prayer of faith will save" our children.

Yes, when we pray, we need to be **expectant** that God will answer our prayers. He said it, "I will save your children. I will bring them from afar" (Isaiah 49:25). We should expect God's answers for Jesus has promised, "If you ask me for anything in my name, and I will do it." (John 14:14). This is God's desire for us. He wants to bless our children. All we need to do is believe and bring our petitions before the throne of grace.

Uniting Together to Pray

It is good to pray individually, but there are times when there needs to be a coming together in prayer, for there is power in communal prayer. When God's children get together and pray things happen. In the book *Parental Legacy*, we have shared an interview from our dad who told that in growing up his children, he used to go to the woods with his brother-in-law to spend much time praying for his children. Here is a great example of how we might get additional support from others. Parent you might need to call a trusted friend, a prayer partner, a special prayer group, a parent or grandparents to intercede with you. Do not be afraid to become vulnerable before others for the battle is real. Do not fight the forces of evil on your own when you can have the power of others to help.

Prayer as the Road to Victory

It is a daunting experience for any parent whose child, no matter how old he/she might be when the child is consciously or unconsciously battling the forces of evil. We have experienced such a situation with our own child and understand fully the need to be on our knees interceding with God to remove the demons. We are convinced that a "love demon" is one of the most difficult entrapments from which one needs release. We share these personal stories, for they are real, and first-hand information.

One of our sons was madly in love with a young woman, many individuals believe was incompatible with his personality and beliefs. But he was "in love" because friends said "You look good together." Both had a love for music, which was probably the only thing they had in common. It would take pages to relate the almost two years of battle before release came, but we will try to give you enough so you can understand how much prayer is needed when the forces of evil are determined to entangle your child.

Yes, our son was in love with a young woman he hadn't even bothered to introduce to us as his special friend. This was quite uncharacteristic of him. In spite of that, we determined to be open-minded to do a fair evaluation. As we looked, God sent us indications from various unsolicited sources. The informants were not even aware that we did not know of the challenges confronting the life of the young woman. We knew by the information that such a match would be disastrous for various reasons. At times we shared insights with our son, and he often wondered if we were psychics, for we had information even when we were far away on vacations. Needless to say, our son just could not see what we were sensing and what others were seeing; he was "love struck." The "love demon" had him; and, therefore, his perceptions were clouded. Our resolve was not to fight with him or to be unkind to the young woman, so our only recourse was prayer. As we prayed, we dialogued; but of course, you know the answer. He didn't see anything wrong, for his friends told him she was cool; and for a time, his siblings thought so too, for they "looked good together."

While the relationship escalated, everything else went wrong for our son. He lost his car, lost his job, and life was just going down the tubes. God was speaking, but he was madly in love, or so he thought, that he could not read signals. We wanted him to come home and pick up the pieces, but of course, we could not say it because his friends would ridicule him. On Thanksgiving morning 1997, we knelt in a circle with his two siblings and interceded on his behalf that God would open his eyes and help him to see the destructiveness of the relationship. His weekly trips of three hundred plus miles were costly. We prayed that he would come home so that we could have more chances for dialogue. We wished he would come over for breakfast, but of course, we left that to him. As soon as we arose from our knees, the phone rang; he was on the line. Dad spoke with him, and our son stated he wanted to come over but needed fifteen minutes to be ready. After hanging up the phone, Dad dropped on the floor and bawled. He was shocked that our instant plea to God brought such quick response. Fifteen minutes later, the phone rang again; he was ready, so Mom picked him up, for Dad was still overwhelmed by the quick connection to heaven's hotline. Breakfast was over, dinner was finished, and our son was still at home. We prayed silently in our hearts that God would continue the miracle, and he certainly did. Before dark, our son left the house with one of his brothers; and about two hours later, they returned with his television and a small bag with toiletries, we presume. He placed them in his room. We asked no questions, but we continued to pray. At worship time we knelt and held hands and just praised God for our Thanksgiving gift.

Our son brought his things home in stages, but the battle had only begun. Satan was not about to release him without a fight. We lent him a car so that he could get to work, but he still insisted on making the three-hundred-mile plus trek to see his lover. During the week, phone calls averaged at least ten per day. This was signal for us of a codependent relationship, which, of course, our son could not agree with. One weekend as he started out on his three-hundred-mile trip, Mom, feeling distressed and pained over our son's blindness, turned her eyes to heaven and prayed that God would smash the transmission of the car. One might say that was a mean prayer, but God heard the cry; and before our son had reached too far from home, yes, you guessed it right, the transmission was gone. A new transmission was placed in the car, and he continued to work. After a few weeks, the three-hundred-mile haunt revived, and our son was determined to go. Again, Mom lifted her eyes to heaven and prayed the same prayer, "God, smash the transmission." Again, the three-week-old transmission went, and this time it was not replaced. We cannot tell what God had saved him from, but we do know that these were clear signals that the relationship was a troubled one.

As we pleaded with God on his behalf, the evil forces were angrier, for as he tried to break the relationship, the young woman tried desperately to hold on to him, by using, what we considered, crafty means. When he would no longer drive to visit her, she would visit a mutual friends' house in the area, and found ways of getting to our son through his youngest sibling. She confided in that sibling that she had to find out the reason our son was breaking off the relationship with her.

On another occasion we noted a somber looks on our son's countenance, and felt that something was not right. As mothers like to do, Mom simply said, "She is here." Our son's response was simple "Yes" with more sadness in his voice. That was the weekend we compared to "Jacob's night of struggle." We knew if our son did not get the victory, the devil was going to finish him off. The Sunday night at midnight, when he came home, we called him into our room, and we dialogued with him and asked him if he mind that we pray with him. He said,

"Oh yes, please do." We took it that he was sincere and formed a guard around him. Dad (DK) prayed, resisting the temptation to say, "Ephraim is joined to idols, let him alone" (Hosea 4:17). Then it was our son's turn to pray. Each time he opened his mouth to pray, we heard only muffled sounds coming forth. We opened our eyes, and what we saw startled us. Each time he tried to pray, froth came from his mouth, and the room began to get dark. Dad grabbed him, held him tight, and asked God to remove the demons as Mom dropped to the floor in loud sobs. Dad continued in prayer for about half an hour until finally, our son had peace and began to pray.

The devil was not finished with him yet, for the young woman began calling the house several times each day and hanging up the phone. If Mom picked up, then the young lady would report to our son that Mom hung up the phone on her. Her complaint allowed our son to lose confidence in her. He knew that such behavior was uncharacteristic of his mom. Additionally, when we reviewed our house phone logs, he noted some thirty incoming calls from her in less than two weeks. He began to realize that he was in a codependent relationship, which he needed to break. He then began to note that she needed help and that he must give her that help. We simply told him to connect her to services that were nearest to her due because he was seeking disconnect. We encouraged him to step back and look at the situation for a while, because if she needed a counselor, she should be able to find one where she lived. In the meantime, our began to spend more time in the reading of Scripture, and a book we had introduced to him called *Messages to Young People,* a compilation of quotes from the writings of Ellen White. We did not bother him much during that time, but simply prayed for him and with him, when he joined us in family worship. As we listened to him, we sensed that he was turning in struggling to take a new direction.

One week our son decided to engage in fasting and prayer for deliverance, while he asked us to join with our prayers. On the weekend following, he decided to drive to New York City. He told us he was going to New York City, but we did not ask why, and did not worry that he was gone. He left late Friday, and early next morning, before we were out of bed, our phone rang. Mom picked up and our was on the other end asking for the exit on the Palisades Parkway, for the recreation area that we hand taken them in 1983. He stated that he wanted to find the spot where when Dad had finished his doctorate, we had spent a Sabbath in praise and thanksgiving. He said that he wanted to spend the day in prayer and fasting because he needed to get the victory. That morning, we prayed with lightened hearts that God would give him the victory he sought. At the close of the day, he returned home and said, "Mom and Dad, it's over, I have gotten the victory." We believed him. But for whatever reason, Dad said. "Son, I have a haunt that that while you say you are finished, the devil is not finished with the situation, for she is going to show up six more times on your radar." We are not sure of what was significant about those numbers, but after counting the number of times, we asked ourselves whether it was related to **666**. We also thanked God when the cycle was broken before the seventh time. Our son confessed that it was only after he stepped away from the relationship that he saw what we had been praying about and what was happening to him. We told him that, we hope that in the process of prayer and effort at intervention, that we were not insensitive. He assured us of his gratitude for our level of support.

We note that there are details that we have omitted, but we admonish all parents to keep close to their children. Be supportive and loving. Your advocacy will best when you assure your child of your unconditional love. If we were not close to our son and had no relationship with him, and a sense of divine dependence, we could have lost him. Today we rejoice knowing that there is power in prayer.

We stand fast in the knowledge that when we lift up our children before God, when we are their prayer advocates, God will not give a deaf ear, but will answer us. Our son is happily married now and has a family of his own, but what excites us most is that he loves the Lord and works tirelessly to help with the stability of many families. It has been gratifying to see him and his wife serving in various ministries including Family Life, in their church. Of interest, is that while our son was in what we call his life struggle, he was still very involved in church. However, it was obvious that his life was falling apart in many other ways. The point that became most clear in the encounter of our son was that belonging to the same church does not mean an instant match. Even in more innocent contexts one should never be unguarded concerning the building of positive relationships. In all relationships and for all of life, we must pray that the Lord will be with our children. Someone rightly says, "No matter how we fight the idea, we are always our parents' child." The old adage "When they are young, you carry them in your arms, and when they get older, you carry them on your heart," is still true. Prayer is one of the most effective tools of advocacy.

QUESTIONS FOR REFLECTION

1. How well do you, as a parent, focus on prayer as a means of advocacy?
2. How beneficial have you found prayer to be when you have confronted stormy times with your child/ren?
3. What kinds of prayer support groups do you have for facilitating your child/ren in times when advocacy is necessary?

Chapter XV

Using Counseling for Advocacy

We had not planned to say anything about counseling as advocacy, but after an agonizing call one evening, just before supper t, we felt a compulsion to include it, even though quite briefly. The call came from a grieving mother whose daughter was sexually molested and who was now suffering profound psychological trauma to the extent that her school performance was being radically compromised. The mother revealed that she had come to the United States and left her daughter in her country of birth with some relatives. She wanted to know whether we were aware of anyone that could get her daughter a counselor in the place where she resided. She also wanted to know what contact could be made with the perpetrator's employer to see what financial help could be obtained to cover the cost of the counseling. As mother she wanted to make clear that she was struggling to care for her daughter otherwise, and would not be able to cover the additional costs.

After praying with the distraught mother and assuring her that we would do everything to give the necessary assistance in contacting the president of the organization that she identified, we began to reflect on the need to speak more explicitly of a subject that is still quite concealed in many cultures. Yes, some persons from some geographical areas of the world hold counseling as suspect. Some minority groups and some religious communities in our metropolitan world are also unenthusiastic about counseling. It might also be a fact of interest that in hard economic times, one area that is looked at as an expendable service is counseling. Finding well-respected counseling services in some place is still a chore.

Therefore, the purpose of this discussion is to emphasize the significance of counseling and to help parents, as advocates, find the kinds of counseling services that can be most helpful. Counseling creates a structured context of particular time commitments through which individuals build supportive relationships. Such relationships are important to help individuals deal with problems that they cannot resolve by themselves. Support and guidance from a counselor often helps individuals to address their problem so that they can regain stasis and return to wholeness and dignity. The following areas are offered as topics that can give a brief overview as to areas that a parent might need to observe as they think whether they need to seek out a counselor.

- Abuse (e.g. substance, physical, emotional, spiritual, rape, molestation, etc.)
- Addictions (e.g. substance - drug, alcohol - sexual, internet, phone, food)
- Developmental challenges – Special needs
- Broken dreams – lack of focus on task completion
- Injustice – (e.g. bullying, racism, classism)
- Unfairness – (discriminations)
- Health challenges (Handicapping conditions)
- Divorce and separation

There are Various Forms of Counseling

School Counseling—Sometimes Called Educational Counseling, Guidance Counseling, or Professional Counseling

- Developmental needs
- Financial aid
- College choice
- Professional or career options

Psychological Counseling (Sometimes Called Therapy)

- Psychological assessments
- Psychological traumas
- Mental health challenges
- Dealing with destructive behaviors

Mental Health Counseling

- Anxiety disorder
- Attention deficit disorder
- Bipolarity
- Borderline personality
- Depression
- Eating disorder
- Generalized anxiety
- Obsessive-compulsive disorder
- Panic disorder
- Post-traumatic stress disorder
- Schizophrenia
- Social phobia

Marriage and Family Counseling

- Building strong interpersonal skills
- Creating clear boundaries
- Having high ethical standards
- Desire to collaborate
- Goal-setting skill
- Conflict management
- Managing divorce
- Resolving abusiveness
- Building positive attitude

- Behavior management (such as aggression)
- Dealing with adolescence

Job Counseling

- Suitable places to find jobs—especially summer jobs
- How to network for a job
- How to apply for jobs
- How to interview for a job
- How to dress for a job
- What to expect from the job?
- What kind of behavior to be carried the job?

Pastoral Counseling

- Spiritual (faith) development
- Character development
- Moral (ethical) development
- Discipleship development

Grief Counseling

- Support
- Encouragement
- Dealing with guilt and shame
- Dealing with trauma
- Dealing with death and dying

Financial Counseling

- Money management
- Making a budget

- How to save
- Purchasing
- Debt management

The Value of Counseling

The outlines above are to show that there are multiple forms of counseling are available and that these are to be sought when appropriate. Although a parent might be able to do many things, there are times when professional advice is of utmost importance. Professionals who have studied the theories of the mind can do much more than those who are "guessing and spelling" – those who are just trying and failing. What counselors basically do is to "get behind" or "get beneath" something that is expressed and seek to interpret or decode it so that proper remedies can be found. The task of the counselor is to engage the mind so that a person can admit the reality of what they are confronting and commit to any necessary changes that might be required. The counselor points the way to what is necessary to change by:

- Listening
- Assessing—reading beneath the surface of behavior or attitudes
- Offering feedback
- Helping to focus on realities
- Addressing weaknesses and strengths
- Supporting
- Directing
- Correcting
- Challenging
- Encouraging
- Empowering
- Helping to find resources

When a counselor identifies frustration, anger, rebellion, exploitation, or manipulation in a child, the counselor will ask why? The counselor will spend much time unearthing any disguised feelings until there can be clarity. A way forward can thus be found for transformation. What is of interest to any effective counselor is transformation. This is to say the goals of parents are the same as the counselor, only that parents sometimes will not take the time to note the correspondence of interest.

Reducing the Resistance to Counseling

If you are a counselor reading this brief presentation, you might wish to pay for the advertising, for that is mostly what we have done here, just noting the constructive benefits of counseling. The point as we have noted at the beginning of the presentation, in many quarters of our world, many persons are still quite cynical about counseling. Such persons might come to "the end of their ropes," but they live in their despairing world rather than find out what are their possible alternatives. The intention for this brief discussion is thus to help parents gain a fresh appreciation for counseling as advocacy or provide another means for parents to recognize how to find resources to deal with their child/ren's personality, career, relationship development so that that the child/ren might have a healthy well-being.

QUESTIONS FOR REFLECTION

1. What views do you have concerning the positive effects of counseling for yourself and your children?
2. What kinds of counseling do you think would be most helpful to you as a parent?
3. How well do you know the kind of counseling services that are available for you and your children?

Chapter XVI

Going Beyond the Rules of the Game for Successful Advocacy

The attitudes, behaviors, and actions of advocates are not just determined by the practice of rules and restrictions that might be placed upon them. That which is known in a theoretical sense must be evaluated by the character on which such attitudes, behaviors and actions rest. This point has been made with regard to the keeping of the commandments. Jesus himself said, "If you love me keep my commandments." (John 14:15). At the end of the Gospel that focuses on this theme, it notes, "Anybody who receives 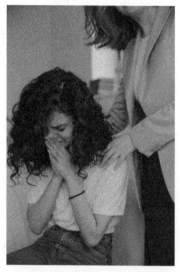 my commandments and keeps them will be one who loves me; and anybody who loves me *will be loved by my Father*, and *I shall love him* and *show myself to him*." An intriguing point of interest is that the very chapter in John that records the words of Jesus "If you love me keep my commandments" (i.e. John 14), also records the promise of Jesus Christ that he would send another advocate, counselor, or helper. This means, it is a fundamental perspective that character is basic to advocacy.

This concept of character as the basic rule for advocacy was made more transparent to me (June) when I taught children with behavioral challenges. Rules were co-constructed and put in place with the view of bringing control to the population under my charge. For the first two or three months, I tried hard to create stability, but somehow, I recognized that rules alone were insufficient. That experience coupled with my reflections of the lessons I learned from home caused me to realize that there weren't enough rules to change poor behaviors, there has to be an inner desire for change. What is needed mot in advocacy is transformation of characters.

Those who think of character education, as priority within the educational curriculum, are certainly wise. In the face page of the character education network, Dr. Thomas Lickona argues, "Character education is the deliberate effort to develop virtues that are good for the individual and good for society. The objective goodness of virtues is based on the fact that they affirm our human dignity, promote the well-being and happiness of the individuals, serve the common good, define our rights and obligations, and the universalizability of all humanity."[72]

What Is Character?

Our understanding is that a proper definition of *character* has to do mostly with *being*, that is followed by *knowing* and *doing*. The American Heritage Dictionary of the English Language, fourth edition 2000 states, "The combination of qualities or features that distinguishes one person, group, or thing from another." *Character* means that which is "engraved" in a person or thing.

---

[72] http://charactered.net/main/traits/asp.assessed on May 21, 2008.

How Is Character Formed?

Character is that which is formed by interaction with one's environment. It is defined by the constant responses that one gives to stimuli, that is practicing to give positive responses.

To form a positive character, one has to respond to life in positive ways and imbibe the values that seek to uplift and ennoble life. To form a negative character, one needs to builds on their negative habits and actions to life.

Actions and Habits

Every action when repeated can become a habit. Habits are formed when actions are repeated. Habits are repeated actions that do not require mental activity; we do them because they have become a part of our life's routine. We do them because they have become engrained in our system. We get up early or late in the mornings because it is our habit. We get to bed early or late at nights because it is our habit. In effect, habits are powerful motivators. If one wants to do anything for a long time, make it a habit, and it will certainly become a part of the character and, eventually, the personality. To break a habit takes hard work. It is therefore important to form good habits. As we create habits for the more mundane chores in life, we must also to create habits for the extraordinary things of life. For example, getting up a few minutes earlier in the mornings, taking time for study and meditation, eating a proper breakfast, taking the stairs instead of the elevator, saving a little money every week, paying bills on time, drinking water throughout the day, staying in touch with friends, exercising, stretching, reading a little every-day, relaxing, writing in a journal, are habits that are very important to life. If you do not practice them, very frequently, they begin to weaken.

Character Traits That Are Very Important for Living

In effect, positive habits must be formed, and the habits must be rooted in principles or traits that are in the structure (character) of one's life. The following principles or list of positive character values are only suggestive:

Positive Character Traits	The Meaning and Importance of Traits
Integrity	Honesty, truthfulness, sincerity, dependability, trustworthy are major components of integrity. These are determinants of how one will be viewed throughout the lifespan. Such traits must be carefully seated in children as they grow so that they can bear good fruits.
Self-discipline	Having restraint, self-esteem, limits, obedience. The sooner one begins to learn the importance of self-discipline, the easier it becomes to restrain oneself.
Service	Giving, sharing, being responsible, having a purpose for being. These values must be grounded in service. To truly understand service, one must first understand the true importance of being responsible, of giving oneself, and being willing to share the self, unswervingly.
Faith	Trusting and believing. The world is filled with doubters and unbelievers. Many have been brought up as skeptics to trust no one and nothing. But faith must be a cornerstone in one's life if one is expected to form relationships. Faith must be nurtured until it matures. It is never too early to encourage and foster faith development in children. The earlier it begins, the stronger it will become, thus, it can be effective in adulthood.
Love	Care, compassion, nurturing, kindness, empathy, adoration are necessary corollaries of love. No one can thrive without love. If one shares it with others, there is immense happiness and a sense of fulfillment. Love allows us to be one with others. One must learn to love the self and be at peace with who he/she is.

	Cultivate a joyful spirit, a spirit of peace, a giving spirit, a spirit of deep feelings for others. Love and loving are not acquired by chance. They are best learned by doing, by practice, by modeling.
Temperance	Being temperate in all things covers every facet of one's life. One must find a balance between two extremes. Moderation, having a balance, demonstrating self-control, avoiding excesses, and exercise restraint. This is a difficult character trait to form, especially because we live in a world where excessiveness is norm—a world in which the media feeds the appetite in every way. However, practicing temperance from the earliest years will heighten the tendency to live a life that is in balance with demonstrating the inner power to control the self and thus have a well-ordered life.
Perseverance	Society moves at such a fast pace that immediacy of action is the ideal. Patience, endurance, confidence, persistence, firmness, stamina, determination, insistence, and steadfastness are values that are declining. But these are important if one must achieve the goals for this life and the next. Never giving up, never giving in, having the drive and the will to forge ahead, the patience necessary to reach the top, the endurance to hold on, and the confidence that it is achievable, need to be a part of the daily menu for being healthy, and developing a character that can withstand the pressures of life.
Respect	Values of courtesy, deference, amazement, awe, reverence, graciousness are quite despised today in certain contexts. Yet there is a general recognition that such values are desirable in order for society to maintain stability. And it is to be remembered that one cannot truly give respect until one learns to have respect for oneself. So, in the work of advocacy, one should be reminded to ask for and give respect.

Accountability	Nearly everybody wants to blame somebody these days. Often many parents get angry when they or their children are being asked to be accountable. Attitudes expressed by parents often lead children to get the view that the problem is not with them but with those who are asking for accountability. Of course, the blame game has been practiced from the earliest days of human history. Nobody wants to be accountable. It is always somebody else's fault. However, success is achieved in one's life when one can be held responsible.
Diligence	Some individuals behave as if slothfulness and carelessness are some of the greatest virtues that have ever been revealed. They even confuse slothfulness with patience and negligence with independence. However, the positive virtues that are built on diligence such as dutifulness, industry, carefulness, thoroughness, attentiveness, and conscientiousness are given little worth. It is therefore imperative that we lift up diligence, give it great emphasis so that we will not need to advocate for that which can be corrected otherwise.
Humility	Often enough, arrogance is considered a *bravura* virtue. However, people are turned off by arrogant individuals. It is important to understand the significance of humility. To be humble is to be modest, meek, mild, rather than be brash, rash, and rude. In the context of advocacy, it needs to be remembered that meekness is not weakness, nor does it lead to accepting subjugation or abuse.
Graciousness	There are many comments from teachers and other adults these days that many children are impolite, unkind, unmannerly, uncouth, and uncultured. Some children will use the most indecent language before an adult. Of interest, we have heard it from indiscrete parents, who do not choose what language they might use, before their children. We emphasize the need to teach politeness, kindness, and culture to children.

	Values that are built on graciousness are vital, especially for those who are involved in advocacy. Therefore, it is crucial that we teach graciousness.
Gratitude	It has been argued that since the middle of the twentieth century, self-interest and self-gratification have become more dominant in the socialization of children. Such qualities of character have even been glorified in the world of politics and ethics at the expense of caring, sharing and appreciation. The spirit of gratitude has been relegated to some old traditional place to be abandoned. However, in the work of advocacy, gratitude leads to positive relationships.
Courage	One of the challenges that many children face is fear. Sometimes fear leads to withdrawal, isolation, a sense inadequacy, or feeling of insufficiency. Fearful people are impatient and easily angered. Some practice bullyish behaviors to cover up their fears. But an advocate should be courage, because courage is essential for success. Without courage people despair. It sometimes takes years to develop courage. We must make every effort to seat courage in our children so that they can have the capacity to be self-advocates.
Loyalty	These are the days in which loyalty is considered of little value, except in the cultures of the underground. Of course, many children and youth who seek to keep negative practices from their parents and teachers, will play the game of loyalty. But the true understanding of loyalty needs to be taught. Loyalty should be offered as that virtue which regards truth and honesty as of paramount importance. To be loyal is to be dependable, faithful, consistent, reliable, and trustworthy.

Morality	The issue of morality is being used to frame the highest ethical behaviors of life. At a time when high government officials and many adults are practicing immorality with little burden of conscience, a new emphasis must be placed on morality. Morality involves the proper stewardship of one's body, the ways in which one practices sexuality and intimacy, and the regard that one has for others on the question of justice. To be moral is to be principled, ethical, and just. The individual who understands morality can become a valuable mentor and an effectiveadvocate.

These are only a few of the multiple values that one needs to adopt or teach as one seeks to become advocacy.

Developing Character for Advocacy

The opportunities to teach character values for advocacy are multiple. Anyone with interest might browse the internet and look at a host of characters whose virtuous lives have left their impress on history. These impressions did not come by chance, but by deliberate actions of individuals who sought to help in the development of positive character values.

The Bible also has examples of individuals such as Daniel, Hananiah, Michaël and Azariah [who were taken to Babylon], Joseph, (who was sold as a slave in Egypt) Josiah (the young king), and other such characters who lived with integrity as youngsters. What is significant is that behind all characters that are studied, it can be noted that their positive characters did not just develop on their own. The Bible is clear about the roles parents played in guiding the qualities that have made these characters exceptional. The point is that parents must provide guidance and advocate for their young ones from the earliest of ages. As a matter of fact, such should begin before the birth of the unborn (prenatally). The attitude of mothers and fathers, the foods children eat, their state of mind, will all impact, in significant ways, the character of their children.

How Can Parents Be Advocates in the Character Development of Children?

Many schools focus on values transference curriculum that is aimed at strengthening the character. Good as that might seem, it should only be supplemental to what is done at home. As a matter of fact, by the time the child is of school age, it is too late to begin the development of certain positive character traits. It is therefore crucial for parents to begin from day one. Here are some advocacy tools that parents can use to begin the character development of their child/ren:

1. **Start early in the process**. Remember that character formation is a life process; the earlier one begins to emphasize positive principles, the more hope there is for a successful end result.
2. **Model the best example**. Children live what they see. Parents who are consistent in modeling positive traits have a tremendous influence on the lives of their children.
3. **Tell good stories**. Share the blessed stories of your life. Many individuals have grown-up on stories that were used to teach values. Also, share stories from nature—the trees, animals. Share stories with the consequences of children who displayed certain positive traits. **Do not dwell on the negative**.
4. **Let your children learn by doing.** Children develop positive character traits by caring for pets, by planting seeds and watching them grow, by doing chores and many other kinds of activities around the home.
5. **Let your children listen to and learn with wholesome music**. Music is a powerful transmitter of values, if music that focus on positive values are utilized. Learning to play an instrument also teaches lessons such as patience, diligence, endurance, creativity, consistency, positive work ethic.

6. **Note the importance of proper precepts.** Precepts might be shared by lectures. Too many lectures are bad. Do not be too preachy. Use discussions, games, problem solving, and other means to share the values you hope will be imbibe.

There Is No Compromise for Effective Character Development

Yes, to see children develop positive character traits bring joy to the hearts of parents, as well as to society. But the frankest reality is that it takes hard work. Parents much be clear about the impact of disciplining. It is not about rules so much as it is about healthy relationship. Relationship building takes hard work, commitment, constant nurturing and the willingness to change.

QUESTIONS FOR REFLECTION

1. What do you understand by the topic "Beyond the Rules of the Games"?
2. How important is character development in the work of advocacy?
3. What character traits would you like your child/ren to strengthen?
4. What habits would you like your child/ren to break?
5. What behavior pattern would you like to see changed in your child?

CONCLUSION

For all the issues to which we have given attention, it is quite evident that we have barely scratched the surface of the topics that might be covered under the caption of parental advocacy. However, we believe that whatever surfaces we have scratched, we have provided some critical insights into aspects of the work of advocacy that will be able to help a lot of parents and children who might otherwise be on a path of destruction. Yes, while as parents, it is impossible to resolve many issues that might come to in the lives of our children, it is necessary for us to work beyond the bounds of our frustrations, doing the best we can to help when those about us need our help. In all our efforts we must remember that we are not going to be parents forever, nor are we going to be children forever. We all mature. But we also need to state the contradiction that once we are parents, we will always be parents, and once we are children, we are children forever. What we have to do is to advocate for our child/ren as we should and they will in turn, advocate for us when they need to. All of us must work as hard at advocacy as we can.

- Be as enthusiastic and energetic as we can.
- Be as positive as we can.
- Be as decisive as we can.
- Take the initiative where we can.
- Be as dependable as we can.
- Be as friendly as we can.
- Be as self-disciplined as we can.

- Be as goal oriented as we can.
- Be as organized as we can.
- Be as detailed as we can.
- Be as creative as we can.
- Be as helpful as we can.
- Be as cooperative as we can.
- Be as punctual as we can.

We need to learn to evaluate all situations before any step is taken.

Advocacy and Listening

A wise and thoughtful advocate will actively listen to those for whom and those with whom the advocacy is being done. It is rightly stated that when we express our wants, feelings, thoughts and opinions clearly and effectively, we have only participated in half of the communication process needed for interpersonal effectiveness. The other half is listening and understanding what others communicate to us. Some of the challenges we face when listening include:

- Being too preoccupied with multiple interests.
- Being so interested in what we have to say that we listen mainly to find an opening to begin speaking.
- Formulating and listening to our own rebuttal to what the speaker is saying.
- Listening to our own personal beliefs about what is being said.
- Evaluating and making judgments about the speaker or the message.
- Not asking for clarification, when we know that we do not understand.[73]

---

[73] Cf. Dr. Larry Nadig's "Tips on Effective Listening," http://www.drnadig.com/listening.htm.

Advocates must be careful of combativeness when listening. We must also be careful about being too passive, so that we believe everything we hear. What is needed is attentive listening, that will allow us to reflect on what is heard so that we can give the right responses.

Advocacy and Negotiation

A significant part of advocacy is negotiation. Negotiation is the exchange of thoughts between two individuals who are trying to work out a solution. Some persons think of negotiation as *Win Lose*, one wins and the other person loses. However, this kind of negotiation has been found to be very unproductive. It leaves the situation of conflict unresolved and those for whom the negotiation is being done feeling betrayed. The other kind of negotiation that is spoken is the *Win Win*. This is the strategy in which both parties come away from the negotiation as winners. When we use negotiation in advocacy it is important to remember the following, (1) learn the positive skills of negotiating, (2) be reminded that what you are seeking to build with the one with whom you are to negotiate is long term relationship, and (3) avoid tricks and manipulation which usually comes back to hurt you.

Advocacy and Mediation

Sometimes those with whom we seek to resolve an issue are not ready to listen to us. It is helpful therefore that we seek the assistance of a mediator. A mediator is a go between two or more individuals in a conflict situations. Such a person needs to have a neutral interest in a situation. When it is not possible to find a trusted friend, one needs to seek the services of a professional. The point is to resolve conflicts in the most positive way so that a child caught in an unresolved situation can find a way to move forward.

Advocacy and Self-Control

Nothing is worse than when one is advocating that one cannot control oneself. Self-control helps a person to make appropriate decisions and respond to stressful situations. The parent whose child was hit on a baseball field, and who decided to kill the baseball coach, was out of control. Frustrations might be great, but control demands that one:

- Is careful to avoid verbal and physical attacks.
- Acknowledges one's frustration and seek to control it.
- Understands the consequences of one's actions.

Advocacy and Protocols

One of the chief reasons many advocates fail is that they do not understand procedures and protocols. To understand them, one needs to learn how to:

- Show some respect/honor to those with whom they are dealing.
- Learn how to cope with authority.
- Learn how to build trust.
- Learn to suspend judgment.
- Learn to be sympathetic.
- Learn to overcome fears.
- Learn to use appropriate praise.

A final word to those who are preparing to be parental advocates:

- Spend more time with your children.
- Listen more carefully to your children.
- Watch for signs of rebellion in your children.
- Watch for any sign of depression or suicidal tendencies.
- Develop friendship with your children.
- Develop trust with your children.

- Love your children for who they are.
- Encourage your children to become involved with positive peers.
- Help your children find a network of dependable adult mentors.
- Attend a church that is balanced in its views of faith and religion with your children.
- Pray for your children.
- Pray with your children.
- Have prayer groups to pray for your children.
- Constantly sensitize your children to your positive expectations.
- Be redemptive with your children when they fail.
- Monitor your children's behavior and habits.
- Get advice from parenting professionals and counselors.
- Seek church support groups for your children.
- Study your child/ren's strengths and weaknesses.
- Have a list of potential mentors for your children.
- Don't blame others for your failures.
- Know the addiction agencies in your community.
- Make a list of job services in your area.
- Become aware of your any social service support agencies that you can.
- Know the after-school support programs in your area.
- Know your parenting assistance agencies (fatherhood, brotherhood, sister to sister, organizations).

We trust that this was a rather helpful orientation as to how it might be possible for you, as a parent, to participate in the work of advocacy in a more constructive way. Advocacy is not easy, but it can be done by anyone who wishes to see positive transformation in the lives of their children.

APPENDIX I

The purpose of the table below is to give a brief overview of some of the multiple challenges facing families today. What is covered is not a complete listing of all challenges but a list that is extensive enough that will draw attention to profound need for parents acting their part as advocates.

VIOLENCE	Violence can be understood in various ways, but among the most dominant views are: • The use of physical force exerted for the purpose of violating, damaging, or abusing someone. • Any behavior, involving untamed force such as the abusive or unjust exercise of power. • Vehemence of feeling or language expressions.
Data	• The average child witnesses 200,000 acts of violence on TV and 16,000 murders before the age of 18. [74] • A population data study for various countries showed homicide rates doubling within 10 to 15 years after introduction of TV, even though TV was introduced at different times in each site examined. [75]

---

[74] Center for Media and Public Affairs, 1992
[75] Centerwall, BS: Exposure to television as a cause of violence. In Comstock G (ed): Public Communication as Behavior. Orlando, Fla.: Academic Press Inc; 1989, 2:1-58.

	• One study showed, 8-year-old boys, who viewed violent programs growing up, were the most likely to engage in aggressive and delinquent behavior by age 18 and serious criminal behavior by age 30. [76] • Estimated 30% of youth in the US (or over 5.7 million) involved in bullying (bully, target of bullying, or both). • In recent national survey of students in grades 6-10, 13% reported bullying others, 11% reported being target of bullies, and another 6% both. [77]
Causes	• TV violence • War games • Wars • Poor models in the home (learned behavior) • Socialization • Oppression • Stress • Certain forms of music
Consequences	• Aggressive attitudes and behaviors • Street fighting • Copy cats • Cultivate fearful or pessimistic attitudes about the non-television world. • Desensitization of real – world and fantasy violence
Resolutions	• Monitor children's exposure to violence • Guard your words and actions before your children • Do not facilitate war games for your children • Know your children's friends • Be a positive role model • Work with anger management programs

---

[76] Dr. Leonard Eron, University of Illinois at Chicago, Testimony before the Senate Committee on Commerce, Science and Transportation, Subcommittee on Communications, June 12, 1995.

[77] http://www.safeyouth.org/scripts/faq/bullying

LACK OF PARENTING	When primary care givers refuse to bare their responsibilities to provide for, adequately supervise and monitor the activities of their child (ren) with a sense of seriousness it is a lack (neglect) of parenting.
Data	In 2011, 73.8 million children under age 18 lived in the United States—representing 25 percent of the country's civilian noninstitutionalized population. In recent decades, the percentage of children living with both parents has dropped, while the percentage living with a single parent has increased (Figure 1). In 2018, 69 percent of children lived with two parents, 65 percent live with two parents who are married, while 23 percent lived with only their mother and 4 percent lived with only their father. No parents were in the household for 4 percent of all children. In 2012, 10 percent of all children under 18 lived in households where at least one grandparent was present. The majority of children living with Grandparents were in households where the grandparents were the householder (68 percent). Three out of every five children living in a grandparent's household had at least one parent present in their home.[78] A little over half of children aged 5 to 14 were in child care arrangements in 2002. Relatives were important care providers. Fathers, grandparents, and other relatives, including siblings, each accounted for about 13 percent of child care for this age group in 2002. Grade-school-aged children were less likely to be cared for by nonrelatives than younger children. Five percent of children this age were in organized facilities, 3 percent were cared for by nonrelatives in their own home, and 5 percent were cared for by nonrelatives in the provider's homes.

---

[78] U.S Census Bureau

	A very high percentage of children were in school (94 percent) and some (16 percent) participated in enrichment activities such as sports, lessons, clubs, and before- or after-school programs. In addition, 15 percent of grade school-aged children cared for themselves on a regular basis without adult supervision. While neglect is the most common type of maltreatment across all age groups, types of maltreatment vary by age. In 2005, 73 percent of substantiated child maltreatment reports for children ages 0–3 involved neglect, compared to 53 percent for teens ages 16 and older. On the other hand, 23 percent of substantiated reports for teens ages 16 and older involved physical abuse and 17 percent involved sexual abuse. Among substantiated reports for children ages 0–3, 12 percent involved physical abuse and 2 percent involved sexual abuse.[79]
Causes	• Work schedules • Lack of preparedness • Absenteeism of fathers • Divorce • Youthful marriage • Poverty • Drug and alcohol use Children acting as parents • No role model
Consequences	• Struggling children • No structure in the lives of the children inconsistencies • Lack of affirmation for teens • Lack of consequences for inappropriate behaviors.
Resolutions	• Take time for your children • Schedule your work so you might have more time with your
DIVORCE	Whether one thinks of divorce as the legal dissolution of a marriage or the destruction of any spousal relationship, where children is involved it can have the most debilitating effects.

---

[79] http://www.childstats.gov/americaschildren/famsoc3.asp

Data	A statistic published on the American divorce rate states that as of 2019, 50 % of marriages will end in divorce. **Custodial mothers** and 56.2% of **custodial fathers** were either **separated or divorced**. In 2002, 7.8 million Americans paid about $40 billion in **child and/or spousal support** (84% of the payers were **male**). The **percentage of the population that is divorced:** 10% (up from 8% in 1990, 6% in 1980). In recent decades many marriage rates seem to be declining. However, that does not tell the truth, because many younger people are not marrying and are opting for other arrangements. The following table can be analyzed for the divorce trends by age since 2019.

	Median age at first marriage:
	     Males: 29.8
	     Females: 27.8
	
	 Median age at first divorce:
	     Males: 30.5
	     Females: 29
	
	 Median age at second marriage:
	     Males: 34
	     Females: 32
	
	 Median age at second divorce:
	     Males: 39.3
	     Females: 37
	
	 Median duration of first marriages that end in divorce:
	     Males: 7.8 years
	     Females: 7.9 years
	
	 Median duration of second marriages that end in divorce:
	     Males: 7.3 years
	     Females: 6.8 years[80]

---

[80] http://www.divorcemag.com/statistics/statsUS.shtml

Causes	- No time for relationship building - Individualism of culture - Lack of communication - Mind set of no permanence - Desecration of marriage - Normalization of divorce (easy to get) - Lower levels of tolerance for mistakes - Unstable economic conditions – Debt pressure - Youthful marriages - Culture of wonder-lusts - Dysfunctional families
Consequences	- Hurting children - Poverty - Resentment - Less parenting - Delinquency - Low academic achievement - High school dropout rate - Suffer from depression, anxiety, and other emotional disorders - Exhibit behavioral problems including hyperactivity aggressiveness, fighting, and hostility; young children especially become depressed and anxious - Become young offenders - Do less well in school and stay less long in school - Children are used as pawns - Have more relationship problems, in part due to their behavioral problems [81] - Girls are more likely to become single mothers.
Resolutions	- Insist on better marriage education and counseling - Learn to be more tolerant and patient - Put away self-centeredness - Reason through the consequences of break up - Stop making choices where the children become irrelevant - Learn to put trust and friendship at the center of your marriage.

---

[81] Furstenberg and Kiernan, 2001; Le Blanc et al., 1995; Sun and Li, 2002

INVASION OF PRIVACY	One of the greatest concerns of our time is the wrongful intrusion into people's private lives by other individuals or by the government. More egregious is the unwarranted exploitation and publicity that is been given people's private lives through the use of internet technology even leading to much mental anguish to the average person. There is a greater need today than at any time in human history to protect the privacy all persons, especially that of our children who are the most vulnerable agents of our society.
Data	In a survey conducted by social researcher Amy Canfield on Teens in Chat rooms and peer pressure, 58% of parents surveyed say they review the content of what their teenager(s) read and/or type in chat rooms or via Instant Messaging; 42% do not.[82]
	In 2019 the U.S. Federal Trade Commission 50% of Americans experience identity theft each year. Their identities are fraudulently used to enter their bank accounts, credit card, or utility accounts. In 2017 businesses lost $50 billion. Consumers lost more than 16 billion.[83]
Causes	• Technology • Terrorism • Search for security • Crime/cyber crime • The availability of personal ids (SS Cards, Credit cards, Debit cards, etc.) • Media publicity on targeted families/persons
Consequences	• Insecurity • Fear/loss of public trust • Identity theft • Depression

---

[82] http://www.articlesbase.com/home-and-family-articles/teen-chat-rooms-peer-pressure-statistics-321938.html - (Teen Chat Rooms, Peer Pressure Statistics - Amy Cainfield.

[83] www.cbnc.com/2017/09/12 workplace-crime.cost.us

Resolutions	• Teach the rules of ethical relationship regarding privacy • Show respect for peoples' property and space • Become about monitoring and protecting your children against ID theft.
VALUES CONFUSION	One of the greatest resources that has kept groups and communities together and allowed for effective education is values. If there is consensus on the values people uphold, they can build community. On the other hand, where there is conflict in values chaos occurs.
Data	As difficult as it is to gain consensus on which are the most fundamental values in a society, so it is difficult to write statistics on values. In any case there is consensus that we are in a world that is very much confused about values. Relativism is being experienced everywhere and the common complaint is that there are breakdown in values.
Causes	• Disregard for law • Lack of tradition • Lack of role model • Lack of focus on God
Consequences	• Lack of accountability • Rebellion • Disrespect • Irresponsibility • Social fragmentation • Losing touch with reality • Confusion between attitude and behavior
Resolutions	• Start early in child's life to teach positive values • Model the Divine Law • Connect your children with persons who model positive values
SOCIAL ISOLATION	Many social scientists have been concerned about the loneliness and separation that is being experienced by many children in society today. Older persons, particularly retirees, are quite vulnerable to isolation, however, because of stigmas regarding certain disabling conditions and the brokenness of society, children are also caught in the frame of isolation and alienation

Data	In 2005, parents reported that older children were more likely to care for themselves before or after school than younger children: 3 percent of children in kindergarten through 3rd-grade and 22 percent of children in 4th- through 8th-grade cared for themselves regularly either before or after school.[84]
Causes	• Rugged autonomous individualism • Brokenness • Fear • Poor self-esteem • Disabilities • Homelessness • Social contact • Family resources • Residential mobility • Divorce • Ageing and loss of friends
Consequences	• Restricted human development • Shyness • Low academic performance • Inability to sustain friendships • Depression • Alterations in mental status • Altered state of wellness • Immature interests • Alterations in physical appearance • Unaccepted social behavior • Inability to engage in satisfying personal relationships • Suicide
Resolutions	• Parents must prioritize their needs to offer up themselves for more time with their children • Teach the significance of positive relationships • Take children to church and communities with positive relationships

---

[84] http://www.childstats.gov/americaschildren/famsoc3.asp

LACK OF TIME FOR RELATIONSHIP BUILDING	Relationships take time: time to build trust, understanding, respect, collaborative experiences and time for conversation. But with the increase of parent's time away from home, there is little time left for relationship building between parents and children.
Data	More than half of children under age 6 ate breakfast with at least one of their parents every day of the week. Those who lived with married parents were more likely to have this meal with a parent than were children who lived with an unmarried parent.

Among children living with married parents, 61 percent ate every day with their mother and 30 percent ate every day with their father, compared with 50 percent of children living with an unmarried mother and 41 percent living with an unmarried father.

In a typical week, children under 6 years old were more likely to eat dinner (79 percent) than breakfast (57 percent) daily with a parent. Among children living with married parents, 81 percent had dinner with their mother every day, while 64 percent had dinner with their father this often. Seventy-five percent of children under 6 living with an unmarried mother ate dinner with her every day, while 66 percent of those living with an unmarried father ate dinner with him this often.

Older children were less likely to eat meals with their parents than younger ones. Among children aged 6 to 11, 37 percent had breakfast with a parent every day and 73 percent had dinner with a parent this often. In a typical week, 24 percent of children aged 12 to 17 ate breakfast with a parent every day and 58 percent of them ate dinner with a parent this often.

Among teenagers living with unmarried parents, eating breakfast and dinner together was more common if they lived with their father rather than their mother. |

	Among children living with unmarried parents, 69 percent of those living with mothers received praise three or more times a day, compared with 57 percent of those living with fathers.

For children under 6 years old, 72 percent were talked to or played with for 5 minutes or more, three or more times every day. Among children of married parents, mothers were more likely than fathers to talk to or play with their children this frequently.

About half (51 percent) of children aged 6 to 11 were praised by a parent three or more times a day, compared with 37 percent of children aged 12 to 17. Forty-nine percent of children aged 6 to 11 and 41 percent of those aged 12 to 17 were talked to or played with three or more times a day.[85] |
| Causes | <ul><li>Lack of trust</li><li>Different expectations</li><li>Lack of commitment to long-term partnership</li><li>Differences in priorities</li><li>Moving through life at different speeds</li><li>Compatibility issues</li><li>Communication challenges – unwillingness to learn how to dialogue – speaking and listening</li><li>Self-love – narcissistic attitudes</li><li>Poor habits – such as unwillingness to deal with addictions</li><li>Money management issues[86]</li><li>Overwork</li><li>Materialism</li></ul> |

---

[85] Source: A Child's Day <http://www.census.gov/Press- Release/www/releases/archives/children/009412.html>

[86] https://www.psychologytoday.com/us/blog/communication-success/201507/top-10-reasons-relationships-fail

Consequences	• Brokenness • Dysfunctional • Isolation • Divorce • Disobedience • Disrespect
Resolutions	• Learn to make sacrifices such as giving up you job if it will cause the destruction of your children • Create more family time – try to eat some meals together each week • Build opportunities for communication
PEER PRESSURE	Children feel social pressure to conform to the peer group with which they socialize. Their dress, music and the games they play are very much determined by the choices they make with friends. Often enough their risky behaviors such as involvement with alcohol, drugs, and sex, have to do with pressure that they have from their peers.
Data	• "The first use of alcohol begins around the age of 13, two thirds of teenagers who drink buy their own alcohol, and junior and senior high school students drink 35% of all wine coolers sold in the US." • Illicit drug use is on the rise for 12-17-year olds.[87] • "If you go back to '92 and forward to '97, it (smoking marijuana) went up 275%."[88]
	• At least 3.1 million adolescents and 25% of 17 and 18-year-olds are current smokers. [89] • "Approximately 9 % of 14-year-olds, 18 % of 15- to 17-year-olds, and 22 % of 18- to 19-year-olds experience a pregnancy each year."[90]

---

[87] The second study, the National Household Survey on Drug Abuse conducted by the Department of Health and Human Services.
[88] Gen. Barry McCaffrey, director of the White House Office on Drug Control Policy.
[89] An American Lung Association Study.
[90] Communities Responding to the Challenge of Adolescent Pregnancy Prevention Report.

Causes	• Normal human development • Desires to blend into culture • A desire to 'fit in.' • To avoid rejection and gain social acceptance. • Hormonal inconsistencies. • Personal/social confusion and/or anxiety. • A lack of structure at home. • Find the love that is absent at homes • Running away from abuse at home • Seeking the protection that is lacking at home.
Consequences	• Choices between one's peers and one's parents • Sexual experimentation • Alcoholism • Drug addiction • Thefts • Murders • Delinquency
Resolutions	• Know your children's friends • Build your children's esteem • Know where your children are and where they are going • Stay close to your children • Control the media that are used to educate the children • Monitoring and supervision of children • Education
SEXUAL ABUSE	Sexual abuse toward children and adolescents is a stark reality worldwide. A common misperception about child sexual abuse (CSA) is that it is a rare event perpetrated against girls by male strangers in poor, inner-city areas. To the contrary, CSA is a much too common occurrence that results in harm to millions of children, boys and girls alike, in large and small communities, and across a range of cultures and socioeconomic backgrounds.

	These acts are perpetrated by many types of offenders, including men and women, strangers, trusted friends or family, and people of all sexual orientations, socioeconomic classes, and cultural backgrounds[91]
	Sexual abuse involves an older person engaging in inappropriate sexual behavior with a child. It can include actual physical contact, such as fondling or rape, but also includes making a child watch sexual acts or pornography, using a child in any aspect of the production of pornography, or making a child look at an adult's genitals.[92]
Some Data	• About 100 thousand children are forced into child prostitution in Taiwan. • Venezuela has around 40 thousand underage prostitutes; • Approximately 25 thousands prostitutes aged 12 to 17 in the Dominican Republic; • Peru has about 500 thousand child prostitutes, • another 500 thousand child prostitutes are in Brazil; • Canada has 200 thousand child prostitutes. • From 300 thousand to 600 thousands of 2 million prostitutes in the USA are children and teenagers under 18. Most of them are under the category of street prostitutes. [93]
Causes	• Dysfunctional homes • Children left unprotected • Lack of parenting • Uncaring society • Amoral individuals • Poverty

---

[91] https://www.ncbi.nlm.nih.gov/pmc/articles/PMC4413451/
[92] http://www.findcounseling.com/journal/child-abuse/sexual-abuse.html
[93] http://english.pravda.ru/society/stories/11-10-2006/84991-child_prostitution-0 and http://www.ncvc.org/ncvc/main.aspx?dbName=DocumentViewer&DocumentID=32360 and http://www.usatoday.com/life/2002/2002-03-12-pedophilia.htm.

Consequences	• Multiple dysfunctions including anger, depression and suicide • STDs • Promiscuity and sexual slavery
Resolutions	• Monitoring and supervision of children • Education on sexual responsibility • Teach about how to report incidents of abuse
TEEN PREGNANCY	Although teen pregnancy rates have declined in the United States from their highest levels since the 1980, teen pregnancy continues to be a problem for many parents in many parts of the world. And it is still a problem even in the USA where poor families exist. Even though abortion and other contraception's are being used, yet wherever a child or teen pregnancy occurs there remain a lot of challenges for parents and teens, as well.
Data	In 2017, the total number of teen pregnancies in the United States was 194,377 (18.8 pregnancies per 1,000 people).[94] Teen pregnancy is viewed to be the cause of many problems. Teen mothers are more likely to not finish high school or college. Additionally, it is estimated that as much as 80% of unwed teen mothers end up welfare. Compared to 25 years ago, pregnant teens are also far less likely to be married.[95]
Causes	• Cycles of teen pregnancy in families • Lack of proper parental guidance • Low self esteem • Absentee fathers • Economic relationship • Peer pressure • Conflict in the home

---

[94] http://www.pregnancy-info.net/teen_pregnancy_statistics.html
[95] http://www.pregnancy-info.net/teen_pregnancy_statistics.html

Consequences	• Childbearing may curtail education and thereby reduce a young woman's employment prospects in a job market that requires ever higher levels of training.[96] • Single parenting • Cycles of dysfunction • Lack of values in society • Loss of the joy of being teenage
Resolutions	• Appropriately communicate with your children on issues of sexuality • Spend more time with your children • Show your children love • Try to understand the challenges your child is facing • Build your child's self esteem
THE SEXUALIZATION OF OUR CHILDREN	The sexualization of children involves exposing children to sexual information that is not appropriate for the developmental stage of a child. Many parents and adults today feel that there is a far-reaching change in the sexual understanding and involvement of children, more than any generation of previous decades. Children have, thus, become the major consumers of the sexualized image being shared through every agency that is available.
Data	**Stats parents should know:** • More than 500,000 predators are online everyday • Kids 12 to 15 are susceptible to being groomed and manipulated by offenders online • FBI stats show that more than 50 percent of victims of online sexual exploitation are 12-15 years old • 89 percent of all sexual advances toward our children take place in internet chat rooms and through instant messaging • In (27 percent) of exploitation incidents, predators ask kids for sexual photos kids for sexual photographs of themselves. • 4 percent of kids get "aggressive" sexual solicitations that include attempt to contact the kids offline.[97]

---

[96] http://www.statcan.ca/english/kits/preg/preg3.htm
[97] http://www.unh.edu/ccrc/pdf/Am%20Psy%202-08.pdf.

Causes	- Media impact
- Child pornography
- Clothing makers who portray little girls as eroticized creatures
- Access to adult culture by the internet
- Media portrayal of sex focused on children
- Lack of parental oversight by parents
Consequences	- Abortion
- STDs
- Promiscuity
- Sexual confusion
- Conflict between parents and children concerning sexual decisions (egg. Contraception
- (such as condoms, birth control pills and Vaccinations (such as HPV))
- Child and teen pregnancies
Resolutions	Control the media that are used to educate the children
SUBSTANCE ABUSE	Over the last four decades the United States has experienced major shifts in substances of abuse that have had dramatic effects on children and families. In this last decade, the increase of opioid misuse has been described by long-time child welfare professionals as having the worst effects on child welfare systems that they have seen. Studies indicate that there is substantial overlap between parents involved in the child welfare and substance use treatment systems.[98]

While unprescribed drugs and Alcohol have led the way among substances that have been abused, the opioid epidemic has revealed that some of the substances being abused today are prescribed. The reality is that substance abuse is one of the foremost challenges facing parents and children today. |

---

[98] https://ncsacw.samhsa.gov/research/child-welfare-and-treatment-statistics.aspx.

| Data | - In US Children account for 11.4% of alcohol use.
- 57% high schoolers are binge drinkers.
- A 2006 study of asked high school seniors, "On how many occasions, if any, have you used drugs or alcohol during the last 12 months or month?"[99] |
|---|---|
| Causes | - Life addiction
- Dysfunctional
- Peer pressure
- Lack of parental guidance
- Bad parental models
- Curiosity and experimentation
- Low self esteem
- Accessibility |
| Consequences | - Poor performance in school
- Delinquency
- Inability to hold jobs
- Becomes ward of society
- Codependency
- Begin cycle of stealing to support habit (theft),
- murders (Kill) |
| Resolutions | - understand that you love them
- Listen to your child.
- Carefully observe your child for changes in his/her life
- Use opportunities for drug counseling and drug rehabilitation
- Be careful about judgmentalism |
| ***EATING DISORDERS*** | Abnormal eating beliefs and behaviors are very widespread among children, as they are present among adults in our world, today. The three leading forms of eating disorders are anorexia, bulimia, and binge eating. There are other forms of named and unnamed disorders observed among children, but the ones named are considered most significant in relation to the psychological impact that they have on the lives of the children who practice them. |

---

[99] Press release: *Teen drug use continues down in 2006, particularly among older teens; but use of prescription-type drugs remains high*, University of Michigan News and Information Services, December 21, 2006. (Acrobat file 576.81KB)

Data	According to US estimates from The National Institute of Mental Health, • between 5 % and 10 % of girls and women (i.e. 5-10 million people)[100] • 1 million boys and men suffer from eating disorders, including anorexia, bulimia, binge eating disorder, or other associated dietary conditions. • Estimates suggest that as many as 15 % of young women adopt unhealthy attitudes and behaviors about food.[101] • Each day Americans spend an average of $109 million on dieting and diet related products. [102] • 42% of 1st-3rd grade girls want to be thinner (Collins, 1991). • 81% of 10-year olds are afraid of being fat (Mellin et al., 1991). • The average American woman is 5'4" tall and weighs 140 pounds. The average American model is 5'11" tall and weighs 117 pounds. • Most fashion models are thinner than 98% of American women (Smolak, 1996). • 51% of 9- and 10-year-old girls feel better about themselves if they are on a diet (Mellin et al., 1991). • 46% of 9-11-year-olds is "sometimes" or "very often" on diets, and 82% of their families are "sometimes" or "very often" on diets (Gustafson-Larson & Terry, 1992). • 91% of women recently surveyed on a college campus had attempted to control their weight through dieting, 22% dieted "often" or "always" (Kurth et al., 1995). • 95% of all dieters will regain their lost weight in 1-5 years (Gradstein, 1996).

---

[100] The National Institute of Mental Health
[101] The National Institute of Mental Health
[102] http://www.annecollins.com/eating-disorders/statistics.htm

	• 35% of "normal dieters" progress to pathological dieting. Of those, 20-25% progress to partial or full-syndrome eating disorders (Shisslak & Cargo, 1995). • 25% of American men and 45% of American women are on a diet on any given day (Smolak, 1996). • Americans spend over $40 billion on dieting and diet-related products each year (Smolak, 1996).[103] • About 31 percent of American teenage girls and 28 percent of boys are somewhat overweight. • An additional 15 % of American teen girls and nearly 14% of teen boys are obese. • A recent study reported in Drugs and Therapy Perspectives reports that about one percent of women in the United States have binge eating disorder, as do thirty percent of women who seek treatment to lose weight. In other studies, up to two percent, or one to two million adults in the U.S., have problems with binge eating. About 72% of alcoholic women younger than 30 also have eating disorders. [104]
Causes	• The media portrayal • Hollywood image • The availability of junk food • Binge eating disorder, • Causes of obesity include fast food, snacks with high sugar and fat content, little physical activity including use of automobiles increased time spent in front of TV sets and computers, and generally more sedentary lifestyles than slimmer peers.

---

[103] http://www.annecollins.com/eating-disorders/statistics.htm; Health magazine, Jan/Feb 2002).

[104] http://www.annecollins.com/eating-disorders/statistics.htm; Health magazine, Jan/Feb 2002).

Consequences	- Dysfunctional personalities
- Depression
- Health Care system overload
- In addition, people with eating disorders often abuse prescription and recreational drugs, sometimes to numb themselves emotionally, to escape misery and depression, and sometimes in the service of weight loss.
Resolutions	- Education on good habits of eating
- Provide the right kinds of food
SINGLE PARENTING	A single parent is one that assumes the role of both parents. Even where a second parent might be tacitly involved, it means that one parent has very much impact in the care of the child. Although it is known that single parents have reported being successful, however there are uncontestable evidences that one parent cannot fulfill the role of both parents.
Data	- There are approximately 14 million single parents in the United States today, and those parents are responsible for raising 21.6 million children.
- 83.1% of custodial parents are mothers
- 16.9% of custodial parents are fathers

Of the mothers who are custodial parents:
- 45.9% are currently divorced or separated
- 30.5% have never been married
- 21.8% are married (In most cases, these numbers represent women who have remarried.)
- 1.7% were widowed

Of the fathers who are custodial parents:
- 56.4% are divorced or separated
- 23.1% are currently married (In most cases, these numbers represent men who have remarried.)
- 19.7% have never married
- 0.8% were widowed
- 80% of custodial single mothers are gainfully employed
- 50.5% work full time, year round
- 29.6% work part-time or part-year |

	• 89.8% of custodial single fathers are gainfully employed • 70.6% work full time, year round • 19.2% work part-time or part-year • 26.1% of custodial single mothers and their children live in poverty • 13.4% of custodial single fathers and their children live in poverty • 30.3% of all single parents receive public assistance • Only 8.4% of single parents receive TANF (Temporary Assistance for Needy Families) • 36.8% of custodial mothers are 40 years old or older[105]
Causes	• Casual sexual behaviors • Divorce • Teen pregnancy • Absent fathers • Wars • Gang violence • Promiscuity
Consequences	• Lack of stability for a future generation. • Lack of mature role models for the next generation • Poverty • Struggle for survival • Inadequate housing and schooling • Multiple jobs • Overload welfare system • Little time for self and children
Resolutions	• Educate and encourage the role of motherhood and fatherhood as normative models for family. • Educate about the challenges of single parenting, even in the most ideal situations • Discourage cycles of teen pregnancy – What mother and father does, a child needs not do • Encourage working with advocacy support groups • Find models for support and mentorship

---

[105] Statistics on *Custodial Mothers and Fathers and Their Child Support: 2003*, released by the U.S. Census Bureau in July, 2006.

STEREOTYPING	Ethnic and racial is a common phenomenon faces by many children, especially in immigrant communities. Many persons can look back to their childhood and think of the labels that have been attributed to them, especially by authority figures. Teachers and social service works are very much aware of the cost of labeling.
Data	According to the Entman-Rojecki Index of Race and Media, 89% of Black female movie characters are shown using vulgar language, while only 17% of White woman are. Black women are shown as being violent in movies 56% of the time compared to the 11% of white women. These types of proportions are consistent throughout this and other studies. Where do they get them? Are blacks really a more violent race? The statistics say no, they are not (www.raceandmedia.com). The Entman-Rojecki Index of Race and Media also shows that the most serious crimes (homicide, rape, robbery, and assault) are only committed by a small percentage of African-Americans in inner cities (around 8% by estimates). Despite this small percentage, Stephan Balkaran of the Yale Political Quarterly claims that, "the tendency to characterize all African-American males continues in our society." After seeing some of these statistics, you can see that African-American people truly are shown unrealistically.[106]
Causes	• Prejudice • Conflict in Intra-cultural communication • Language barriers • Cultural differences • Gender rules of conduct • Conflict in values

---

[106] http://www.associatedcontent.com/article/33262/racial_stereotypes_in_the_media.html

Consequences	• Ghettoization • Hatred • Distrust • Suspicion
Resolutions	• Educate your children about others • Expose your children to groups that might not understand them • Let them dialogue about issues that confront them • Build self-esteem
CULTURAL UPROOTEDNESS	While the phenomenon of cultural uprootedness is not so contemporary, the conditions of life today have left a lot of feeling profoundly socially and culturally displaced, and such displacement or uprootedness has been causing profound crisis between parents and their children
Data	• The United States admits between 700,000 and 900,000 legal immigrants each year ("green cards" recipients). • http://www.cis.org/topics/legalimmigration.html • 7 million illegal aliens living in the United States, a number that is growing by half a million a year. Thus, the illegal-alien population in 2003 stood at least 8 million. • For the illegal population to have reached 8 million by 2000, the net increase had to be 400,000 to 500,000 per year during the 1990s. [107]
Causes	• Immigration and migration • Wars • Economic dislocation
Consequences	• Conflict in values • Communication gaps • Conflicts in ways of disciplining • Lack of support • Economic instability • Parents/child struggles

---

[107] http://www.census.gov/population/www/socdemo/immigration.html

Resolutions	• Try to get educated about the new culture into which your children must survive • Be more open to the view of the new culture • Be more understanding of your children
PASSIVE/ AGGRESSIVENESS	Passive-Aggressive Personality types are just as it sounds. They often are passive outward and aggressive inwards. The Passive-Aggressive types often anger others around them, yet the other person may feel wrong since they are not clear on the foundation that caused the anger. Children are very good at using passive-aggressiveness, or what is called "sulk" behavior to manipulate or intimidate their parents or other authority figures. Among adults passive aggressiveness is most often seen in the work environment, where people sulk, or act our other negative behaviors to show their rebellion against the perceived authority. There has been ongoing debate in the social sciences as to whether passive aggressiveness is a personality disorder or a defense mechanism. Whatever it is, when it is not dealt with in childhood, it often becomes a problem for one's adult life.
Data	• The latest data from the Centers for Disease Control shows: "In the United States every year, about 1.5 million women and more than 800,000 men are raped or physically assaulted by an intimate partner," that makes men 36% of victims. • A recent 32-nation study by the University of New Hampshire found female students initiate partner violence as often as male students and controlling behavior exists equally in perpetrators of both sexes.[108]
Causes	Likely from personality disorders Development of antisocial behaviors Fear of conflict Abuse

---

[108] http://www.nlm.nih.gov/medlineplus/rape.html; http://endabuse.org/resources/facts/

Consequences	- Resent responsibility - The struggle for attention - Procrastination - Intentional inefficiency - Unresolved conflicts - Anger - Verbal abusive - Manipulativeness - Arrogance - Blame others
Resolutions	- Use personality and gift tests to help your children learn who they are. - Teach positive self-worth - Teach how to use positive systems of self-advocacy, mediation and negotiation
CONFUSED EXPECTATIONS	Many children live conflicted lives because they are confused by the expectations they receive from their parents. Parents express confusion between healthful, nurturing behavior and overindulgence. While nurturing behavior leads to high self-esteem, integrity and healthy relationships between parents and children, overindulgence breeds self-centeredness and immaturity in children.
Data	A sample of students in grades 6 through 12 who represented some 28,182,000 students in grades 6 through 12 in the United States in early 2003 revealed that roughly nine out of every 10 students (91 percent) in grades 6 through 12 had parents who expected them to continue their education beyond high school, with about two-thirds (65 percent) having had parents who expected them to finish college. Other findings presented in this report show that about one-third (32 percent) of students had parents who perceived that their child's school did very well at providing information to help their child plan for postsecondary education.

	Finally, among students whose parents expected them to continue their education after high school, 82 percent had parents who reported that the family was planning on helping to pay for their child's postsecondary education costs, and among those whose parents reported that the family was planning on helping to pay the costs, 66 percent had parents who reported that they had enough information about postsecondary education costs to begin planning.[109]
Causes	<ul><li>The understanding as to what is valuable</li><li>Role modeling</li><li>Double messages from parents</li><li>Identity problems</li></ul>
Consequences	<ul><li>Problems with communication and relationship skills Problems with decision-making and time management. Problems educational achievement</li><li>Apathy and complacency</li><li>Hopelessness</li><li>Helplessness</li><li>Over compensation</li><li>Depression</li><li>Hatred</li><li>Disassociation</li><li>Low performance</li></ul>
Resolutions	<ul><li>Make all expectations clear – whether it is about going to college or reading</li><li>Teach the children how to prioritize goals and objectives</li><li>Create a world of reality through mentoring, role modeling, and peer intervention</li></ul>
INTERGENERATIONAL GAPS	Conflict is a common phenomenon between generations. However, when cultural conditioning makes portray a lack of regard for the one generation over against another the conflicts can be severe.

---

[109] http://nces.ed.gov/pubsearch/pubsinfo.asp?pubid=2008079

Data	In developing countries nearly 70 percent of older persons live with family members. In developed countries, such as the United States, many elderly prefer to live independently and can afford to do so. Many countries are strengthening laws on family responsibility for care of the elderly and regulations for nursing homes and other care facilities. Although statistics might not be quoted for this area, yet it is clear that the reality exists in very profound ways. Ask any pastor or teacher who will make it clear that a part of their task has been to bring about conflict resolution between many parents and their children, especially adolescent who think that their way is better than any.
Causes	• Immigration • Poor models • Pressure to over perform • Variations in cultural values • Identity problems
Consequences	• Increasing parent–child conflict, which in turn weakens positive parent–child bonding • Educational failure • Identity confusion • Apathy and complacency • Hopelessness • Helplessness • Over compensation • Depression • Hatred • Disassociation • Low performance
Resolutions	• Teach how to prioritize goals and purpose • Create world of reality through mentoring, role modeling and peer intervention • Work with school and other types of helpful counselors to bridge the generational gaps

Parental Advocacy

FAMILY ESTRANGEMENT	Although statistics are not available on this area, yet a lot of therapists, other social service workers and pastors have stated to us that this is a growing area of crisis among American families today. Children are not talking to their parents and vice versa. The Dr. Phil's show has gained a lot of popularity by identifying this as a problem and trying to fix it. The estrangement is not just with families of "the well to do" or with children of Hollywood stars, but with children of ordinary folks, like us.
Data	Author Nancy Richards focuses on the fact that while statistics might not be easily available for family estrangement, it is of interest that countless individuals seeking help with family cut-off's can be found on the internet. Google lists 776,000. Yahoo lists 890,000! Such lists reveal that estrangement can be seen in the families of celebrities, friends, co-workers, and neighbors.[110]
Causes	• Divorce • Uprootedness • Self-centeredness • Destructive behaviors • Unacceptability of those with whom children associate
Consequences	• Intolerance • Frustration • Cycle of divorce • Step parenting • Workaholism • Immigration • Criticism • Judgmentalism • Legalism

---

[110] Nancy Richards, Healing from Child Abuse and Family Estrangement, http://www.squidoo.com/healandforgive

	- Alcoholism
- Lack of generosity
- Bigotry
- Drug abuse
- Anger
- Aggressiveness
- Self-abuse
- Violence
- Isolation
- Disrespect
- Low esteem
- Juvenile delinquency
Resolutions	- Learning the power of forgiveness
- Don't ever close the door to reconciliation. Even if the other person is unresponsive, send cards, gifts, e-mails whatever you can
- Use positive mentoring to bring healing
- Have enough courage and love to initiate contact
- Once you begin communicating again, resist any impulse to rehash every detail of the situation that precipitated the estrangement
SCHOOL DROPOUTS	With just over fifty percent of American high school students finishing within the prescribed four or five years, one need to be aware that school dropout is a big problem in America. Dropouts include:
- Students who just leave school for undefined reasons.
- Students from special education, upgraded, or alternative education programs who just leave school
- Students who leave school and enter a program not qualifying as an elementary/secondary school (e.g., cosmetology school)
- Students enrolled as migrants and whose whereabouts are unknown
- Students who enter the military before graduation

Data	• The U.S. high school dropout rate may be as high as 30 percent, almost three times higher than government estimates, with men accounting for 60 percent or more of dropouts, according to a study commissioned by the business Roundtable and conducted by the Center for Labor Market Studies (CLMS) at Northeastern University. • Between 50 to 60 percent of students in some of the nation's largest school districts—including those in Los Angeles, Detroit and New York — fail to graduate from high school. • Government statistics show that on average there are 120 to 130 male high school dropouts for every 100 female dropouts, but CLMS analysts say the true ratio is likely to be even higher because males are more likely to be undercounted by the U.S. Census Bureau and are much more likely to be incarcerated than women. • Nearly two million more women are now attending college than men and are acquiring far more associates, bachelors and master's degrees. The disparity is highest among African Americans (166 women per 100 men in college in 2000), with Hispanics second (130-100) and whites third (126-100).[111]
Causes	• Lack of models • Lack of parental involvement • Disabilities misunderstood • Lack of awareness of how to advocate for children • Low expectations for children of certain communities • Drug addictions • Career dislocation

---

[111] - Chart: "National graduation rates," *Pittsburgh Post-Gazette,* Source: Rand Corp.; The Manhattan Institute, 13 July 2006, http://www.post-gazette.com/pg/06194/705557-298.stm

	• Lack of goal achievement • Feelings of failure • Poverty • Pressure from parents • Health problems
Consequences	• Joblessness • Low paying dead-end jobs • High rates of incarceration • Social outcasts • Poverty
Resolutions	• Early counseling • Positive encouragement • Build esteem • Provide climate for incremental success
ACADEMIC ACHIEVEMENT GAP	The reality of an academic achievement gap has been spoken of by educators and politicians so often that some persons might pass it off with little concern. However, the gap is a reality without discrimination and has had a profound impact on many parents and their children today.
Data	Academic gap is evidenced by discrepancies in statistics such as standardized test scores, high school graduation rates, college success rates particularly between Whites and their Black and Latino peers. It is noted that although the racial academic achievement gap refers to a crucial issue in today's education sector, the gap is by no means a concern exclusive to education. Others areas where the gap can be felt is in economics and jobs.[112] Multiple studies have been done nationally and on a state by state; city by city basis that show many variations in the gaps. One only needs look at the various reports available on the web to see the gaps[113]

---

[112] http://www.blackstarproject.org/home/index.php?Itemid=46&id=31&option=com_content&task=view

[113] As example look at http://iume.tc.columbia.edu/pathways/achieve3/academic.asp

Causes	- Low family expectations
- Lack of understanding of developmental stages
- School systems and teacher
- Lack of school resources
- social class
- social capital
Consequences	- Low motivation
- Poor self-image
- Teen pregnancy
Resolutions	- Have realistic expectations
- Give support
- Ascertain that your child is in an equitable educational system
- Provide mentorships and tutorials
SELF ESTEEM ISSUES	The issue of self-esteem has been studied for over a hundred years, and it has been argued that it has positive or negative impact on children. Thus no one would wish to go through life without it, so it forms a strong component of every school curriculum.
Data	- Although no exact statistics many be presented on self-esteem, yet it is known that certain children, families and their communities are very low in esteem and that such communities suffer profound negative consequences. What relationships might one find between the following statistics found on the internet and self-esteem?
- 75% of teen girls 15-19 agree that society tells girls that attracting boys and acting sexy is one of the most important things girls can do
- By age 18, a U.S. youth will have seen 16,000 simulated murders and 200,000 acts of violence
- 81% of the women in the United States think that the media set an unrealistic norm for beauty that most of the women won't be able to reach.
- Today's "beauty ideals" create "appearance anxiety" for 86.9% of all teenage-aged girls.

Causes	• False images of the body and personality shown in magazines and on TV • Abusiveness in home and family • Family rejection • Depression • Failure • Overweight • Prejudice and discrimination
Consequences	• Poor academic performance • Inability to form stable friendships • Bullyism • Isolation • Depression • Lack of motivation
Resolutions	• Affirm children • Practice positive role-modeling • Teach self-appreciation Make clear that character counts about all external beauty
ECONOMIC INSTABILITY	In a global economy that is unstable as it presently is the question of economic instability has to be an interest of the most thoughtless person. The reality is that economic instability is not just a problem for poor people, but at some stage or the other, it has negative potential for the most secure.

Data	• Frequency of child support reported by fathers 15-44 years of age who have at least one child under 19 years of age who does not live with him, 2002:
	
	   o Does not contribute: **15.3%**
	   o Contributes once in a while: **8.9%**
	   o Contributes on a regular basis: **75.8%**
	
	Note: Men with nonresident children were asked if they contributed money or child support in the last 12 months for those children.[114]

---

[114] http://www.cdc.gov/.nchs/data/series.

	• Amount of child support given in the last 12 months by fathers 15-44 years of age who have at least one child under 19 years of age who does not live with him, 2002:
	
	   o Median amount: **$4,250**
	   o $3,000 or less: **36.0%**
	   o $3,001-$5,000: **22.9%**
	   o $5,001-$9,000: **23.5%**
	   o More than $9,000: **17.6%**42[115]
	
	• In 2004, 14 percent of children in two-parent families lived in households with an annual income below $30,000.3 Thirty-nine percent of children living with a single father, 62 percent living with a single mother, and 59 percent living without either parent were in households with incomes below $30,000.

Causes	• Poverty • Immigration • War and violence • General economic downturns • Lack of vocational and professional skills
Consequences	• Brokenness • Physical Abuse • Homelessness • Indebtedness • Family dysfunction and dislocation • Lack of basic life's needs
Resolutions	• Get training in self-advocacy • Counseling and debt management • Skills training – Children need to learn survival skills

---

[115] http://www.cdc.gov/.nchs/data/series.

TECHNOLOGICAL DEVELOPMENT	There was a time when parents had great control over their children, but with the adventure of the internet and telephone, many are feeling like they have lost total control.

The point is that as technology continues to develop and as software proliferates young children will receive more exposure to technology. One the one hand this is good, but on the other hand it makes us all anxious for the destruction of our children.[116] |
| Data | • A 1999 survey reports that 71 percent of U.S. households with children ages 8-17 have computers and 67 percent of those computers connect to the Internet (Annenberg Public Policy Center, 2000). A separate study of "on-line households" with children ages 6 through 12 showed that 81.2 percent of the parents or guardians had post-graduate degrees, 75 percent had college degrees, and 42 percent had high school degrees.
• Overall totals: During 2006, consumers filed 207,492 complaints. Complainants said they lost $198.4 million, the highest total ever.
• Types of fraud: Nearly 45 percent of the complaints involved **online auction fraud** -- such as getting a different product than you expected -- making it the largest category; more than 19 percent **concerned undelivered merchandise or payments**. Another pervasive scheme last year involved an **e-mail threat of murder**. Others include identity theft, investment fraud, cyber stalking, phishing, spoofing, spamming, and others. |

---

[116] My intention is not to present our present technological development as a problem but to demonstrate its positive and negative impacts on our development and what we need to do to understand it.

	• The perpetrators: Three-quarters were men. Nearly 61 percent lived in the U.S., with half in one of seven states. Other top countries included the U.K., Nigeria, Canada, Romania, and Italy. But the report shows that the "average" complainant was a man between 30 and 40 living in California, Texas, Florida, or New York. Individuals who reported losing money lost an average of $724; the highest losses involved Nigerian letter fraud, with a median loss of $5,100. Nearly 74 percent of the complaints said they were contacted through e-mail, and 36 percent complained of fraud through Web sites, highlighting the anonymous nature of the Web.[117]
Causes	• Misuse and abuse of technology • Overwhelmed by technology • Babies created by technology – donor parents
Consequences	• Generation gap • Unethical behaviors • Over-expenditures • Intergenerational conflicts • Isolation • Values erosion • Invasion of privacy • Identity theft • Lack of belonging • Identity crisis • Anonymous fathers
Resolutions	• Give guidance • Teach values and responsibility • Carefully monitor • Use the blockers that are provided

---

[117] http://search.findtarget.com/beaucoup/search.php?q=Computer+Ownership+Statistics

WITCHCRAFT AND THE OCCULT	A great struggle is being developed between persons who claim that witchcraft hysteria has become a dominating theme in the lives of children in the west since with the publications of Harry Potter's works, and those who think that Harry Potter is a simple portrayal of the struggle between good and evil. At one time when one thought of witchcraft one thought of Africa, the Caribbean, South America, especially Haiti, Jamaica, Guyana, Cuba and Brazil and a few other places that have been involved in ritual witchcraft. Today however, the argument is that witchcraft is being popularized through Harry Potter and Wicca religion.
Data	In a commentary written by Matt Nesbit, published on the net, it is argued that there is a growing national fascination with witchcraft here in the United States. It also states that while estimates vary, but there are between 400,000 to 3 million practitioners of Wicca in the United States. Adherents to the religion, male and female, call themselves witches or Wiccans, and are actively battling for religious acceptance and tolerance for their beliefs. Some claim that Wicca is the fastest growing religion in the United States.[118]
Causes	<ul><li>Recruiting from religious groups that accept the spiritualistic values.</li><li>Games</li><li>Books</li><li>Cult behavior</li><li>Soap opera</li><li>Movies DVD</li><li>Popularization of Wicca and other religions of the genre that offer the non-traditional path to power, knowledge and light.</li></ul>

---

[118] http://www.jesus-is-savior.com/False%20Religions/Wicca%20&%20Witchcraft/witchcraft_and_tv.htm

Consequences	- Children becoming initiates of witchcraft - Children getting out of touch with reality - Children withdrawing from mainstream society - Children getting depressed - Children getting involved in violence
Resolutions	- Find out whether the reality of witchcraft is being forced on children. - Know various of forces - Be informed about its intent for our children - Read about it - Know the games children play - Take active role in what they are doing - Point out dangers
HEALTH ISSUES	For several years now various countries and organization have been demonstrating that they have a profound concern for the health of their children. However, a striking reality that many researchers are reflecting is that the good health of our children leaves much to be desired. Many children are still suffering obesity, many sexually transmissible diseases and other health issues associated with the negative health habits that are pervading our world.
Data	In Africa, in 2003, some 26.6 million people were living with HIV, 3.2 million people became infected, and AIDS killed 2.3 million.
Causes	- Environmental challenges (pollution) - Dietary – poor food choices - Prohibitive costs of or lack of health care - Promiscuous lifestyles - Displacement
Consequences	- Poor development (physically, mentally, socially) - Poor educational performance - Poor job skills
Resolutions	- Monitor your children's health - Finding ways of providing financial support

APPENDIX II

Call the **DEPARTMENTS OF CHILDREN & FAMILY SERVICES** in your state for the help or hotline for abuse, neglect, safety or anyone challenges you need to resolve that is beyond the resources that are easily accessible to you.

Here are a few examples of the lines as per telephone numbers. These are national line lines.

DRUGS AND ALOHOL	1-877-855-8758
HIV/AIDS	1-800-342-2437
NARCOTICS ANONYMOUS	1-844-326-4685
GAMBLING	1-800-522-4700
EMEMGENCY SERVICES	911
DOMESTIC VIOLENCE	1-800-799-SAFE (7233
FAMILY HELPLINE	1-800-222-1222
CHILD ABUSE	1-480-922-8212
POISON CONTROL CENTER	1-800-222-1222
NATIONAL SUICIDE PREVENTION	1-800-273-8255

Whatever challenges you have there is a hotline that can assist you. Check online

A FEW HELPFUL BOOKS AND OTHER RESEARCH RESOURCES TO POINT THE WAY TO MORE EFFECTIVE PARENTING IN THE CONTEMPORARY AGE

Special Issues of the Journal Early Child Development & Care. Volume 50, Issue 1 1989.

Arendell, Terry, editor (1997), *Contemporary Parenting: Challenges & Issues*, Thousand Oaks, CA: Sage Publishers.

Bayley, N. (1993). *Bayley Scales of Infant Development* (2nd ed.). New York: Psychological Corp.

Bruce, Robert & Debra (1999), *The ABCs of Christian Parenting*, St. Louis, MO.: Concordia Publishing House.

Clare, L., and H. Garnier. (2000). "Parents' goals for adolescents diagnosed with developmental delays in early childhood," *Journal of Early Adolescence*, 20(4), 442-446.

Cordes, Colleen, and Edward Miller, editors (1999), *Fools' Gold: A Critical Look at Computers in Childhood.* New York: Alliance for Childhood.

Croyle, John with Abraham, Ken. (1997), *Bringing out the winner in your child*, Nashville, TN.: Cumberland House.

Firestone, R.W. (1997), *Compassionate Child-Rearing: An Approach to Optimal Parenting).* New York: Insight Books, Plenum Press.

Glennon, Will. (1999), *200 ways to raise a girl's self-esteem: an indispensable guide for parents, teachers, & other concerned caregivers*, Berkley, CA.: Conari Press.

Goldstein, Robin. *Everyday Parenting* – Look up the books under the varying by Robin Goldstein who is considered to be one an excellent contemporary author, who is very helpful to parents raising children through their varied stages of development.

Hammet, C.T. (1992). *Movement Activities for Early Childhood.* Champaign, Ill.: Human Kinetics.

http://www.cs.cmu.edu/afs/cs.cmu.edu/user/bam/www/numbers.html.

http://www.ed.gov/Technology/TechConf/1999/whitepapers/paper6.html#1

http://www.usnews.com/usnews/issue/000925/nycu/computers.htm

Kelly, Katy. "False Promise." *U.S. News and World Report.* 25 Sept. 2000.

Kristensen, N. (2001). *Basic Parenting Focus Issue: Motor Development.* Minneapolis, Minn.: Family Information Services.

Mann, Dale. "Documenting the Effects of Instructional Technology: A Fly-Over of

McDowell, Josh. (1987) *How to Help Your Child Say NO to Sexual Pressures,* Dallas,

Meltz, Barbara F. "Computers, software can harm emotional, social development." *The Boston Globe.* 01 Oct. 1998. http://www.boston.com/globe/columns/meltz/100198.htm

Mike Murphy and Victoria Johnson. (2002), *Raising Kids in a Violent Culture, Cook Communications Ministries. Colorado Springs, CO. This publisher has multiple resources for parents and children.*

Myers, Brad A. *Computer Almanac: Interesting and Useful Numbers About Computers.* 2nd ed. New York: Random House, 1997. 271.

Narmore, Bruce. (1980), *Adolescence is not an illness.* Old Tappan, NJ: Revel.

Omartian, Stormie. (2007), *The Power of a Praying Parent, Irvine, CA.:* Harvest House.

Paquette, Penny. (2000), *Parenting for A Child with A Behavior Problem, US.* Contemporary Books.

Payne, V. G., and L.D. Isaacs. (1987). *Human Motor Development: A Lifespan Approach.* Mountain View, Calif.: Mayfield.

Policy Questions." *The Secretary's Conference on Educational Technology.* New

Porter, Glenn. "Industrial Revolution." *Encarta Encyclopedia 2000 on CD-ROM.*

Schwartzman, Michael & Judith Sachs. (1990), *The Anxious Parent: Freeing.*

RESOURCES ON SOCIAL MEDIA: WHAT PARENTS SHOULD KNOW

https://www.caringforkids.cps.ca/handouts/social_media
https://kidshelpphone.ca/get-info/what-sexting
*https://www.pinegrovedaycamp.com/prospective-families/
what-our-families-say/10-tips-keep-kids-safe-social-media/*
*https://www.pewresearch.org/internet/2018/09/27/a-majority-of-teens-
have-experienced-some-form-of-cyberbullying/*
https://www.helpguide.org/articles/abuse/bullying-and-cyberbullying.htm
https://www.internetmatters.org/resources/social-media-advice-hub/

THE FOLLOWING ARE TOPICS THAT HAVE BEEN PUBLISHED BY THE NATIONAL RESEARCH COUNCIL. I HAVE SELECTED A FEW THAT ARE CONSIDERED MOST SIGNIFICANT TO ORIENT ANY INTERESTED PARENT CONCERNING THE VARIETY OF RESEARCH THAT IS AVAILABLE CONCERNING THE CHALLENGES THAT ARE LISTED IN THE FIRST APPENDIX

A Common Destiny: Blacks and American Society (1989) (ISBN 0309039983) *Gerald David Jaynes and Robin M. Williams, Jr., Editors; Committee on the Status of Black Americans, National Research Council*

Children of Immigrants: Health, Adjustment, and Public Assistance (1999) (ISBN 0309065453) Donald J. Hernandez, Editor; Committee on the Health and Adjustment of Immigrant Children and Families, National Research Council

Children's Health, the Nation's Wealth: Assessing and Improving Child Health (2004) (ISBN 0309091187) *Committee on Evaluation of Children's Health, National Research Council*

Development During Middle Childhood: The Years from Six to Twelve (1984) (ISBN 0309034787) *Panel to Review the Status of Basic Research on School-Age Children, Committee on Child Development Research and Public Policy*

From Generation to Generation: The Health and Well-Being of Children in Immigrant Families (1998) (ISBN 0309065615) *Donald J. Hernandez and Evan Charney, Editors; Committee on the Health and Adjustment of Immigrant Children and Families, National Research Council and Institute of Medicine*

Growing Up Global: The Changing Transitions to Adulthood in Developing Countries (2005) (ISBN 030909528X) *Cynthia B. Lloyd, Editor, Panel on Transitions to Adulthood in Developing Countries, National Research Council*

Health Insurance is a Family Matter (2002) (ISBN 0309085187) Committee on the Consequences of Uninsurance

Inner-City Poverty in the United States (1990) (ISBN 0309042798) *Committee on National Urban Policy, National Research Council*

Integrating Federal Statistics on Children: Report of a Workshop (1995) (ISBN 0309052491) Committee on National Statistics and Board on Children and Families, National Research Council and Institute of Medicine

Juvenile Crime, Juvenile Justice (2001) (ISBN 0309068428) *Panel on Juvenile Crime: Prevention, Treatment, and Control, Committee on Law and Justice, and Board on Children, Youth, and Families, National Research Council, and Institute of Medicine*

Losing Generations: Adolescents in High-Risk Settings (1993) (ISBN 0309052343) *Panel on High-Risk Youth, National Research Council*

Minority Students in Special and Gifted Education (2002) (ISBN 0309074398) *Committee on Minority Representation in Special*

Education, M. Suzanne Donovan and Christopher T. Cross, Editors, National Research Council

New Findings on Poverty and Child Health and Nutrition: Summary of a Research Briefing (1998) (ISBN 0309060850) *Anne Bridgman and Deborah Phillips, Editors; Board on Children, Youth, and Families, National Research Council and Institute of Medicine*

Promoting Health: Intervention Strategies from Social and Behavioral Research (2000) (ISBN 0309071755) *Brian D. Smedley and S. Leonard Syme, Editors; Committee on Capitalizing on Social Science and Behavioral Research to Improve the Public's Health, Division of Health Promotion and Disease Prevention*

Risking the Future: Adolescent Sexuality, Pregnancy, and Childbearing (1987) (ISBN 0309036984) Cheryl D. Hayes, Editor; Panel on Adolescent Pregnancy and Childbearing, National Research Council

Schools and Health: Our Nation's Investment (1997) (ISBN 0309054354) *Diane Allensworth, Elaine Lawson, Lois Nicholson, and James Wyche, Editors; Committee on Comprehensive School Health Programs in Grades K-12, Institute of Medicine*

The Best Intentions: Unintended Pregnancy and the Well-Being of Children and Families (1995) (ISBN 0309052300) Sarah S. Brown and Leon Eisenberg, Editors; Committee on Unintended Pregnancy, Institute of Medicine

The Immigration Debate: Studies on the Economic, Demographic, and Fiscal Effects of Immigration (1998) (ISBN 0309059984) *James P. Smith and Barry Edmonston, Editors; Panel on the Demographic and Economic Impacts of Immigration, National Research Council*

Understanding and Preventing Violence, Volume 1 (1993) (ISBN 0309054761) *Albert J. Reiss, Jr., and Jeffrey A. Roth, Editors; Panel on the Understanding and Control of Violent Behavior, National Research Council*

Understanding and Preventing Violence, Volume 3: Social Influences (1994) (ISBN 0309050804) *Albert J. Reiss, Jr. and Jeffrey A. Roth, Editors, Panel on the Understanding and Control of Violent Behavior, National Research Council*

Understanding and Preventing Violence, Volume 4: Consequences and Control (1994) (ISBN 0309050790) Albert J. Reiss, Jr. and Jeffrey A. Roth, Editors, Panel on the Understanding and Control of Violent Behavior, National Research Council

Understanding Child Abuse and Neglect (1993) (ISBN 0309048893) *Panel on Research on Child Abuse and Neglect, National Research Council*

Violence in Families: Assessing Prevention and Treatment Programs (1998) (ISBN 0309054966) Rosemary Chalk and Patricia A. King, Editors; Committee on the Assessment of Family Violence Interventions, National Research Council and Institute of Medicine

Welfare, the Family, and Reproductive Behavior: Research Perspectives (1998) (ISBN 0309061253) *Robert A. Moffitt, Editor; Committee on Population, National Research Council*

Who Cares for America's Children? (1990) (ISBN 0309040329) *Cheryl D. Hayes, John L. Palmer, and Martha J. Zaslow, Editors; Panel on Child Care Policy, National Research Council*

Working Families and Growing Kids: Caring for Children and Adolescents (2003) (ISBN 0309087031) *Eugene Smolensky and Jennifer Appleton Gootman, Editors, Committee on Family and Work Policies, National Research Council.*

CPSIA information can be obtained
at www.ICGtesting.com
Printed in the USA
LVHW091659160820
663340LV00009B/338/J

9 781649 453686